Everybody Here Is Kin

Everybody Here Is Kin

BettyJoyce Nash

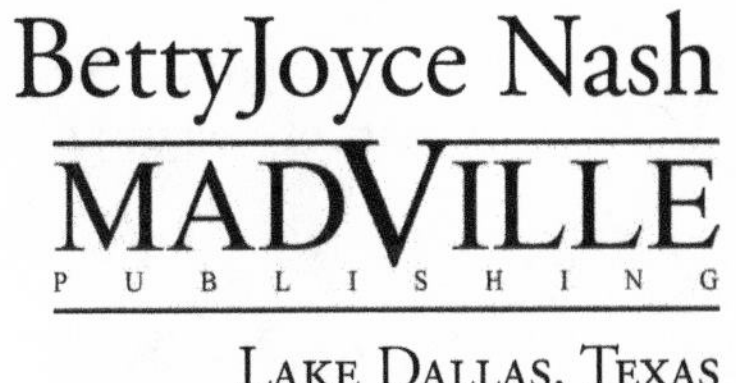

Lake Dallas, Texas

FIRST EDITION

Requests for permission to reprint or reuse material
from this work should be sent to:

Permissions
Madville Publishing
PO Box 358
Lake Dallas, TX 75065

Cover Art & Design: Gentry Lessman
Author Photo: Maguire Neblett Photography

ISBN: 978-1-956440-35-5 paper; 978-1-956440-36-2 ebook
Library of Congress Control Number: 2022944380

We truly are all kin. This book is especially for

Bill & Charlie & Alec & Charlene & Jim & C.H. & B.W.

1

Body Surf

Naomi and I slogged through sand so hot it scalded our tender feet, lugging two rusted lounge chairs and a bag between us—her Coppertone tanning oil, my SPF 35; her Thermos of Pinot Grigio, my lemon water.

The little kids stayed inside the cottage to finish *Star Wars* on the old-school VCR, but I couldn't miss what came next: Naomi, my mom, had arranged to meet her high school sweetheart here at Boneyard Beach, where they hung out as teenagers. We only got here last night.

We pried apart our chairs, and I sat cross-legged, sipping water, while the Atlantic Ocean licked and nibbled the earth. I chewed bitter pulp. He was why we'd stopped in Georgia—not Dad's ashes—instead of beating it to Key West, which I needed to see before it became Atlantis. Supposedly my fourteenth birthday present.

I gulped salt air. It stung my raw heart.

Naomi unhooked her top, and stretched belly down, facing the ocean. "It's been twenty years since graduation."

For sure, he's changed. So has she. "How come he's not married?"

"Divorced. He's a developer, Lucille. Remember that billboard we saw advertising a condo development in Savannah?"

That's what developers do? Tear up paradise? I'd hoped Naomi and I would lie side by side, almost-but-not-quite touching, and talk about Dad, scatter his ashes here, where they got married, and leave. These ashes have burdened our mantel for ten years. Boneyard was a sweet island, OK, I saw that now, but it was not Key West. And now, my trip had become Naomi's trip. This polluted things.

I hated swimsuits, I wore track shorts and T-shirts. Middle school had messed with me, turned me long-legged, and no-hipped, but overnight, at thirteen, my breastless chest had ballooned. Having no hips helped me slide into small spaces when Naomi panicked or got moody, but I hadn't found breasts useful.

She propped herself on an elbow and swallowed a Xanax with wine. She was fortyish, maybe pre-menopause? I'd researched mood swings on WebMD and come up with that.

She oiled her arms and chest, trying to keep her top from slipping.

"Georgia's definitely a red zone." No need to discuss UV rays and ozone, why overwhelm her? I coated my arms and legs and face with SPF 35, though I wouldn't mind the sun healing my pimples.

"Sun's good for you—food for your bones." She plugged in ear buds—another dose of *Ten Days to Enlightenment*. She'd listened daily since dumping Marco last spring.

"Before Tom shows up, quick: Why'd you even bring Dad if you were planning this meetup?" I rushed the words out of my mouth, and why did she hate talking about him?

She rested her head on folded arms.

My eyes drifted shut, and I'd gotten halfway to a trance when her voice, dreamy, remembered out loud the golden hairs on my father's legs. She shut up and went back to her happy place, but I stayed, paralyzed in Naomi's memory, imagining his hairy, sun-glittery arms and legs, his teeth with the space in the middle, and his shaved head glowing with red-orange stubble, same color hair as mine. I swung my feet to the sand and straightened, still unspooling the movie of Dad.

"Re-hook me?" Naomi's regular-mom voice sliced my thoughts.

I re-clasped her top and walked to the water, where people played, little and big, young and old. Friends. Families. They splashed. Launched Frisbees. Lofted beach balls.

Back at our chairs, two guys had settled coolers and towels

nearby. One actually unfurled a ratty Confederate-flag beach towel. I'd seen three real ones flying in Tennessee and Virginia on our way down here. I blinked and stared at these men, one trim but stocky, the other, lean and muscly. Hairy and hot—but—conventional looking. They took beers from a cooler; and Bicep, the hot one, offered Naomi a beer; I hoped I'd get one, too. But no.

Naomi got up. "Luce, meet Tom." Bicep squeezed her waist, kissed her cheek, and whispered in her ear. He didn't let go.

Tom introduced Mike, dark like Marco, Naomi's latest ex, who had immigrated from Mexico. Tom turned and gazed down at me with a benevolent smile.

Naomi beamed. "*This* is my Lucille, my eldest, my right arm." She loved us, for real, but that bit about the right arm made elder-daughter me shiver.

"You look like an athlete, Lucille, strong. You're thirteen, your mother tells me."

"I turn fourteen one week from tomorrow. Labor Day"

Naomi often talked about how great men in the South treat women. "Like chattel?" I would ask in my pretend-innocent voice. This time I said nothing.

Naomi and Tom exchanged names of people they remembered from high school. Naomi barely remembered anyone; she often talked about "back home," but I'd never seen her write a Christmas card or heard her phone anyone down here. Tom must've stirred buried memories. Naomi had always confused me. Why'd "Amazing Grace" make her cry? Why'd she prefer labor-and-delivery drama to a quiet medical office? Now, I worried why she took *indefinite* leave from the hospital.

The men removed their shirts. The naked man-chests reminded me I'd need to watch her every second. I'd been careful around Naomi's men, too, since the one, pre-Marco, who came into the bathroom while I showered; Naomi ditched him fast. Marco, the best of the bunch, was history because he really loved her and that probably scared her. I read on the Internet about fear of intimacy, a grownup condition that makes no sense. How much more intimate than having sex and two kids with a man could you get?

Tom invited Naomi to the water. They ambled, hand-in-hand.

"She has a *July* birthday. She's a *lion*. Cats do *not* like getting wet."

She glared at me over her shoulder. "Luce, shh, I need to cool off."

They'd been high school sweethearts; he was class president four years running; they'd dated two years. I didn't like this meet-up; we were driving to Key West in three days.

Mike rolled, on the ragged towel, closer to my chair. I looked down. "This isn't 1850," I told him. "The enslaved have been freed, supposedly. I can't stand to even look at that towel. Where are you from? I mean, originally?"

He moved to Naomi's empty chair and sat sideways facing me. "My parents are from El Salvador."

"Why would you display that towel in public? Are you *trying* to make people mad?"

"It's only a towel I got cheap from Goodwill."

"Jack and Mayzie, my halvsies? They're part-Mexican. I'd hate for them to see it."

"But it's nothing against Mexicans. Or anybody."

"It's a symbol." I *so* couldn't tolerate that towel, I yanked it out from under the cooler, which fell over, spilling beers. I set the beers upright, gripped a towel edge and tried to rip, but, no, too sturdy.

"Let me." Mike tried using his teeth to fray the thick edge.

He handed it back. He'd started a tear, so I gave it all I had, but the fabric failed to give. Finally, he took one end, I took the other, and we pulled together. Nothing.

"See? How strong racism is?"

He tried not to laugh. "Wait. I know." He dug in the cooler and found a pointy-tipped bottle opener. "Here."

I laid the towel on the beach, and poked it a bunch of times with the opener. We took opposite sides and tore until the pile of towel strips grew.

"Happy now?"

"Why would this make me happy? I like the towel shredded, but, what does that accomplish?" One symbol down, a zillion to go. The flag, and what it meant, was another battle, like ignorance about the overheated world, problems that *killed*. I tried to forget, but the stupids of the world confronted me even on vacation.

At the waterline, even little kids jumped waves and mounted floats or boards and rode them ashore. Waded. Collected shells and driftwood. A bearded guy chainsawed a washed-up tree. The world was having fun while I policed beach racists.

But Mike was OK.

I dropped my head back and checked out the milky atmosphere, sweat pooling in all my cracks and crevices, legs, armpits; even my eyeballs felt too hot for their sockets.

Mike's voice interrupted. "Ever see the ocean before? Tom said you came from Detroit. Wanna ride some waves?" he asked. "Oh, come on. Race ya!"

In the scary, sucking ocean, the beast that must be fed? But to a runner, even a scaredy-cat like me, the words popped like a starting pistol. I beat him easily to the water where I spotted Tom behind Naomi, pulling her arms over her head, holding her by the waist, and plunging her into a foamy curl.

My body stiffened. My legs backed me away; Naomi went under and came up spluttering. Surely she knew how to ride waves. She grew up down here. Big rollers crashed. Mike tugged my hand, but I fought that and the water sucking at my knees.

"It's a blast." Mike pulled me to him, fast, like dancing, then grabbed me, and tossed me at a wave. The water trapped me with no breath. I came up screaming, Mike yelling, "You can touch bottom! Stand up!"

I scrambled to my feet. Oh. Another wave slapped me down, and soon I caught the rhythm—jump-and-fall, jump-and-fall. He fell and surfaced behind me. A wave smacked me and gouged my face into sand. For a second, I forgot Naomi and Tom and Jack and Mayzie, even Dad, but only a nanosecond. Bet Dad loved body surfing; we'd loved all the same stuff.

My ears closed up like I had a cold, and from far away, I saw watery Naomi, waist deep, Tom gripping her hands while she held her head lopsided, angling her chin in *that way* I'd seen too often to not worry.

I sprinted back to the chairs, grabbed our SpongeBob towel, and hurried away. "Nice to meet you," my teeth chattered, feet pounding the shallows, making for Naomi. "Let's go!"

"You run ahead without me, Luce. I'll be along." A long while was what she meant. I knew that. I shivered inside SpongeBob while the ocean snatched sand from under my feet.

2

Hunger

Saturday night, Will Altman whipped around at the sound of that voice. Belva, his date, a word that unnerved him. Plain brown hair swept across her forehead, a thick braid halfway down her back, only the one. Belva.

He'd lurched late into civilian life. This was only his second date since he'd climbed out of the sandpit ten years ago, not counting uninspired sex with guests at the tourist court he managed.

"I wondered whether you'd show. I'm so glad you did."

The sincerity of her tone didn't quite square with the vibe of the mock-rustic dining spot outside Pinesboro, duded up like a pretend sharecropper's cabin.

They took in the décor and exchanged a look.

"Memorializing, I see, the good old days." Will despised the rusted tractor seats, sepia photographs, weathered washboards, and metal signs. "Makes you want to run right out and pick cotton."

"My grandmother picked cotton. Other grandmother picked tobacco."

"No lie? Let's stop this, or we'll lose our appetites." Will's grandmother had also picked cotton, but Belva didn't need to know. The banter jacked his nerves. He finger-combed his beard. The place had been his idea, but he'd seen it only from the road, hoping no one from the old days would be here, people whose names he couldn't unscramble from his fuzzy-to-shot memory.

A waitress showed them to a table and lit a tiny candle lantern.

He scanned the crowd. The noise—raucous talk and twangy country music—didn't sit well. The floor-to-ceiling windows didn't help, neither did CNN on the TV screen behind the bar, showing a photo of the truth-telling journalist ISIS had beheaded. That's when his thoughts truly went haywire, running him to hell but not quite all the way back.

"Any open tables on the porch?" He managed six words to save the evening.

"You sure? Hotter'n floogens," the waitress said. "No one's out there."

"Good."

"How hot *is* floogens?" Will asked the waitress as they walked out the door. The girl was so young she still wore braces. Wasn't child labor illegal?

The girl grinned. "No clue. Hot."

"I don't care about the heat. Do you?" He had to get out.

Belva shook her head. On the porch, she claimed the seat beside him, rather than across, and sat so close their arm hairs mingled, and distracted him. The waitress lit the candle and switched on the ceiling fan to confound the bugs. The air flickered the flame.

Will sniffed the stink of decay. "Smells like home."

Belva pushed her hair off her forehead and tucked loose strands behind her ears.

"You *are* a marsh rat." She smiled.

"For real. Washed in the mud." Will saw her every Friday and Saturday because she managed the old slave market downtown where farmers sold homegrown vegetables and artists sold art. Will offered his hand-carved sculptures. Yesterday, at check-in, she'd asked Will on a date. Whatever was going on between her and her doctor-husband was her business. But she'd invited him. He was here.

She ordered wine. Fizzy water for him, determined to divorce alcohol for good. Out there, the night noise, the gurgle of mud and water, seized his attention so thoroughly that when the waitress appeared with Belva's wine and his water and menus he was shocked to find himself alive, at a restaurant, not on his porch, and with a woman, not his tomcat.

God. The prices. He checked both pockets. He'd forgotten to transfer cash to his dress khakis, and now, scanning the menu, wait, was this a joke? Rattlesnake? He faked a smile.

She broke into a laugh.

"On the menu? That's plain wrong. Wild should stay wild."

"Have you ever encountered a rattlesnake?"

"Hell yes, Boneyard crawls with rattler dens. Once, in the refuge, I nearly stepped on one. Someone had killed it and coiled it at the end of a log over Chicken Creek. I didn't know it was dead. Bet I jumped ten feet. Took me hours to calm my blood." His first trip, post-sandpit, into real nature. The experience had scared him so badly that he'd not returned except for occasional trips to the native shell heaps or to work on his homeplace, or to shake loose from the grind of daily life. That nature scare had formed a creepy brew of shame and fear that a thirty-year-old could and should conquer. Fear of snakes? After you'd caused deaths? Illogical. Silly.

The waitress reappeared. Belva ordered the rattlesnake fajitas.

He closed the menu.

"Same for me." If that's how she wanted to play things—ordering food that conjured a frightful memory—she was welcome to. He wasn't exactly *afraid* of snakes, anyway, the critters had as much right to existence on earth as careless humans.

"Tell you what, if I'd caught the person who'd arranged it, so deliberately, well, he'd be . . . ," wanting to shock her, but he was the one breaking a sweat. He cut his eyes to her face and stared into her irises, fracturing in the jumpy candlelight. What he wanted that look to say, he wasn't sure, maybe it was a warning.

A moment passed.

"Will, I didn't mean to upset you. I'm sorry."

"I'm fine. I'm a big boy, mostly." He smiled into her irises. He sipped ice water until his tongue numbed so he couldn't use it. Minutes passed, whether he wanted them to or not, and then more minutes passed. Years later, the waitress brought the fajitas. Should he own up about the cash?

She sipped wine. "I've enjoyed seeing your variety of pieces over the summer—you've scaled up your sculptures. Carving such big hunks of wood must be hard."

His tongue thawed. He chewed a chunk of rattler, tasting suspiciously like chicken.

So. She'd noticed. "It's the 'art' part that's hard, not the actual carving."

"Did you study art in college? Or what?"

He hated talking about himself.

"Well? I love hearing what inspires artists."

"Accidental artist, that's me. I worked construction, and one day some customer wanted to replace a rotten capital for a Corinthian column—the ones with leaves and flowers—and that led to historical projects in Savannah. When I came home, I started cruising beaches and marshes for driftwood and forest snags." He took a bite of snake.

Her eyes caught fire; he'd say almost anything to goose that fire, so he finished chewing and told her how copying historical designs came easy, but cutting into plain old wood challenged him, how he wasn't sure he had any imagination. "I'm forced to sit awhile, let the grain and any bumps and bulges in the raw wood supply ideas—driftwood's best, because the sea has already sanded and shaped it."

"You love the work, don't you? I can tell."

Did he? He smiled his thanks, to cover his shame at this revelation, if true, but the smile turned to nervous laughter. Will feared talk would sap his work energy. He couldn't discuss *love* at all—of anything or anybody. Love only led to change or death. People, places, things.

She bit into the fajita. "Pretty good. Tastes like chicken." She laughed.

"Eating a serpent? That's plain unnatural. They're sacred symbols in native cultures, sometimes evil, sometimes kind." Steering the conversation away from poisonous snakes or art, he added, "Great name, by the way, Belva. Means what?"

She made a face. "My grandmother's. Beautiful something, the 'Bel' part. I've hated it for years, but lately, I've accepted it. Accepted myself."

"Why? I mean, the 'accept yourself' part. Why now?"

"I'm too old to hate my name or pretend to be someone I'm not. Right?" She dropped her eyes and stared at her plate, cutting her fajitas into chunks.

"Right. OK, full disclosure: I left my cash at home, in my jeans." He was a cash-only guy, one reason he couldn't get a loan, that and no steady income.

"So?" Her face tensed. "My husband left me—loaded."

She lifted a forkful and chewed. Eyes on her plate, she swallowed and then smiled a strained smile. She raised her eyes, glistening.

Stupefied, Will couldn't think, much less speak. It wasn't the news, it was her tear-shiny eyes after she'd delivered the news. He tasted nothing.

Her face soon relaxed. She went on chewing and swallowing. "I've been so starved, how about you? Aren't you going to eat?"

"Can't." Will slid his plate toward Belva, whose eyes now spilled hunger. Did his?

She finished her fajitas and his, then ordered peach ice cream. Her appetite floored him. Besides PB&J, he survived on leftovers from a weekly fish fry, his specialty, the one meal he cooked from scratch, and barbecue takeout where he regularly overate. She spooned the last of her ice cream, scraping the bowl as the waitress laid the bill on the table. Silently, Belva opened her purse, a rainbow of primary colors woven in the third world. He'd lusted after the beautiful woman, Perdita, who, he guessed, imported, then sold the goods at the Saturday market.

"My treat, my pleasure. Maybe sometime you could cook for me."

Couldn't picture any woman in his closet-sized kitchen. "Anything could happen."

The sky could fall.

Belva pulled twenties from a handstitched leather wallet, probably crafted by the market's lone leatherworker, Don, and placed them on the table.

"All you need to do is ask." She added a twenty to the pile.

He parked Pearl in the middle of the block, away from streetlights, away from her house, and waited. What he knew about Belva: two years behind him in school, long-legged, with those tomboy braids, the girl every guy wanted to date, even though she wasn't pretty, not with that razor-sharp chin, those big shoulders; later, they'd studied government together at Georgia Southern; she crossed the classroom to say goodbye after she heard he'd enlisted; the sun lit her up that day, kaleidescoping her irises into shapes so complex he'd nearly lost his balance; she'd married a doctor, also a classmate—the husband was money; they lived in this old Victorian in town, spitting distance from the market that, even in a hick outpost like Pinesboro, must be worth half-a-million. He pictured handmade doors and lintels, carved columns. Antique furniture.

The skinny on her as market manager was impressive, too, according to exhibitor scuttlebutt. Efficient and dedicated, she did every job solo, from PR to accounting. The exhibitor fees, along with donations, generated the funds for a hospital charity that helped families struggling with financial fallout from grave illness. Even he was better off because of her efforts. This year, sales had inched up. Gallery owners from New York to Miami were occasionally buying, though none had yet shown interest in his sculptures.

Her porch light flicked on. Inside the old house, Belva shooed him upstairs. He climbed the steps, but slowed as he approached the light spilling from her bedroom, dread forming in his gut. A garden of floral pillows softened the edges of a hand-carved loveseat. Magnolia blossoms. Clover. Trumpet vines. The botanical theme buzzed his brain.

Her feet hit the steps. He turned and she grinned from the doorway, out of breath. She hurried into the bathroom. He slipped his clothes off and himself under the covers; the circumstance felt bizarre, him naked with a woman in a girly bedroom with lights. He hadn't had sex since the Court's Memorial Day fireworks, a one-off with a tenant, and wasn't sure what he wanted—too much too soon? Maybe not for her. To keep his mind off his hard-on, he silently recited the Latin names of the wildflowers—helianthus, verbena buonariensis—his mother had taught him those while they weeded.

Belva emerged, much too long later, and he forced himself to look away from the glow moving toward him, from the gauzy gown and into the yellow coreopsis, the sky-blue verbena. That long, audible exhale, he understood, was his.

"What have you been doing in there?"

She stretched out beside him, a nervous smile playing around her mouth. He took in her healthy shoulders, freckles, and unruly hair, unbraided, unbridled. He resisted twisting it. Propping herself on a giant dahlia cushion, she took his free hand and turned up his raw palm.

"What's this?" She lifted both palms to the light.

"Me, slicing and dicing. Gouges slip, so do knives."

His hands felt large and alive. Her inspection of them embarrassed him.

A moment later, she dropped both. "I like your work. We're really on the map, drawing people, dealers, even, from Savannah, Jacksonville, Charleston, New York, Miami."

Her eyes were on fire—with work. He pressed his fingertips to her mouth. "Market research? Now?"

"But, it's so cool, all that's going on."

He pulled her close, until her shoulder nestled inside his armpit, his lips to her ear. "You're Wonder Woman. Everyone says so."

"For the record, I never sleep with exhibitors."

"And I never sleep with management. I'm honored, but I suppose you couldn't sleep with all of us, you'd need to add 'sex worker' to your CV, and imagine, that old guy with the . . ."

She grabbed a pillow and threw it at him but he managed to gasp, "watermelons."

He ditched the pillow, flopped back and caught his breath. "One more tiny detail: What's your deal with your husband?"

She stayed silent for a minute. "We're still married."

"Oh." He climbed out of bed and found his pants.

"I told you Nelson moved out."

"But you're still, officially, married." He tuned into his ringing ears.

She reached for him and missed. "He and I—we are *not* together."

One trouser leg in, he stopped. "Do you sleep together?"

"No. You and Joneen?"

Joneen had broken up with him while he was deployed. He got back in Belva's bed and covered up, but said nothing, his thoughts not so much drifting as fighting.

Belva shifted onto her side and squeezed his bicep.

"It's been over." He tracked the pale green leaves trailing the ceiling. At one corner, jasmine flowers unfurled below dental molding. He pointed. "That your handiwork?"

She rested her palm on his chest—this slight pressure arrested his breath.

"Those leaves took a month of me choking on paint fumes. As I highlighted the last shadow on the final, corner tendril . . . right . . . there . . ." she pointed to an obvious smear, "he said he was leaving. I said, 'Where are you going?' I thought he meant the hardware or grocery store. He said, 'You. I'm leaving you.' I should touch up that spot."

A motionless moment passed. Will's heart twisted, for Belva, and for his own prospects with a woman so newly-hurt, that much he'd seen in her face at dinner. She'd just told him again, but he couldn't bear to leave.

When he finally spoke, he made his voice low and neutral. "Without mistakes, though, it wouldn't look real. The Japanese call that 'wabi-sabi.'" Will reached for her, and brought her gown over her head, hoping his thoughts of Monk, the high priest of wabi sabi in his unit, would fade. Will shivered, even as Belva's warmth seeped into his skin, even as he tasted her minty mouth, her tongue. Monk had found detachment, even, and maybe especially, in full battle rattle. "Nothing lasts, nothing's perfect, nothing's finished. No words in our language describe it."

She repeated the words, moving her hips, and climbed on, settling herself. A split-second of panic and Will's head stopped buzzing.

Over too soon. He woke with his head on her belly.

He quietly dressed and tiptoed out, taking each step slowly. A lamp in a corner of the living room laid down weak light that left the off-kilter corners shadowed; somehow this amplified distinct groans from the heart pine floors that spooked him, for an interminable second. Inside, the house looked exactly as he'd pictured.

"Graceful old place, isn't she?"

He turned. Her hair, loose, her in an oversized terrycloth robe, probably her husband's—these domestic details reminded him that she was not divorced, and that he was trespassing.

"Didn't mean to wake you."

"I'm sure you didn't. You figured you'd sneak out before morning. Do you turn into a vampire at midnight?" She checked her watch. "Too late, go ahead." She lifted her chin, exposing her neck and throat.

The most vulnerable part of a human—*aim for the throat, aim for the jugular*—how many times had he heard those words, joke or threat? He brooded, chilled inside the close air of her home, opened his mouth, and out came trite talk.

"Got things to do. Let me scoot. Thanks for the . . ." What? Sex?

"For dinner? Let's go out again." She rescued him and walked past him to the kitchen.

She did that at the market, too, somehow made artists feel good, even if she only checked them in and wished them luck. He'd overheard her concerned questions—"How are your sales?

Do you need sunscreen? Have you brought change?"—when high-strung artists whined.

He followed her, searching for her back door while she ran tap water into a glass and drank it down. "Thirsty?"

He shook his head.

She selected another glass from the cabinet and filled it anyway. "Are you in that big a hurry?" She pushed on his chest, same as she had upstairs, with the same heart-stopping result, and handed him water.

He sipped and swallowed, dredging his mind for a quip, but said only, "Yeah." He studied the drop-leaf table he'd seen on the way into the house earlier, a maple beauty with hand-turned legs. He sat at the edge of a chair, clutching the glass.

"You coming back or what?" She pulled out a chair, sat, and knotted the robe's belt.

Yes and no both scared him.

She shrugged.

"Figured you didn't—," how to tell her he couldn't imagine them together, especially if her husband still lurked in the wings? "Everybody in town will find out when they see Pearl parked. FYI, I didn't park the truck right in front of the house."

She laughed. "Like I care."

"What *do* you care about?"

"My hometown, the hospital. Pulling myself together, building a life. You?"

Maybe he was paranoid but questions like hers made him feel like he suddenly needed to be somehow respectable, in a nine-to-five way. OK, so he should have himself more together.

Words clogged his throat.

"I've got to get going. I'll pay you for dinner."

"I don't need or want money. I hope we can go out again. It'll be your turn to pay, if you like, but I don't care. And, one more thing: I admire you, Will Altman. I remember when I heard you'd enlisted; you stepped up and that took guts. Why did you?"

"We'd been attacked. I wanted to fight something. Seems like I was born fighting. But it wasn't—what I thought—it felt wrong."

She absorbed the words, he could tell, by her lively eyes.

"Thank you—"

"Please don't thank me for my service." He rose and leaned on the door jamb, trying to shake the scene upstairs.

"See you Friday."

"Yes." She smiled. "Don't forget to register, you. It's *a rule*."

God. *Rule*? This could never work.

He drove Pearl along quiet town streets to the four-lane, windows down, the cab filling with dead air. He pulled into the Gas King. The sign said to pay first. He scrounged around the floorboard and collected two quarters. Between the seats, he found enough ones for two gallons.

The window attendant was too old for the graveyard shift, poor guy, and when Will deposited the puny cash in the tray, the guy didn't blink at the amount. Two minutes later, he fired the engine and waved. The attendant rapped the glass. "You have a good one, too." Will puttered away, chewing on the evening. Belva's hair had glistened, even in the dim light. Oh. That parting smile, the way she emphasized the word *rule*? Was she joking? He laughed out loud, at his own idiot-self.

A clatter. An intermittent clack. His salt-corroded muffler finally had dropped. He pulled onto the shoulder and got out. The pump nozzle and hose sat on the highway. He loaded the contraption and drove back to the station. The attendant said it happened all the time. Will promised the fifty dollars by Friday, market day, the one day of the week he had cash.

3

Mud

Daybreak, Sunday. Will sniffed, to suss out rain. Dazed, spacey, but with no hangover or regret. He clanked the tailgate shut. The marsh reek rode in on a breeze, spiked with soot and thick enough to chew. That stink had staying power.

He surveyed his heap of house, the *Loblolly*, a native word meaning mudhole. Sunrise soon torched the loblollies, longleafs, and live oaks, and bronzed the creeks writhing toward the Atlantic. He tarped the planks, so they'd stay dry, while his buddy Trip punched a shovel in dirt, digging the last of the workshop's four footings. He and Trip both had that rangy, rawboned look and ramrod posture that said army.

"Altman, gear up your wiry ass, we need to pour footings. I gotta leave by noon." Trip flipped aside fire-cooked soil, stopped, and dragged his eyes over Will. "The house doesn't look too awful bad."

Will swabbed his beard with his shirttail. "Money, money, money-money," he falsettoed. By the time the VFD churned the forest roads last June, the blaze had crumpled the place. Sheet metal roof slumped into buckled walls. Charcoaled timbers stabbed the sky.

"Let's get this workshop done, then chip away at the house rubble on weekends." Trip settled a cinderblock in a corner hole. "We'll raise her up one layer at a time."

He shook his head. Last person he wanted to owe was Trip.

"Money's not my motive and you know it." Trip fixed him with his lawman stare. "First we finish the workshop, then I call around for a used lathe. There's a market for hand-turned furniture and I need a hobby. Sheriff-burnout is killer."

Will played along. Trip was a gym rat, dog crazy, and, once he'd gotten elected sheriff, he got up in other people's business, like Will's, which occupied what little free time Trip had. He even practiced yoga at Boneyard Community Center. Trip owned the Palmetto Tourist Court and Will managed it in exchange for rent. Veterans helping veterans. Trip was big on that.

"I've discovered useless objects sell. I've pawned my rookie carvings off on tourists from Atlanta, Savannah, even New York." But Labor Day's next week; the Court would keep Will too busy for woodcarving. Too bad; he needed the money.

Will dumped concrete into a fifty-five-gallon drum, the powder blinded and choked him, filthied his hair and skin. He turned from the dirty cloud, knotted a bandanna behind his head, and shoved it over his mouth and nose. He hauled well water up by hand and sloshed it in by the bucketful, raising even more dust.

"Dump the powder in the water, not the other way around. It'll settle on its own."

"Yeah, yeah." Will grabbed a two-by-four and stirred till the slurry was perfect: thick and gray and moody. He tipped the drum while Trip scooped spadefuls and emptied them around the upended cinderblocks.

"Let her cure," Trip said. "Start on her floor tomorrow, or later next week. I'll get real busy Labor Day weekend. You frame her up."

Will hadn't built jack since high school. In the army, everything was pre-fab and pop up. Just add soldiers, blend, and shoot, no reward nowadays in working something the right way. He stirred the slurry around the block, and his rant spewed.

"Nothing makes sense. Prime property, and nobody will lend me money on the land, so I can rebuild." After his mother died, he'd let the insurance lapse; lightning sparked the fire.

Trip flooded the last hole.

"Fact: takes money to borrow money. Lose the attitude. You got to be your own worst enemy, a chip on your shoulder big as this drum."

Will was not only broke, but, according to Trip, broken.

Trip stooped and reworked each cinderblock in each corner. "This high enough off the ground? For real, let's raise her up. Sea level's a wild card."

"*Loblolly's* six, maybe nine feet, above the marsh." Will's ancestors had built the place, felling cypresses and pines, shaping them with drawknives, if family legend had credence. True or false, the story suited Will. "Survived a hundred and fifty years. The marsh soaks up water and wind and copes with whatever nature throws at it."

Trip repositioned the cinderblocks. Will handed him the level and leaned, palms on knees, watching the veins on Trip's bald skull, his heron tattoo spreading along his biceps. The bubble tilted. "See? Off kilter."

"Son of a bitch." Will kneeled and eyeballed one. Sweat filmed his vision and turned it wavy, Trip's face in his.

Trip stood. "I've got calibrated eyeballs, so would you if you'd shot as much as me. Hand me that level."

What did he just say? Will tossed him the old spirit level; it landed in wet concrete. Trip plucked the level from the slurry, wiped it clean, and placed it on the cinderblock. The bubble settled way off the mark.

Will leaned in. "At least I've got sense enough to keep quiet about shooting people."

Trip drew back. His voice went soft. "Hell, did I say *people*, Will? I didn't mean people."

His calm tone made Will want to grab him, but he reined himself in.

"I meant the dummies we shoot at target practice. You're a far better marksman than me, I remember from the way back. Now help me up, asshole."

Will stared out at the marsh, where the sun blazed the grasses, waving ass-high.

"Help me up."

"How come? You're twice as fit as me. Get up by yourself." But Will stuck out his hand, hoping it wasn't a trick and Trip wouldn't flip him with some cop maneuver. He didn't. He got up and pounded the block with a brick.

Will replaced the level. The bubble rested between the two lines. "On the money."

"You're welcome." He looked at Will. "Doing OK? No backsliding?"

"You drive that nasty rut-road all the way from town to lecture me?"

"No. Yeah. That and make sure you actually finish this workshop. Seriously, I need down time. The DUIs, yeah, you know about those, but the domestic calls and the crimes of sheer stupidity? The other day—"

"Shut." Will had no stomach for tales of human folly. He'd seen it firsthand. Trip was pitching in, claiming he wanted to build the workshop right and share the space, but he was keeping an eye on Will, who knew how he must look to Trip. Disorganized hair and beard, haphazard habits, and, though he prided himself on his neat workbench, Will got how Trip might see him as someone who needed saving. And how Trip might think he was the guy to do it.

4

The Palmetto Republic

My dream cracked when my sore muscles woke me, trying to escape Mayzie's arms and legs, flung in four directions. Last night, Dad and I floated peacefully, our arms and legs waving like tentacles; in this dreamy underworld, we were jellies.

Jack and Mayzie got up too and flipped TV channels, scarfing dry bowls of a previous tenant's Cheerios. Strange sounds came from Naomi's bedroom, so I turned up the TV, praying Tom would leave early so we could tend our family business of Dad.

I slipped out before the kids could beg to come. The sun had already heated the clogged parking lot, jammed with old trucks, cars, and vans made before I was born. A staticky speaker coming from a cottage blared some song about *believing in magic.*

Up close, the Court's cracked foundations scared me. Fishing poles and floats pooched out porch screens. Doors squeaked open and popped shut. Outside the office, an ice machine plopped perfect pellets into its silver gut. From clotheslines between cottages, beach towels and bathing suits flew like flags of family republics. Something touched my shoulder, and I jumped. A medicinal stink drifted past.

A thin, sharp voice said, "Tourists can be so trashy." An old woman with hair like dryer lint pushed a wheelbarrow filled with cans. She stared at me with sunken black eyes, her face, a dried dark prune.

"My, you're a pretty girl, but take care of that milk skin, you hear? World's hotting up." Vinegar. Mixed with what? A sweet herb. A straw visor shadowed her face. A starched-and-ironed man's shirt covered her arms, its tail stuffed inside field-pants like scientists wore on nature TV; knee-high rubber boots swallowed her pants-legs.

I took, then dropped her bony hand.

"I'm Lucille. Nice to meet you, Miss . . ."

"Queen. You'll see plenty of me if you stick around."

"Queen. Is that your title?"

She about died laughing. "Believe it or not, girl, Queen was my mother's name, but I am a queen. A turtle queen. I monitor the sea turtle nests on the beach." Still snorting with laughter and shaking her head, she bumped her load over the shells.

The sand was so dry it squeaked under my runners. A sign told people to stay off because dunes are fragile. Another warning: *Turn off outside lights between dusk and dawn. Turtle hatchlings rely on natural light to find the ocean.* Cool. Queen reigned over the turtle nests. The turtles needed guardians—I'd watched TV specials—everybody knew they were in trouble. I trotted close to the dunelets, hoping to spot the fresh nest, but saw no evidence.

Shell collectors, old and fat and friendly, dominated the shoreline, waving and calling, "Hey." I waved, and started my workout with an easy jog, high knees, butt kicks, and backward skips, and sprinted to the high tide line again, farther down the beach, where I stopped and poked around, searching stakes marking turtle nests. I found three wound with orange caution tape. I'd never have guessed eggs existed without the tape and posts. On one knee, sun beating my back, I pressed my palms together and prayed at each nest for the eggs to stay safe until the baby turtles hatched and found the sea. I'd memorized facts: females mate with more than one male until all her eggs got fertilized, males never left the ocean, females homed in on the same nesting sites. Turtles survived the big asteroids and the bust-up of continents. For all time, maybe. Who really knew?

A moment later, I took off. Running was how I claimed new

places. Running tranquilized me like Naomi's pills must calm her. I sped up until my hair shot out, a red torch firing these rocket legs, wind whooshing past. I concentrated on the forward lean, foot strikes, legs lifting and dropping until I floated free and loose, barely grazing the sand. I flat-out flew, tearing around the end of the island, water on three sides, then back, past a creek that could be a river, behind houses, and only then sensed somebody hurtling behind me. I poured on speed, half-scared, half-pissed. Probably a guy trying and dying to beat me.

On the beach, I stopped so fast he couldn't. We collided, our four long legs, splat!—in sand. Studying the sea, waves pounding, tide swallowing the beach, I could swear the island moved, but that could've been me, knocked cockeyed.

Shiny and dark, this guy panted, "God"—pant—"so sorry"—pant—"you OK?"

I was breathless but fine.

"Tried to catch you, but am I out of shape. I'm Renaldo."

I got up and gave this beanpole Renaldo a hand.

"No one beats me." I loped across the road to the Court.

But he did beat me there, switched on a hose, and drenched himself. Tilting his face to the sky, he drank. "Want some?" he burbled. "I live out back, in the original cottage, me and my Grandma. Queen."

"Oh. The turtle lady."

He nodded and watered me. First I got pissed, then grateful for the cool stream. In the office, I dripped on the vinyl floor and froze in the A/C, staring at another extra-tall guy—what, everyone down here descended from Amazon warriors?—this one's rusty brown beard matched his skin; that beard ate half his face, same guy I'd seen yesterday on the beach, slicing wood with a chainsaw. He yawned, stacking towels, obviously trying to keep his eyes open. When he blinked and widened his eyes, except for the beard and hair, he looked a little like Dad first thing in the morning.

"What time is it?" I practically yelled over the boisterous A/C unit. "I ran the whole island, so I'm thirsty." My hands went to my hair, a mess, like, who cared, but still. "Must be noon."

He nodded. "Just after." He smoothed rectangles of white terrycloth, folding once, twice, three times into a neat stack.

"I run a six-minute mile."

He stopped folding, reached under the counter, and produced a bottle of water. "Costs a dollar. The beach is six miles long. Did you really run it in thirty-six minutes?"

I uncapped and drained the bottle. "Didn't time it. I beat some guy following me. Pay you later. Ugh, plastic. Have you heard about the plastic accumulation zones? Five in the Pacific."

He shook his head.

"I started slow, warmed up, and ran around the back side, so, no, it took an hour. Checked out turtle nests along the way, but jetted by so fast forgot to count."

"Five."

I wagged the empty. "Recycling?"

He pointed to a corner bin. I tossed the bottle. Swish.

"Here's the spiel." He loaded a plastic laundry tub. "Welcome to the Palmetto Republic, my own little kingdom, where supreme power rests with natives."

"What's there to do in your kingdom? I'm surprised this place even showed up on Google."

He pushed a brochure across the counter. I studied it.

"Gotta know where to look. On the back side, there's a native shell civiliz—"

"Not much to see, though, is there? Dirt. Trees. Bushes."

"It's *there*. It's *been* there. Before high-minded Europeans ever washed up. You know it all if you know about that. Maybe you didn't realize our reputation for rattlesnake dens. The Rice County Chamber of Commerce won't print *that* in tourist brochures. I like it because it keeps out the riff raff. The snakes and the alligators."

Snakes. Alligators.

"They won't bother you if you don't bother them." At the door, loaded with laundry, he stopped and turned. "Here's what we don't got: water parks, pirate-themed putt putts, corporate hotels, five-star restaurants—make that no restaurants, but Patty's Pizza delivers for ten dollars, a dollar a mile from Pinesboro, the nearest town."

What kind of place was this? It was not 1950. And whoever heard of a motel manager doing laundry? Didn't they have maids?

"Gotta go. I'm swamped. Changeover day. Some people stay Sunday to Sunday."

"We're only here three days. Key West is my birthday gift, not Boneyard Beach. I need to see the Keys before they disappear. This place, too, it's going fast."

"Where's it going?" He shouldered the laundry basket and headed out, bending his knees, too tall for the door. Bet he bumped his head a lot.

"*Under*. Glaciers melting." I followed him, unsure whether he'd heard.

"No offense, but I work alone," he called over his shoulder. "Nothing personal, easier that way." He stared ahead. "Shut the door. We don't need to air condition the whole effing island."

Like I never heard the F-word. He worked alone, OK, but I didn't want to go back inside the cottage; the little kids would still be watching TV, and Naomi and Tom would be doing each other. I wanted to explore. Meet people. Plus Will seemed like what little I remembered of Dad. Naomi's boyfriends, all nice, were always not-Dads. But Will was tall. Like Dad. Gruff, on the outside. Like Dad. Maybe Dad's age. *If* Dad had survived the IED.

At the next cottage, a woman answered his knock smoking a cigarette.

"I'll take that, Mrs. Pitts." She handed it over, he puffed, and tossed it into the seashells, stomped it, and shoved clean towels at her. He dropped the dirties.

I grabbed her dirty towels to make myself useful, they were thick as the air down here, and draped them over one arm.

"No smoking in these firetraps." Will gave me a strange look for taking the towels.

"You love stealing drags from me, Altman."

"And you're too generous with the opportunities, Mrs. P." Will walked on.

"Will, wait." I jogged to keep up. "I'm Lucille. I'll be fourteen Labor Day."

He kept his pace. "Labor Day's the best day of the year. Everybody leaves but me."

At Cottage Ten, ours, Jack, in his Superman shirt, his hair crumb-infested, tossed his Frisbee and caught it, a one-boy game. He threw and threw until the Frisbee landed on the roof.

Will placed clean towels and sheets at the doorstep even though we just got here and nobody'd showered.

Jack stared up at Will. "You're tall."

"But Superman flies. Go ahead."

Jack made a pouty face. Will squatted. "Oh, all right. Crawl up."

Jack threw one leg then the other over Will's shoulders, grabbing Will's hair.

"My head, Superman, not my hair." Will glued his hands to Jack's bony thighs, rose, and walked till he stood under the roof's edge. "Can you reach that?"

Jack leaned toward the roof, Will hanging onto his legs. "Nope."

Will edged Jack closer, Jack threw his torso forward, practically onto the roof, clutching the gutter. "Got it?"

"Almost."

My nerves tightened while Jack swayed from Will's shoulders to the roof, Will holding Jack by his calves, not his thighs, Jack, midair, hands still on the gutter. Were we insured while Naomi was on leave from work? Probably not. Jack could even die if he fell and hit his head on a concrete step. I took little hops to calm myself.

Mayzie slammed our screen door, dressed like a cross between a stripper and a princess—sequined spaghetti-strap top and pink ruffled skirt. Her clothes were too small. Nobody but me had noticed.

"Wow. Is it hot or what?" Mayzie glanced up, saw Jack, and screamed her scream, which is what I felt like doing but, as substitute grownup, never did. She was right, though, the Court was on broil. These smells—fumes reeking of bleach, sunscreen, and sickly-sweet bug spray—made my stomach spin.

Moments later, Jack sat safely on Will's shoulders again, waving his Frisbee. Will lowered himself and Jack climbed down.

“Thanks!” Jack said.

“Last time.” Will walked away.

“You’ve outgrown that top, Mayzie—go change.”

“I ain’t no suit-wearing . . .”

“Shh. Do not quote *The Wire* in public.” She did this all the time.

Will passed us going the opposite way, carrying a plunger like a rifle over his shoulder.

“Lucille!” Will turned around and walked backward, away from us. “Do me a favor? Unwind the hose and water the hibiscuses?” He pointed at wilted flowers.

“You work alone, remember?”

He turned and kept walking.

Flowers drooped at doorsteps—heat-smashed. They weren’t exactly dead but they weren’t fully alive either. I switched on the outside spigot. The hose jumped to life and flooded the seashells around the plants, and soon the humpback stems stood taller—that was their capillaries drinking—their leaves fattened and their fallen heads turned fleshy. Their broad pink petals opened wide, soaking up the sun.

5

Stranded

See you Wednesday. I need this, I'm burned out. I'll text or call. Here's seventy-five dollars—be careful—. She and that guy. A posh resort. Another island.

Last night Tom had treated everybody except Mike, who rushed home, to dinner at a marina in the middle of nowhere. Yachts and tall-masted sailboats and rigged fishing boats rocked inside watery parking spaces beside a place that served seafood fresh off a boat. I drank wine mixed with water and ate salad with fresh figs. I'd never seen much less eaten a fresh fig—its pink flesh cheered my tongue. And these tiny grease bombs, hushpuppies. I could've eaten a dozen. The kids ate flounder and shrimp and red snapper but I stuck to the veggie burger. The ocean was overfished and I hated eating dead animals.

Later, half asleep, I'd heard Naomi in the tiny kitchen. Was that when she wrote this note? That possibility soured my stomach—I figured Tom had included us because he liked us, but, no, it was an adult trap.

Filling my lungs with heavy salt air, I straightened, and smoothed the skirt of my sundress, clean and white. After finding the note, I'd dressed up and laced these runners—my only shoes—and killed the run. Duh, the sibs couldn't wake up and find me gone, too. What would I tell them? The downside of being Naomi's right arm. Even if I wanted to act out, teach her a lesson—drink, smoke dope, even have sex—I couldn't because of Mayzie and Jack—plus I hated those stupid behaviors girls gossiped about.

I'd like to pretend-choke Naomi. Shake her up. But she was so fragile she'd even asked for a leave. My father's death nine years ago nearly killed her, Marco said, but she's ditched him.

The ocean crashed nearby, loud but not loud enough to drown my thoughts: You're not surprised, I told myself, Naomi'll be back and you'll shape her yellow hair into a tiny crown. It'll be just you four again. This one can't last.

What about Key West? What about My Birthday?

I switched on the hose and dragged it to the hibiscuses, offering them drinks because they'd soon wilt. "Party on, flowers. Live it up." Why hadn't I set my alarm? By the time I checked the room—her bag gaped open like a big mouth—it was too late. What did she even take? She traveled light, she always said, claiming she needed no possessions. "The things of the spirit are the most important, things you can't see or touch," she'd said, pausing while we packed, pressing her palms together at her heart and bowing her head. "Yeah, like love," I'd said, folding T-shirts and underwear and stashing them in duffels like the dutiful daughter.

"Exactly." She'd smiled like the plastic Buddha at the bottom of her purse. "We carry our important possessions in our hearts. They're our intangibles."

If possessions were so intangible, why nurse double shifts for extra money, only to change neighborhoods every May, never making a down payment on a house? She believed some perfect Naomi-place existed, someplace all full of new. This worried me and my perfect place, too: a somewhere-in-the-sun place where I could garden and plan for species survival. Naomi dragged us along as she searched, but would she even know when she got there? And new friends. Men. They made Naomi hungry, too, but I hated how she was with men. Marco was the one until . . . last spring? She got bored—or scared?—when he proposed. Namaste, Naomi, good luck—to us.

I re-read the note and inhaled sea air the way Naomi did, but couldn't hear myself because the ocean breathed the same way, only louder, sounding like Naomi's *ujayi* breath. A wave churning the ocean's ragged edge into foam. Yoga, yoga, all that talk about letting go—Naomi really had detached this time, from her own flesh and blood.

Here came Queen, slow-moving, like she was underwater, face hidden under the straw visor, tied under her chin with a leather string. "The girl with flame coming out her head."

I nodded politely. "Lucille." I wanted to brag, but didn't feel up to it, about how I beat her grandson running.

She stuck out her leather palm. "Queen. Science teacher, retired. Turtle guardian. Trash picker."

We'd met, but, whatever. "I checked out the spots where the turtle nests are."

Queen raised her head. She beamed into my face. "You don't say. You like science?"

I grabbed Queen's hand, hoping the old woman could look deeper inside me and tell me not only more about turtles, but more about myself. I held onto the withered claw, wondering how much of what she once knew Queen could remember, because it was never too early to think about next year's science fair. I tested her: "How old are turtles, Miss Queen, compared to dinosaurs?"

"Dinosaurs came first but died out 65 million years ago."

I struggled to dream myself into what little prehistory I knew.

Queen finished my sentence: "Survived whatever killed the dinos, but they've got new trouble. Could kill 'em all. We guard the nests, to make sure the babies hatch and crawl to sea. Oh, I could tell you stories . . . if you've a mind to listen. Sea turtles were related to reptile fossils, thirteen feet long and sixteen feet wide, that turned up in South Dakota when the U.S. of A. was mostly ocean." Her blue eyes shone from deep slits in her dark face.

"It'll be ocean again—soon."

"We hope for the best, don't we?" Queen waited.

Was I supposed to agree?

"Don't we, young lady?" A school teacher voice.

Hope? Nope. I tipped my head—a nod was less of a lie.

"Tonight, we'll sit awhile outside. Meantime, do me one favor.

Don't catch the air on fire with that hair." She trooped across the seashells with her load, hooting at her own joke.

I assumed mountain pose—eyes shut, palms out—breathing in sync with each neon beat, trying to gain detachment. Someone started whistling "Rock You Like a Hurricane." Another day, I'd twirl circles and shut out the world. Not today.

When I opened my eyes, here was Beard, hair sticking out like nerve endings.

"I'm getting the paper. Need anything?"

I could have enlightened him, but opted for no comment. Who still read newspapers?

He stood, without a word, pointing at the dunes across the road. Finally, he said, "Great day coming."

My eyes followed his finger. The sun had hauled itself up and now dripped orange over the grasses, the scrubby bushes, the sandy path, even the water was on fire.

"I know where the ocean is." I clenched my teeth.

He slapped his forehead. "Right. You're not dressed for the beach. Church? You missed it—today's Monday."

I crossed my eyes and chewed my bottom lip.

"You're right. Me? Commenting on clothes? Not the way I dress." He looked down at his T-shirt and cutoffs. "Sorry, Lucille."

"Stop calling me Lucille. I hate that name. I wish the ocean would jump the dune and swallow Boneyard, get it over with. This big glacier in Antarctica's melting from underneath. I hate everything."

"Whoa, ease up. Everything?"

"Not turtles. Why didn't you switch off the neon sign?"

"Timer. Off at dusk, on at dawn. Let's start over. What's the deal with hating your name? Old fashioned, but Lucille beats Bree, Brittany, Briana—all the renters' kids this year had B names."

"It's a grandma name."

"Nah. It's yours. You're no grandma." He knitted the two furry caterpillars crawling above his eyes.

I didn't even have one, not one I knew.

"Your brother and sister sleeping?"

"That or watching TV. FYI, I'm skipping my run due to circumstances beyond my control. FYI, I run with the boys."

Will mouthed *Wow.* "FYI, maybe you're right about a new name." He scratched his beard. "How about Lucky?"

I didn't know what to make of that word. Luck mattered. Naomi and Dad had needed luck. I needed luck to survive childhood. The planet needed luck. But luck required work.

"Well? Lucky?"

"Speed is discipline not luck." My feet tingled. Sprints. Miles. I couldn't dump Jack and Mayzie while I ran. Too many beach oddballs. Queen roaming the beach monitoring turtles and trash, all for the good, sure, but normal? No. And Will? The hermit with no face?

"Do kids drink coffee? Want some?" Will started toward his cottage.

I never drank coffee. I should fix the kids' cereal. I knew zip about the guy. He looked like old pictures I'd seen of that Unabomber dude, but that was just the beard. He was fine, right?

6

Mortimer

Will held the door for Lucille, his dimwit antennae vibrating—was it kosher for a guy his age to be alone with this teenage girl? She was upset. Fuck what people thought. He'd heard their Voyager roll out earlier.

She walked to the far end of the porch and stared.

"You can see Cottage Ten from here." At his workbench, an old picnic table, he reflexively wiped condensation from a knife and three gouges.

"I need to hydrate."

Hydrate? Will went inside for water. Why didn't people just say "drink water" anymore? He brought back coffee and water. "H2O for the athlete."

She drained the glass, set it down, and toed off first one athletic shoe, then the other, while he sipped a scorched mouthful, alternately eyeing her and the paper's headline about some fools destroying turtle nests. Her forehead showed wavy lines she was way too young for, and two marks dented the corners of her frowning mouth.

She opened her fist and offered him a paper wad. He smoothed it and read the loopy scrawl, then handed it back. Sweat ran from his pits and collected at his waist. He stalled, waiting for decent words.

"Well, gosh." Brilliant.

"They're going to Cumb-er-land." Lucille enunciated each syllable. "A native word?"

"Nah. Some British royal who probably never set foot on the sand."

She balanced on one leg, then the other, and peeled off her socks. "Boneyard's a weird name, too, like a cemetery."

"Tree cemetery. The tides wash deadfall—trees, limbs, and what have you, in and out, sand buries and unburies, and the sun bleaches this driftwood—huge oaks, hickory, sometimes complete with roots—till it's skeletal-looking."

He checked his watch. "You missed your run, why not go? I'll watch for your brother and sis." He offered, even as he scowled at his unfinished sculptures. Lucille looked suspicious; she, at least, saw through his fake-kind offer.

"I'm not dressed out. I changed after I read the note, half-expecting something like this after Tom stayed over."

She took a deep breath. Told him how this guy Tom took them to dinner, how they ordered every single thing they wanted, and how they ate *hush puppies*, had he, Will, ever eaten *hush puppies*, best food ever, and sweet potato fries. She'd heard her mother in the night.

"I should've gotten up," and here she raised her eyes, cut them left, right, then stared straight at Will. "How was I supposed to know she was writing that note?"

Silence. He shook his head and swallowed hard.

"I dressed because I might need to explain, to you, or somebody, maybe even the police—," she stopped and gave him another look, with ice blue eyes. "Wanted to look grownup, in case I had to go somewhere or do something to contact them. And the cell service here—doesn't work with our phones. Wi-Fi fades in and out. Mostly out."

He had no excuse. "Dead zone."

Even in her dress, Lucille executed a round of perfect squats, her eyes on their cottage.

Will counted twenty before she paused.

"Relax. She *will* be back." He remembered the woman—she wouldn't remember him—from fourteen years ago—hard-on material for a sixteen-year-old, but the way that military man, presumably Lucille's father, stayed at her side, marked him as an officer Will wouldn't have messed with.

She bobbed her head. Nerves and anger seemed to fuel the squats. His own pushup-jogging workouts happened too few and too far between, and, this minute, her circumstance fanned the embers inside his own cauldron of crazy. Why'd he imagine he could help?

"Y'all go ahead and take care of yourselves, fine with me, and, seeing as you're nearly fourteen, you're plenty grown."

She squatted low and held, pulsing. Girl must have quads of iron.

Still pulsing, she said, "Who would care?"

"State's got 'guidelines' about how old you gotta be to stay overnight with kids, even siblings." Neglect was not uncommon at the Court. Parenting styles ran from overprotective—kids with no freedom—to kids that ran wild. It was the latter worrying Will. Lucille seemed responsible, but looks were just that—appearances.

She finally stood from her marathon squat. "I'm not lucky."

He leaned, palms flat on his workbench, trying to think wise thoughts. He stretched both legs behind him. Yesterday, he'd noticed her gumption. "You're tough, too badass to mess with. You're smart. You got nervous when your brother climbed on my shoulders, that's your lucky brain genes. And, you gave a rip about your sister's clothes, which makes her lucky." What the hell, he was no psychologist. Does that come with a manager title?

"Besides, we're a full-service establishment here at Palmetto Tourist Court, though babysitting's extra." He was joking, but, on second thought, *could* he charge a fee? Will knew this Tom, a developer salivating over the last available morsel of Cumberland, a few hundred acres.

"We? Who's we?" She hurled the words.

Will dropped down to earth. "Me and the 'team' here in the Palmetto Republic. We'll keep an eye on y'all."

Uh oh. More squats.

"Don't you dare tell," she managed on the inhale, and, "I'm used to this," on the exhale.

Poor kid hadn't learned to control her facial expressions, though, which said she was shocked he was telling her. She'd be wrecked if she knew he'd calculated cost of care.

She froze. "This is *not your* problem. We don't need your *eye*."

"You're not a problem, but you're missing one crucial detail. Sheriff Trip, my buddy, owns this place. He and I are tight; it would be easy for me to inform him, maybe even illegal if I didn't, that your mother left you kids, minors, alone."

She processed this intel on her face: scrunched mouth and twitching brows.

"I've been the family grownup since my father got IED'd. I was five. I'm not and never have been a kid.

"My mother needs me. She nurses overnight, a lot, or used to before she took leave from her job in labor and delivery, so crazy-hard she takes *coping* pills. When I'm sixteen, I'll get a real job with real pay, but till then I'm in charge of the family, if that makes sense."

Will was ready to charge a widow for his silence about the kids' staying alone? Altman, you asshole. Not the mother, Tom, but still.

"So, you're saying Georgia's made independence illegal."

"Guess that's right. Like I said . . ."

Lucille resumed her squats. "She"—inhale—"needs me"—exhale—"more than ever."

"Yeah? How come?"

Lucille clammed up.

He was on the hook. Unlike Lucille, Will was allergic to responsibility, a noble gig until you had other people's lives in your hands, which is what his manager title was earning him. The market would start Friday morning. He needed to make art or a reasonable facsimile. He hunched over the workbench, hiding his expression, his fear of screwing up his watch and work, and consulted the three-foot-by-five-foot slab, waiting for whatever attention he could muster.

"Oh, she'll be back. We're going to Key West Wednesday. You'll have lots of time to work. We're fine on our own till then. Perfectly fine. Perfectly."

Will saved the polite smile until later when he'd really need it. This girl may be a master manager of her siblings, more power to her, but what the hell? He dropped to the concrete and pumped out a dozen anxiety-killing pushups. His racing pulse reminded him he was alive, all by itself a responsibility. He got up. Refolding the newspaper, he caught the sea turtle headline again—what was wrong with people, stealing turtle eggs? People sometimes stole children, too.

She stopped moving, eyes on him, jaw open. "Pushups are hard."

"Nah. Just practice." In his prime—when *was* that anyway?—he'd done a hundred a day.

A moisture-loaded breeze pushed at the screen. Will caught and inhaled it; clammy air struggled through his lungs. He exhaled, picked up the half-inch gouge, and quickly fluted the edges of the slab, once a fat live oak limb, 100-year-old barn salvage, rich with bloodstains, wormways and sweet-swirling grain. He'd stored more at the *Loblolly*, but now it was char.

Next, he drove the quarter-inch gouge partway in, hung fire, waiting for the wood to guide him.

The girl's eyes stayed on him—he felt her cold stare and looked up. "See here, I'm no parent." Her eyes bored holes in his, and, for a moment, their eyes, hers as cold and blue as he knew his were, clashed.

"But I know about distraction: ketchup on broccoli, wipes, Band-Aids, Benadryl but no aspirin. All I don't know is how we'll make it to Key West and back before school starts."

She made her caretaking case, or maybe she was teaching him.

"Key West is paradise. Jimmy Buffett said so back before I was born. I need to snorkel and see the Florida Reef—third biggest coral reef in the *world*, biggest in the continental U.S.—before everything dies."

He wished she'd shut up. She did. Neither said anything for some minutes. The silence intensified the sounds of the surf spilling and draining, the slam of cans in the Coke machine. Kid-voices crescendoed outside. Mayzie and Jack trooped onto the porch. Mayzie, thumb in her mouth, handed Lucille an oversized orange tote bag.

"How'd you find me?" Lucille stashed the bag under the workbench.

Mayzie removed her thumb. Today, she wore two T-shirts and an orange skirt-thing over shorts. "Wanted mom. Came outside and heard you and him talking. Court's filling up, huh?"

"Don't remind me," Will said. "Labor Day insanity. Things won't calm down till a week from today. Labor Day brings out the crazy tourists—punched-in screens and punched-out people, I fix both. People crank up on booze or pills and disturb the peace or wreck cottages."

He traced the grooves he'd cut, wondering what to do next, half-dreaming, since Mayzie'd brought it up, of fall. After Labor Day, people desert the island, leaving him solo, his native state.

He glanced up. Mayzie stared at him. She slipped her thumb back in her mouth. "Where IS Mom?"

"Here, try mine." Will extended his thumb. "A little dirty, but . . ." Why didn't they try Tabasco or mittens? This kid had to be at least seven.

Mayzie turned away. "You're mean. Besides, that is the biggest, dirtiest thumb I ever saw!" She folded herself into a beat-up wicker armchair and opened the newspaper, but he saw it shaking with the girl's laughter.

"You're an intelligent kid—and you don't even know me yet."

"Yeah, where's Mom?" Jack clutched the corner of Will's workbench, squatted, and shot into the air, squealing.

"Quit it," Lucille said. "How can Will work if you wiggle the table? Mom'll be back."

"Oh. With who? From where?" Jack asked.

"How about carving a pterodactyl, Jack?" What was it to Will if Jack knew his mother ran off? It just felt like something the kid didn't need to hear. "My grandfather taught me to carve when I was five—you're at least five, am I right?" Will sandpapered the tip of a small knife, dulling it, and stood behind Jack, his arms around Jack's skinny shoulders, his hands covering Jack's tiny hands. "Carve away from your body, like this." Jack peeled a few curls from the pine.

"Pterodactyls get big as this house at night." Jack clumped the wood scrap across the workbench.

Will drew back. "Do they bust open roofs?"

"Nope, they stick their heads out the windows till the sun gets up."

"Whew. Otherwise, I'd have a ton of work."

Jack lost interest and dropped to all fours, sneaking up on Monk, Will's cat, who hightailed it outside.

Lucille picked among scraps, and selected an eight-inch, rough-cut piece of sycamore.

"What were you thinking when you carved this? It looks like a bird, dazed and hurt, with its wings glued shut. I'll feather it, carve little lines. Free its wings so it can fly." She palmed the wood. "You could've imagined it differently."

"Did I ask for a critique? How old did you say you were?"

She grinned. "Fourteen, one week from today. Labor Day."

"You sure are opinionated for fourteen."

Mayzie lowered the paper and nodded vigorously.

Lucille said nothing. She rubbed her fingers over what she called a bird. Pointing at the work under his hands, she said, "Those marks around the edge? That border? It traps the image, whatever's waiting to come out."

He'd penciled a crude sketch of a dock, a boat, a tree.

"That does not make the grade. Why copy nature? Go abstract. Don't try so hard to make it look all real." She tossed her hair. "The thing about nature is making people notice it. Like those birds in oil? They didn't even look like birds once they got all gooed-up. When they turned into black freaks with wings stuck to their bodies, people started looking close. We were shocked by how unreal reality really is. Like Jack's pterodactyl? Doesn't look real."

"Pterodactyls was real!" Jack shouted.

"As I was saying, it's better than reality because it makes people wonder and dream about dinosaurs." Lucille went back to her bird.

Will retreated inside his head, mulling her words, which reminded him of his Army buddy Monk. Lucille's philosophy was different, but her idea was the same—touch the soul. For Monk, a mistake reminded you of your humanity. These thoughts set off flashes, not of Monk for a change, but of Belva's leaf, the one she'd smeared when her husband left her. Will wished he could smile, but this day, this moment, with dust motes billowing inside random sun patches, felt rickety, the air held potential for chaos. He needed to put the workbench, his alt-reality, to rights and get to work.

Mayzie snapped the newspaper.

"Lucky, that bird looks good."

"Good! I've hardly started." She selected his *special,* curved-blade knife, the Flex-Cut, and dug "C" shapes into the wings.

He wanted to tell her about wabi-sabi and Monk, but language failed him like when he first mustered out, when he cussed and ranted. Behind the wheel, he'd threaten to kill tailgaters, or drivers who cut him off.

Lucille's voice broke his thought pattern. "Suggestions?"

He held his breath and swallowed hard. Her bird looked more fiction than fact. Speckled wings. She was polka-dotting the bird with the awl; its round eyes looked sadly out at the world.

She laid down the awl and got up, squatted, stepped side-to-side, and curled her hamstrings. She scooped up her bird and perched it on her palm. "The big heavy bird is ready to fly." She put the bird to her cheek. "Your name's Mortimer."

Mayzie whipped her braids side-to-side. "He looks lonely."

"Everything looks lonely to you, Mayzie." Lucille spoke gently.

A moment of silence. "Sorry, Will. I can't help taking charge. I'm the smartest kid in my grade, too smart to follow stupid rules like getting a permission slip to use the bathroom. And my bio teacher? Mrs. Kelly's got a mustache, and she skipped frog dissection after kids complained about cruelty, never mind that frog biology could help future scientists preserve habitat. Frogs are losing their homes. What's more important than habitat?"

She paused for breath, staring at Mortimer.

Will had no comment on habitat or home. Did his own shell of a place count? As home? Or habitat? Outside, the wind was a faraway noise, faint and harmless, but who could say what was coming?

"People need to wake up. Otherwise, we'll be extinct, sooner, not later."

"I sympathize, I really do." He'd contributed. "Believe me, you have my full attention."

"You're lying."

Will bowed and rose, sweeping both arms up.

"Welcome to the world of grownups."

7

Habitat

We trailed Will across the Court, me carrying my orange tote, past two gi-normous trees with big fat limb-legs sprawling on the ground, down the bank, and dropped inside the creek's bed. Low tide. I'd run past this sea of grass yesterday, when it was full of water.

Tramping around the edges of cordgrass clumps, *Spartina alterniflora*—I'd read the plant name in the brochure—the muck sucked at our feet and splattered my dress.

I gripped Jack's and Mayzie's hands. A gun handle poked from Will's back pocket. The sight dizzied and nauseated me. This was America, where men who seemed nice shoot people for no reason. Plus, guns *accidentally* kill people all the time. Would Naomi come back if she saw us on TV dead?

"What's that gun for? Want me to carry it? Stick it in my bag." This way, I'd be in control.

"Nah." He stopped, we stopped, first me, Jack, then Mayzie. Will turned toward us. "Rattlers. Gun making you nervous? Or is it only me? It's loaded but I'd have to cock it and pull the trigger to fire. You'd have time to run."

Mayzie and Jack laughed. Me, too, but mine was fake.

Will about-faced and plodded forward. Behind me, Mayzie and Jack chattered. I caught words: *loaded* and *cock it* and *pull the trigger*. Keeping my voice low, I told Will Naomi mourned war-damaged Dad—after nine years. "We brought his ashes so we can scatter them."

Will turned his head enough for me to see his face fall. Even his beard seemed to wilt.

None of this information should've escaped my big mouth.

He marched us forward.

At first, I'd gotten pumped about crossing to the wild side of the island; though the clouds were scooting across wide sky, the grasses stayed golden. But the gun had played with my mind. These creeks flood with tide, every six hours. This trip struck me as a looming disaster. On TV, during storms, cars even slid off bridges and into rivers. This creek qualified as a river. People could die. When *exactly* would the tide fill the creek to the brim? Here we were, stuck in the mud between the strip of barrier beach and the thick forest.

Yards and yards later, we reached the other side. Will scrambled up the bank first. He pulled Jack, then Mayzie, their feet dragging mud. I grabbed handfuls of sharp grasses, hauled up my own self, and ruined my dress. We followed him down a path—trees and shrubs and tangly vines with prickles—ending at a set of rotted steps that led to a boardwalk skirting the marsh. A dented brown sign topped a metal pole. Somebody'd scraped out the word "Indians" and replaced it with "Native Americans."

"Right. People are so stupid." I couldn't resist.

Will shot me a dumb look, then smile-smirked. "OK. I get it." He read out loud:

Native American shell rings harbor the debris of daily living: oyster shells, bones, potshards, and more. They're located above the highest daily tides. The calcium in shells and bones—

Wait. Bones? What was this place?

— acidify the soil and preserve nearly four thousand years of civilization, recording the first human architecture on the East Coast. Natives inhabited the Orcoosa Shell Rings until the estuary's salinity levels changed, forcing them to migrate after about 200 years.

Salinity. Salt.

Jack frowned. "You said we were going someplace cool!"

"Did you build this, Will?" Mayzie squinted. "Wow. How long did that take?"

Will shook his head. "It's a trash pile. Inside the dirt, you can see what Native Americans, or whoever they were, made or trashed—broken pots, oyster shells, beads."

"Gross," Jack said, in his automatic way.

Will scowled.

Mayzie saw her chance to get in good with Will. "How old is it again, Will? You didn't build it? Somebody built it."

"Yeah." Will sat on the boardwalk and dangled his legs over the mud. "That somebody would be four, maybe five thousand years old. My family used to picnic out here, and look for antlers and bones and shells and pottery made into beads. No idea how or why these people built these rings—two soccer fields big, Jack. You can't see how big because of the trees and bushes and vines growing inside."

Jack dribbled an imaginary soccer ball. "They played soccer?"

"No, idiot." Mayzie glanced at Will and corrected him, too. "You probably aren't allowed to take stuff home from here. That's what Lucille is always telling us."

She stared at me and so did the others, maybe because I hadn't said a single syllable. My mouth opened but nothing bubbled out. Too hot inside. How can brain-formed words make sense of a place where everything is buried but alive? The wide open marsh on one side, the tall, chattering trees on the other, the sculpted earth, these shells shooting to the surface like something dying to get out. Native spirits were down there. Fishing and eating and living lives I couldn't imagine and making me, my sister, my brother, even my mother and Will, and Dad, seem *related*. Queen, too, and her grandson. These people. Here. Like us. Spirits.

"How many shell rings have they found?" I ducked under the railing and dropped to the dirt, scooped two handfuls of black, rich soil, and sifted it through my fingers; I found broken shells and whole ones, too. How did those natives live? "What kind are these?" I held up a large shell, pearly inside—ugly and rough on the outside.

"Oysters. Bury it back, so it won't decompose."

Does anyone even know what those people looked like? Who wrote their stories? Anybody? All we knew was what archaelogists learned from the dirt. I had tons of questions, but Will probably didn't know many answers.

"Hundreds of these exist, up and down the South Atlantic coast, other places in the world, too," Will said, "three here, but water's already swallowed one; this is the biggest."

"What are potshards?" Mayzie asked.

"Bits of pottery. Pieces," Will said.

"But, Will, Native Americans? It's just wrong. We're not in India or wherever Columbus thought he was headed. Native Americans makes it sound like they lived in America, but there was no America then."

"It's an old sign." Will said this like he was sorry.

"Not that old. They ate berries, nuts, seeds, fruits, and shellfish. Wait. It *was* a trash pile."

"Yep. But is it only a trash heap?" Will asked. "Native Americans didn't waste much. Maybe they used the trash."

"What for?" Mayzie plopped down beside Will. "Necklaces? Made from shells?"

"Yeah, maybe art, or ceremonial stuff. The place took your breath away when you realized what it was, right?"

Mayzie nodded.

"Maybe they lived inside the ring of shells, maybe the shells protected them. This big one's full of sparkleberry, holly, sassafras, pines, and sycamores, but, back in their day, the land was probably clear. The calcium in the shells changes the soil, and that's how archaeologists know so much even after thousands of years. They drill the shells and analyze the dust to find out how old the shells are. They can even tell what season they were harvested. Without the calcium, the shells would've disintegrated."

"So the natives *are* telling us how they lived! And the civilization lasted four thousand years?" I had to know.

"Two hundred." Will twisted to look at me. "They left; we're not sure why."

"I know! Sea levels changed salt concentrations, the sign said so. That hurt fish harvests. It's happened before. It's happening today."

"Maybe. Two hundred years in this place, then people moved on."

"Like we'll be forced to do. I give us maybe three years before this place is underwater." I shouted. I paced the boardwalk, minding the gaps. This wasn't history, this was now. We'd go extinct. Maybe in my lifetime. Didn't anyone care? Why did everyone act like nothing was wrong?

"Native Americans! We named them. We killed them. And now we're killing the earth."

"We didn't kill these Indians, did we, Will? She's wrong, isn't she?" Mayzie was crying.

"Nah. These Indians came before we did." Will got up. "The tribe's descendants who called this place home, Queen's ancestors, mine, too, cause we're related, practically everybody who lives here's kin to everybody else—they were from here, maybe a dozen tribes came after the people who built these shell rings—middens, that's another name for the rings."

Clicking and buzzing blended with the swish of tree branches and leaves rubbing leaves. Antsy. All life down here was antsy.

"At least," Will paused, "they didn't flatten them with bulldozers."

"Who did that?" Mayzie stared down.

Will didn't answer. He turned us around, and down the disintegrating boards we stepped.

At the bottom, he faced us, flipped his palms to the sky, and said, "Our tribe."

Low tide had emptied the creek, so, OK, the tide wouldn't strand us, but Will forked onto a whole 'nother path, in the opposite direction. "I'll show you guys my habitat—interested?" But by the time he explained, we'd snarled ourselves in barbed vines, and Will had to lift twisted stems and knife away razor fronds that scratched our legs and made us itch, muttering, "Damn doghobble."

My sundress? Ruined, briar-snagged. I didn't care. The magic of the shell rings had mutated into ugly feelings that fought inside me because I could not believe this world passed for civilization. Even smart people acted stupid. OK, so I paid *too* much attention, read *too* much, how else would I know important facts like how it takes twenty-five tons of compressed ocean life—minute sea animals like periwinkles, millions of years old—to produce one *quart* of *gasoline*? The thought of peoples' stupidity still sickened me so much I thought I might throw up, but I hadn't eaten much today, none of us had. Will must exist on air.

In no time—no spacey warp, no fuzzy edges—we'd entered Will's World, which I saw could double as a setting for an end-of-time movie, starring a gun-toting good guy. At least, I hoped he'd play the good guy and not suddenly go . . . well, crazy.

A clearing. Dirt. Black on top with spots of green poking up; in the surrounding woods stood wounded and dead trees, sooty and still smelling of fire. Flame had licked the ground and burned the bark of trees deep into the forest. At the edge of the woods, away from the fire-ruined house, I spotted a rectangle staked off with wire, cinderblocks at each corner. Bright blue plastic, weighed down with more blocks, covered a bulky load.

A shell of a house sat in the middle, its only surviving feature a set of concrete steps that led to nothing but caved-in walls and a melted roof.

In the apocalypse movie I ran in my head, characters belly-crawled, dug roots, picked berries and ate them or dirt, but we plopped on the steps and shared our six stale PB&J halves four ways. Even Will ate a half.

"Feast your eyes on the nothing left of the *Loblolly*."

Will said this sadly, I thought.

The name meant mudhole, he said, and his great-great somebody built it from cypress and pine trees with axes. They used drawknives. I'd never heard of a drawknife, but could imagine the house sheltering generations of somebodies.

"*Mudhole*. Cool name."

"Think so?" Will smiled at me.

How many years was a generation? And how'd it feel to even have a home? And then a wrecked home?

"What started the fire?" Did they even have a fire department around here? In Detroit, I heard sirens day and night.

"Lightning."

"Are you sure?" Mayzie twisted her braids, her black eyes darted from the house to Will, playing detective. "Maybe you burned it to get insurance money? Or hired someone to burn it? Anybody hate you? How come there's no fire department down here?"

"I'd been living at the Court awhile; after my mother died, I rarely came over here. Except for giving her clothes away, I hadn't dealt with the household goods. By the time I found out about the fire—someone reported smoke to Trip—fire trucks came, but too late. And," he looked at Mayzie, "I'd let the homeowners' insurance policy lapse. Bad luck, bad decisions."

"Couldn't you see the smoke?" Jack asked.

"Smelled it, too late. Wind blew landward that day—'cause of a thunderstorm."

Jack and Mayzie finished eating and tore around the clearing. Jack peeked under the blue tarp. "What're you hiding under there?"

"Lumber. I'm rebuilding the workshop first, and the house when I get enough money."

"Everything? Burned?" This seemed impossible.

He nodded, his face expressionless, maybe he felt dazed.

"What was the worst thing you lost? You been inside?" I stare at the glassless windows.

They stare back.

He shook his head. "Nothing left."

"How do you know if you haven't been inside?"

"I've nosed around. Biggest loss was the old turtle shell, a loggerhead that belonged to my father, caught before that was illegal."

Wow. People caught and killed sea turtles? I shook my head.

Jack raced from the workshop site to a falling-down wire fence around rotting vegetable plants. Shriveled tomatoes on vines. The whole place stank of dying plants, wood, earth. A sweet smell, rich, even with the fire stench locked in everything. Dead plant life was fertilizer.

"Weeds." Will saw me staring at the garden. "Nobody's planted there for three years."

"Plants are growing." I pointed to a blooming sunflower.

"They reseed themselves. Plants do that."

"We do, too. Humans."

"So we do." His voice sounded surprised.

Mayzie ran over and tried to climb the fence.

"Mayzie, stay in the clearing. Who knows what kind of varmints lurk in those tall weeds? Snakes." Will patted his gun. "My mother knew Latin names for plants."

"Why don't you grow food? You could come over and tend plants, harvest fresh vegetables. Five a day, like the food pyramid says."

"Too many deer. They break fences, eat everything. And wild hogs."

Hogs! Hadn't considered hogs. "Not sunflowers. Not rotten tomatoes." That giant yellow blossom wobbled, too huge for the stalk. "This sunflower needs water. It hasn't rained since we landed here."

Will took giant steps to a low, round concrete structure and slid off its cover.

"Here's my well. I haven't had electricity to run the pump since the fire, right, so I uncover the well when Trip and I use water to mix concrete."

We'd never seen a well. We studied its depth. We couldn't see water.

"How far down does it go?" Does the well reach into an aquifer?

"I'd need to look that up but the paperwork burned."

Jack could barely see over the edge so Will lifted him. Jack hollered his name into the deep and his voice bounced back as though another boy was calling Jack. We took turns playing echo. It was eerie, and I wondered whether those underground aquifers were clean. Or did chemicals leak down and down?

Will wrapped his hands around the rope and lowered the bucket. It took a minute to hit water. A few minutes later, he hauled the bucket to the edge.

"How'd you know it was full?" Mayzie reached into to the bucket. "Cold."

"Feel, it's heavy," Will said.

We took turns feeling the weight of water. I found out about heavy water when I struggled out from under that wave. Mayzie and I together lugged the bucket to the sunflower and dumped it.

"How long did you live here, Will?" Mayzie returned the bucket to Will. "Your whole life? You're old. You'll be dead by the time I'm your age."

"Shh. He will not." Will might die before Mayzie reached his age but I hoped not.

Will only grinned and raised his eyes to the sky. "Thirty next March. I lived here till about three years ago, minus six years in the army. But this place is five times my age. It's my—as Lucille would say—habitat. I've gotta rebuild, don't I?"

Habitat: *The place where a person or thing is usually found.* This seemed truer of Will than anyone I'd met—where was my habitat? Detroit didn't feel like habitat, even though it was where I was usually found. For Will, though I'd known him, like, not even two days, he was a tree, maybe not a tree, but an endangered species in the forest, a man, no, not a man, a creature—not only the beard, but the way he had no real job you go to every day, but worked alone in his habitat, with materials he gathered from his habitat. He'd never leave this marsh place. It belonged to him and he belonged to the marsh. *Loblolly. Mudhole.* It was him.

"We could help. I like carving. And I can hammer." Jack bounced on tiptoes.

"Thanks, pal, but it's too big a job even for me, and I've framed whole houses. Trip's helping."

"Sheriff Trip?" Uh oh. I shivered. What if Will told him about Naomi leaving?

Will nodded.

I walked slowly around the clearing, inhaling the sooty smell mixed with the fresh summery smell—trees and dirt, memorizing the light streaming through the trees. In case I never came back. Even wrecked and roasted, Loblolly was mysteriously magic.

"Let's go, Will. Tide'll be in soon." I'd hate to get stuck here overnight.

On the narrow path back to the creek, Will led, Mayzie, then Jack and I brought up the rear. Now Jack stopped fast, and I nearly knocked him down. Mayzie ran back to us. *Choum*. A fat, loud pop. God. Gunshot. *Choum*. I clapped both my hands over Jack's ears.

The shot shut out the world.

"What? What's going on? What is wrong with you?" I screamed louder than I ever had.

Will, without turning, called, "No worries. Rattler."

Jack ran to Will. "Get back. He can still bite."

"You shot it dead. Can I have the skin?" Jack squatted nearby.

From a couple of yards away, Mayzie and I froze and stared. It was big, not only long, but thick. First snake I'd seen except on TV; a snake's nervous system took time to register death. How long would it take a person to die?

"Let's let the skin go back to nature," Will said.

I couldn't, but wanted, to see Will's face. His voice cracked; that told me to stay quiet.

Finally Will said, "Y'all, I hate to kill a living thing—that rattler was defending his territory. Instinct for both of us."

Mayzie's dark face went ashy, and Jack danced around, hyper. A few moments later, when we passed, we walked around the carcass, leaving space between us and the snake, its black skin patterned with diamond shapes. Will had blown its head off.

"Necessary." He motioned us around. "Native cultures worshipped snakes, makes sense around here because rattlers are everywhere. Snakes protect sacred spaces. The rattles, in some cultures, were used to heal."

We trudged to the creek. "Will, can I fire that gun?" Mayzie opened her palm.

"No." I stepped between her and Will.

"Take it." He placed it in Mayzie's hand. "It's a revolver."

She stared. Jack's mouth fell open. I did not like this.

"My turn, my turn." Jack glued his eyes to Mayzie's palm.

"It's heavy."

"Put it away." I did not like the gun, but the gun even fascinated me; Dad would've had one, maybe not this make, but he would've carried a service handgun. I'd read all about the weapons my father used.

"Can I shoot?" Mayzie asked.

Will pocketed the revolver and guided Mayzie, then Jack, down the creek bank. "OK, down here, there'll be no stray bullets. Everybody gets one shot, then I'll have two left in case I see another varmint."

"What's a varmint?" I asked.

"Critters you don't like or who don't like you. Or get underfoot, like y'all."

"If we killed every animal that bothered us, we'd kill useful parts of the food chain."

"Lucky, you are so right."

An odd look crossed his face as he showed Mayzie to hold the gun two-handed, and clamped his oversized ones over her small ones.

"Never point a gun at anything you don't mean to shoot. Usually guns have safeties, but this is a revolver, there's no need for a safety because it's got a hammer. See?" Will pulled back a small lever on top. "Aim into the bank, aim at that grass clump."

"There's life in there." I yelled in a weak voice.

"There's life everywhere, you're smashing some with your feet. Stand back, Jack, you, too, Lucille. Mayzie, there's a bad guy in the grass. Tell him to scram."

Mayzie took a deep breath and spit, then called, "*I do dirt, too, but never shot nobody not in the game.*"

How she memorized these *Wire* lines I'd never know.

"Pretty good." Will squinted into the distance, the jumble of forest. "How about this? *Get your ass out, this is American democracy, let's show 'em how it's done.*"

Silence. Mayzie was the first to laugh, why? Was this a line from *The Wire*? She screamed, "What he said!"

Will moved her pointer finger into the trigger place. "Pull. Steady, smooth."

"I'm trying."

Will slid his finger over hers. Together they fired.

End of the world loud.

This time, the ringing in my ears didn't fade. Why hadn't I clapped my hands over Mayzie's ears?

"Next time, we'll use ear protection. It's no big deal for me, my hearing's shot, but you kids are young. Can you hear nature? She makes a beautiful racket. You ought to listen to a cricket symphony."

We shook our heads, not knowing what to make of this sudden music lecture. Dad had gone nearly deaf. Naomi hadn't been able to talk to him anymore, "but it wasn't only his hearing," she'd told me, "it was his brain, scrambled." How scrambled was Will's brain?

Will took Jack's hands in his own, and I clamped my arms over Jack's ears and stuck my fingers in mine. Mayzie stuffed her ears, too, with both thumbs, but even before Jack and Will fired, I shook all over, though I hadn't touched the gun. The noise—I couldn't describe that any better than I could spill my hot feelings about the shell civilization.

I didn't want a turn. The sky clouded. The breeze died. My ears could still hear the trickle of the tide coming in. I dragged my feet forward, and kept going, leading us along the roots of the grasses. We slapped mosquitoes spearing our bare flesh and sucking our blood. What would come next, West Nile? Worse?

Will took Mayzie's and Jack's hands; inside the creek bed, sun behind the clouds, I sensed, rather than saw the paths threading through the grassy banks, leading to the Court. We neared land, and the massive cloud broke. The sun spewed rays like lava.

That night in our cottage, we picked at our fried bologna sandwiches. We, too, were fried. Mayzie took a forever tub-soak and Jack fell asleep before he cleaned up and without brushing his teeth; I didn't dare comb his tangles and wake him. I watched Mayzie wipe steam from the bathroom mirror and primp: She undid her braids and fluffed her long, black hair. Later, I caught her using my iPad trying to reach Marco. "Don't tell him Naomi's not here, OK? He'd worry, and he needs to prepare for the new school year. We'll be home next week. You'll have lots of time. And we're fine, aren't we?"

She climbed in bed. I tucked her in tight.

"Shouldn't I tell him since there's no grownup?" She put her thumb in her mouth.

I pretended to consider her idea. "I'm the one you always have, just like when Naomi's working. But suppose you do tell Marco. Suppose he drives down. He wouldn't arrive till tomorrow night. And Naomi's coming back the very next day, Wednesday, when we go to Key West. But Marco starts school Thursday. See? How long and hard that drive would be for him? Besides, Naomi and Marco broke up."

Tears laced her lashes. I'll be kinder tomorrow, I told myself, wondering if Naomi found what she wanted on Cumberland Island.

On the porch, I curled into a rocker and watched the night fall. Batwings fluffed the air and fireflies sparked in bushes and trees.

Queen, without her hat, white hair aglow, opened the screen, and silently took a seat, leaned forward, and rasped-croaked. Awwk. Or something. Was she sick? A moment later, a creature from outside sounded the same call.

"What was that noise?" I asked.

She *awwked* again. Animal talk.

I mimicked Queen's voice, sound I dragged from deep in my chest. In the quarter-moon, perched in that chair, she seemed prehistoric, and, for a minute, the sight of her warped the world. Boneyard was surreal, a word I'd only learned last year. Beyond real.

"What's out there?" I stage whispered.

"Night heron. Hunting." Crouched on the big rocker's seat, old and shriveled, Queen seemed more animal than human, wings, not arms, at her ribs. Soon she turned and talked turtles, her out-loud words conjuring pictures of a mom waddling from summer depths, settling above the high tide line, flipping and digging, and dropping eggs. Sweeping sand over her babies.

Under moonlight, my arms and legs paled, but Queen's dark skin purpled. Was she a witch or what? Everything and everyone down here struck me as, well, alien. Was that only me? Tired, and now half-asleep? Paranoid, after Naomi's treachery? And who was Will? Marsh-man, gun-guy, rattlesnake-shooter?

8

Empty

Watering the hibiscuses Tuesday morning, I overheard Will talking with Monk, who meowed back. That was weird. After last night's meeting with Queen, this seemed extra-spooky. I'd never had a dog or cat, was this normal? What were Will's actual words?

I was dying to see Mortimer, but didn't want Will to get sick of us, and we had tons to see and do on the beach. I swabbed our bites with cotton balls soaked in alcohol, which at least seemed familiar, the smell, the burn, and stopped our itching. We gooped ourselves with sunscreen, head to toe, packed lunch, and money. We marched to the beach.

Showing them a staked-off turtle nest, I explained, "After she fills the hole with eggs, she sweeps it clean to fool her enemies. Neat?"

Mayzie looked around. "What else? Besides stakes and orange tape? *It ain't no crime scene yet.*" This was my reality, Mayzie quoting *The Wire*; the surreality was in my head. Jack faked interest—I could visualize the embryo-filled eggs, but they couldn't—and zigzagged to and from the water. Who could blame them? Besides city parks and the schoolyard, when could they run free? My feet hadn't pounded the beach since Sunday.

We walked, counting ten palmetto trees before reaching Boneyard Bait and Grocery, a rough square of concrete blocks, obviously mortared by a moron, that leaned beside a community center mortared by the same moron. Inside the tiny store, floor-to-ceiling food lined shelves: canned and cartoned, boxed and bagged. A glass-front freezer advertised creatures and pieces of creatures. Bait. Chicken necks. Gizzards. Shrimp. Fishing lures dangled from a rack, shimmering like Naomi's earrings. I selected two rubbery fish, with rainbow-colored curls dangling from their bellies. I'd make them into earrings.

Inside, the clerk hollered, "Welcome to Boneyard. I'm Linda. What'll you have?"

"Ice cream."

Linda grinned. She wasn't old or young, but wonderfully strange looking, with spiky blue hair and a missing tooth. "Fell off my perch the other day, but I'm getting a new chopper. Your family at the Court?" Linda stuck out her palm, callused and hard, and shook with Jack and then Mayzie and then me. The kids chose nutty buddies while I found feminine hygiene products. Linda shoved a brown paper sack over the counter. I was grateful.

"Hey." Linda spoke to the kids. "Make you a deal. You unload these two boxes of potato chips and hang each bag on that stupid rack right there—I got no patience for it—and I'll give you these treats free. Shouldn't take smart kids like you longer than twenty minutes."

She turned to me. "I see you got your track suit on—run now before it gets too hot. Take your time. We'll have fun."

I hesitated. Was she real or surreal?— but Linda shook her head and waved me on. "Go on, everybody here's kin to everybody. We look out for each other, after a fashion."

"OK. I'll be quick." Starting with eight 45-second runs, I stopped, sprinted, stopped. I did maybe two thousand meters, to the end of the island. My spirits soared and allowed me to even dip myself in the ocean, calm and stable for once, but I didn't go far, only waded, fell, and let gentle waves rock and roll over me. By the time I hiked back for the kids, the sun and breeze had dried my clothes, and it was noon. Surprise.

Time here seemed spastic; I never knew how long anything might take. Some minutes flew, others stretched but never broke, like a clock strangling to move its hour hand past the twelve or the six. I made the kids walk with me to the end of the island, and we tromped along the back side, where the dark dirt seemed more soil than sand. The tide filled the creek; people in little boats dangled lines or hauled up wire cages with crabs inside.

I once saw a faded color photo of Naomi wearing a floppy hat, a shirt and rubber boots, her bikini bottom showing part of her skinny butt. What was *she* was fishing for? In the picture, she was all hair gone loose and excited in the wind, half-turned, with the crooked "I-see-you" grin she wore Sunday with Tom. A spidey sense jangled me. What if he beat her up? What if she beat him up? Naomi wasn't weak that way—she'd broken up, I reminded myself, now that dark thoughts had started to descend, with the guy who spied on me in the shower. She stared down anybody who even looked at her the wrong way. *Don't worry.* But I did. All the time.

She told me stories about Boneyard—creek crabs, fishing, air and mud and water that brewed magic. I wished hard for Dad now, in my deep self, deep as Will's well.

OK. Burying Dad was on me. I'd do it this week. He'd rest with the natives in Orcoosa. If I left the ritual to Naomi, nothing would happen—or the something that could would upset her.

That night after showers, I doctored our six scratched-and-bug-bit legs and fixed a spaghetti-fish-sticks-applesauce dinner. I read the kids *Horton Hatches the Egg.* "A promise is a promise," Jack chanted. They crashed.

In Naomi's room, I opened the window to catch a breeze, wondering why Mayzie and Jack took me, but not Naomi, for granted. When they wanted food, I fixed healthy snacks and make-do meals like fish sticks, apples, carrots, or even, yesterday, a can of Vienna sausages left by the previous tenants. Yuck. I hated but they loved the little pink cylinders, even though I couldn't read the label without gagging. At home, I cooked meatless spaghetti, stir-fried veggies, and eggplant parmigiana. When either sib needed to pee at the beach, we sneaked behind a dune and I screened them with my towel. When Jack tired of walking, I kneeled, and he climbed on my back, toes gripping my hipbones, chin digging my neck, and heart beating under my shoulder blades. I was there. Every day.

And who did I take for granted?

Wind, soft and hot, sifted through the screen. Outside, doors slammed. Insect voices hummed and chirped and croaked. That nature symphony. The tide traveled out, noisily. I imagined the creatures the ocean swept in and out twice a day, every day. With no limit to its energy, ocean claimed more and more of earth. Sucking and swallowing.

I propped myself against pillows on Naomi's bed. The moon spooked the clothes, strewn on doorknobs and across a chair, into strange, empty shapes. Naomi in shadow. Dresses, yoga pants, and a bra. Her slippery rayon robe lay in corpse pose on the carpet. I crawled to the end of the bed, hung my head off the edge, and yanked up the robe. Empty. I slipped into the slick fabric. The robe fell to my thighs because I was taller by four inches than Naomi. I belted it and checked the pockets: Ambien, Xanax, a handful of generics. Thought she'd quit Xanax, at least, but hadn't asked, not lately. Hopefully, since she wasn't working, she was off Adderall. The robe smelled of lavender, like her; it electrified the hair on my arms and my head. I shucked it off. In the moonlit room, the mirrored me looked nothing like Naomi. She was pretty but hated pretty. "Gets you nowhere," she always said.

But I was *pretty* sure *pretty* got her this jaunt to Cumberland Island.

I opened dresser drawers. Empty. I dropped to all fours, felt for loose change, but found only dimes and nickels, enough for a Coke. Money was not what I'd been searching, though, money was no clue to adult behavior. I longed to understand adults. Why wouldn't she talk about Dad? Why was she addicted to yoga? Why'd she refuse Marco's marriage proposal and then disappear with a man she loved at eighteen? She'd leave this hot Tom, too, assuming he stayed interested. She'd find herself alone—we would grow up. Why run from people who loved her?

The sea breeze picked up speed and flapped the blinds until

they beat on each other. I peeked between slats: outside, the parking lot glowed, an ocean of shells where cars floated like boats. Imagine driving on shells that once housed live creatures.

I tried Naomi on FaceTime but got no signal. In her bed, the rumpled sheets smelled of lavender, too—and Tom's cologne had stunk the pillow even though they'd left more than twenty-four hours ago. Imagine Naomi rising that early on vacation. The big bed made me feel small. I'd figured on luxuriating in all the space, without Mayzie planting her feet in my back, but the space only made me itch. I pulled the plug on the phone and shut the door.

Naomi wasn't home even when she was home. I missed her less and less. The trip down here marked a new low; we could barely afford gas for the Voyager. Naomi wasn't herself—as if I even knew that "self." I was five when dad died, but never forgot the social worker or the off-the-charts, spaced-out Naomi. This "taking off," with this so-called good guy, was this hitting bottom? Sure, we stayed alone once Marco moved out, while she worked overnight shifts, but that was different—inside our apartment in a city where cell phones connected. Would she come back tomorrow like she promised? Maybe she'd let me drive. This year, I'll take driver's ed. I can get my learner's at fourteen years and nine months.

On Labor Day, I'll be fourteen. Joan of Arc had her first vision at thirteen. My only visions were of some kind of home—I didn't want to be a martyr.

9

Better Breed of Man

Jack crawled, belly down, and sneaked up on Monk, who fled. Smart cat. Mayzie jammed a gouge into a linoleum scrap, "for a print," she said, "like in third grade." Lucille scraped, feathered, and chiseled Mortimer, loving that bird to death. Busy kids—OK, so why the jitters in Will's gut? Yesterday he'd listened for them—worried, too, but watched them come and go from the beach. They'd waved and called, "Hey, how's it going?"

But he needed today and tomorrow to finish carving enough work for a decent show.

"OK. Listen." A minute then two passed. He massaged his jaw like words might fall out if he rubbed hard enough. They looked up and stared.

Mayzie flipped her braids. "What's your problem? Cat got your tongue?"

Clever, this one, repeating phrases grownups probably used on her; that way adults could dial in how stupid they sounded. Will drained his glass of water and cleared his throat. "This week going OK? So far, so good? Wednesday, hump day."

"Are you feeling OK?" Lucille asked.

"I'm serious. Sorry if that embarrasses you."

"Not me. Looks like it's embarrassing you." She turned back to Mortimer. "We appreciate you taking us to Orcoosa, oh, and the *Loblolly*, way cool, especially the garden, the way the tomatoes and sunflowers sowed themselves—but the place looks like a tornado touched down. Also, that rattler. And crossing the creek while the tide poured back in? I've read how water can sweep you off your feet even if . . ."

As Lucille described the day's adventures, they sounded perilous, but he'd done that stuff all his life; it was all the kid-entertainment he knew. That or worse—diving off the bridge or surfing during thunderstorms.

"And here I thought I'd been a good host. What should we have done, played video games?" His insides emptied.

"I'm joking, Will. We loved, loved, loved all that. Seriously, I was kidding—nobody's ever showed us cooler or more dangerous places."

Lucille sent him a big smile dedicated to mending his hurt feelings, which touched him. He feasted his eyes on Jack, who'd whittled a crude cylinder, small in diameter and length.

"What's that you're making?"

"A penis." Jack concentrated.

"Thought so. What are you guys up to today? Gotta put my nose to the grindstone, shoulder to the wheel. Market starts Friday."

Lucille spouted ideas. "You need help finishing pieces, and, oh, by the way, I've titled these three for you." She gestured at the relief, in progress, and two freestanding monstrosities.

He swallowed hard and spoke slowly. "Glad you're interested, but I've got my own ideas." A lie. He simply didn't want her—what? Thinking better than he could? Come on, Altman, lighten up. The work came easily for her and hard for him. That wasn't it, not really; he needed more time to work without distraction.

"Don't you want to hear the titles? Artists name pieces because names help people understand the artist's concept, of reality or whatever world the artist created."

"What are you talking about?"

"How you see the world. *Art is your vision*. Of course, it's not that simple."

His insides churned. "Who died and made you queen of art?" He should've bitten back the juvenile words.

Lucille threw the Flexcut on the work table. “Are you in third grade?”

“What’s wrong with third graders? I’m going into third grade,” Mayzie yelled.

“Shut up, Mayzie.” Lucille glared at her then Will. “You are a real artist, you’ve got everything you need—you’re grown, for one thing. Do you have any idea what it’s like to be a kid at the mercy of adults? Also, you have a truck. OK, so you should get off fossil fuel, but that’s a different question. Third, you can gather driftwood, those tree ‘bones’ on the beach, and more. Last, you better enjoy living here on this crazy-cool island while you can because soon it’ll be underwater. We’re drowning. It’s our fault. But, I’ve told you all that.”

She paused and fastened her eyes into the outside distance, chest heaving; why, she hadn’t even gotten this worked up when she found out her mother and Tom went AWOL. This girl and Will had something in common he hadn’t even recognized in himself: They were wedded to the natural world.

She gulped air and continued. “We’ll be leaving, maybe even today, and before I go, you need to understand.”

He leaned across the workbench, palms pressing into sharp gouges, though he felt nothing. He bit his lower lip until he tasted blood. She riveted her eyes to his until their depths met. All the while, her hands worked the bird, while she glanced up-down-up-down, giving Will the stink-eye on the up. His eyes roamed the porch, silent except for the scrape of Jack’s and Lucille’s knives. Mayzie popped her thumb in her mouth.

“What I meant was,” she dropped her voice, “you should be grateful.”

He couldn’t trust his voice. He picked up Monk, lounging on the cool concrete, and cuddled the cat to his chest, then set him down. “I’ll consider your suggestion about naming my pieces. Now, I’ve got to get these done. I need—” he paused—“alone time.”

“Sure, let’s get out of here. Mayzie, come on, Jack, finish later. Mortimer’s mostly done.”

At the door, she threw this: “You’re the one who invited us

in. You're the one who showed us Orcoosa and the *Mudhole*. We didn't ask."

Ten minutes later they crossed the shells, Lucille lugging her giant orange tote. True, he'd reached out first, but they didn't need him. Why'd they hang around his workshop? They formed their own unit. All for one, one for all. A family. A tribe. They made their own home. Did they secretly need a grownup and didn't want to show it? Kids. Inscrutable. Will stepped outside, calling, "Never turn your back on the ocean! And don't go in above your knees."

No response. "Knees! Knees! Waves can drag you under, you hear?"

Jack turned and waved and called back, "OK. Come to the beach when you're done."

Inside, Will inventoried tools, hoping to put himself in work-mode. Glues, finishes, and a stack of sandpaper sat on a wall-mounted shelf. Files, scrapers, T-square, calipers, and a roll of wire hung from hooks. A wall cabinet held a can of air to blow dust from tight corners. On the workbench—Jack's pretend-penis, Mayzie's lino-cut petals, and Lucille's bird, detailed down to its fantasy topknot. Nice, but how and why did she think up a macabre name like Mortimer?

Six pieces of his "oeuvre" crouched in a corner like animals; he'd sold a small gnome-like thing last weekend, a practice exercise from a magazine, happy to get the money and happier to see it go, that and a half-assed abstract piece some fool mistook for a human figure.

He'd lost touch with his work. The disconnect jarred his mojo. He'd sculpted half-starts before summer crowds hit the island, before these kids had worked their way under his skin. He tried to keep an inventory of twelve pieces, ranging from fifty to three hundred dollars, though he'd yet to sell a piece that pricey.

He was no artist who thought up abstract titles and charged real money the way he would for building a cabinet or replacing stairs or reproducing a Corinthian capital. Making art took more than skill—the wood showed *him* how to shape *it*, not the other way around. The grain and his instincts gave it life, or afterlife. Staying power, like the mud and the marsh reek. He itched to carve forms that would stick with people. The harvest pleased him most, cruising beaches or the national wildlife refuge with a chainsaw, ripping slabs, stalking snags on his own acreage at *Loblolly*. These sites held strange finds, even the dead, standing in the forest like old men.

Clear the bench. Set aside the kids' pieces, keep them safe, ready for their return, probably dinnertime. Dinner. He'd carve all day, clean up, and jog to the market for a slab of flounder. He was a master fryer. What, he wondered, had the kids been eating? His table barely seated four, and it was Trip's night to check on Will, his personal project, which made five. Face it, Will, you are one lonely mother. Sinking. Literally. Funny to live with the rising ocean underfoot, but never consider the phenomenon while Lucille couldn't shut up about it. Her words about the ocean and its gallop to swallow the shoreline finally hit him where he lived.

He whisked shavings and dust from the table, organized tools by size, all the while eyeing the relief. Big. Flat. Meant to hang in a home and call forth all outdoors, all of nature. How do the great artists—he's seen pictures: Picasso's abstract paintings and sculptures convey big ideas through wood or clay or metal or on canvas. How?

Out There. That's what he'll name it, hoping to do the concept justice.

Monk pranced on top of the relief, his motor running.

"What do you think so far?" Monk rubbed against his belly, crawled up his chest, then climbed up and across his shoulders. Will cupped the cat's skinny mid-section and set him down on the cement. He plugged in the pad sander and ground into the original image, obscuring but not erasing. Choosing among gouges, he selected and ran the No. 6, the biggest, in as free an arc as possible, again, again, until scattered fronds, thick stems, narrowing at the tips, cut the plane, joining the deeper undulations he'd gouged earlier this morning. He carved delicate shoots.

Sweat dropped and deposited salt stains. "That's OK, too, right Monk?"

Wabi sabi. The original Monk's words filled his head. That guy was a better breed of man. And now, the long submerged day or nightmare, never far from Will's horizon, lowered its anvil. The trailer to this cliché of a movie featured farmers tending tiny stands of wheat, like pioneer forefathers, trying only to feed families, then the supposed good guys kick open doors, shatter glass, aim 50-cals at kids, insult wives and women just by looking.

He jammed two gouges in the wood with savage strokes—dreams, random phantasms—and, though he fought to surface, slashed the pretty arcs, the peaceful, waving grasses. Chaos grabbed his hands, his bruised fingers moved across the wood, painting with blood and sweat, full of their own adrenaline, muscles and tendons jumping, wreaking the havoc playing in his head, taking revenge on the wood. Muscles aching. Ears ringing.

Ringing. The phone.

The down side of management: forwarded office calls.

"How are they?"

He fell into silence. How was who?

"It's Naomi. How're my kids?" Now her words merged in a way he did recognize.

Why was she suddenly calling, and why would he know where they were?

He paused and tried to construct an answer that implied an occasion she ought to rise to.

"Could be anywhere. Maybe at the beach. Alone. By the way, how are you calling?"

"A telephone. At the desk. That's great, I'm glad they're . . ."

Her voice trailed and died, as though they'd gotten disconnected, but it wasn't that. Her voice, the words, lacked life. The voice of what? Eternal grief? Lucille's dad was a vet; though dead a decade, dead was dead. The grieving never stopped.

"Don't sweat." A stab of sudden sympathy. "I told them not to go in the ocean over their knees. Lucille's plenty competent. But, your children need—you."

Silence. Why'd he tell her *not* to *sweat*, when, actually, she should sweat?

"Mrs. Lamb? When will you return?"

"Friday? What's today?" She laughed.

Was she serious? Days melted by, but her slurs—*whatsh*—meant she was fucked up.

"Look it up. It's on all calendars. Remember Lucille's counting on Key West. She thinks you're leaving tonight for the *Keys*." He doubted it would hit home.

"Tomorrow?"

"Tonight. She thinks you're leaving *tonight*. Today is Wednesday."

"This trip has done me good, I needed rest. We'll make the Keys—someday."

"The sheriff may have something to say about your absence." Lucille would, too.

"Tom's got meetings—we need a few extra days."

"Put Tom on the line." At one time, Tom Barnes had wanted *Loblolly's* fifty acres, but he'd lowballed Will, who now wished he'd sold.

"He is meeting with architects. Please don't keep asking."

Fantastic. Development on the one island where nature had stayed halfway wild. But, the Great Inundation would devour Cumberland, too, once Arctic ice dams and glaciers disappeared.

"FYI, your reservation runs only through tonight; I'll need to move them."

Will threw the Flexcut into the pine, yanked it free, threw it again, harder. It lodged and twanged.

"Good. Will, sorry, should've asked, can we pay you? Things are—have been—rough."

"Only one room, without A/C. An oven."

"They'll be fine. Lucille won't mind moving my luggage."

"Ask her yourself. Be a parent in person."

"Will? I'm not—well. My job's—."

What? Her job was what? The cryptic phrases sounded familiar; Will was no stranger to alcohol's twisted tongue, and her words failed to move him. He had no sympathy, no patience. Still, a widow—Jesus, how the grit from the sandpit must've burrowed into their lives and bodies. Will's own father had survived Khe Sanh, but part of him died in 'Nam, maybe the best part. Will's own girlfriend had sensibly avoided the problem of living with a combat veteran. She'd broken up with him.

Lucille worried him the most. She'd bear the brunt. Could he help Naomi? No. But Lucille and her siblings? Somehow, he'd help. Or die trying.

That afternoon, needing a break, Will showered and drove to Belva's. On her porch, his clean, soapy scent evaporated until he smelled like his tainted mix of mud-reek, body odor, and sawdust. He pressed the doorbell. It chimed. He jumped. At his feet, a jumble of droopy black-eyed Susans stared at him through the railing. Under his left sneaker, a rotten porch plank gave.

She opened the door.

Why was he here? He should've thought through his unplanned trip.

"Could I maybe—?" He dropped his eyes, pointed, and stomped the deteriorating slat.

"Fix this?" He'd need to hit the lumberyard, unless they'd kept spares.

Her appearance overwhelmed him—tangled hair, no neat braid, at her collarbones, a wrinkled, shapeless dress grazing her calves.

"It's too hot, isn't it? For physical labor?"

He shook his head. "Got any spare wood?"

"Why would you repair my porch? Is that why you drove to town?" She seemed dazed by his offer. "If you replace the one you're standing on, you'd need to replace the others."

"I can do that. Maybe not today, but soon."

"I would love to watch you work." At last, a smile. "But not now," her eyes dropped to his hands, "your hands tell me you've already had a rough day in the studio. What have you carved besides your fingers?"

He laughed at his nightmarish day, now that he realized it had led him here. "A *relief* sculpture that gave me grief, and no relief." What did he want? To drink her in. She didn't even need to talk; Will specialized in silence. He didn't need to sleep with her again, either, not now, though, he wouldn't turn down an opportunity, despite her uncertain marital status. He waited for what might happen next, bouncing on the problem plank.

"OK."

He jogged to Pearl for his toolbox, found spare slats in her garage, and carried them to the porch. He pried off the weak wood, which splintered the adjacent planks, but not so badly they'd need replacing. He settled and nailed the new piece, obviously overstock from the last repair, and it nestled nicely in the vacant space, with only an inch of overage. He ran his extension cord to the door, walked it inside, and plugged it into an outlet. The saw's whine destroyed the quiet; he dropped the overage in a second. He plugged in the sander, mounted coarse-grit paper, and smoothed the replacement and its raw edge.

"I'll need to match the paint."

"Don't worry about that." Belva spoke from the step, where she'd moved, and seated herself sideways, legs crossed and stretched along its length. She half-turned and faced him; the sun streamed through cloud cover, overexposing her. He couldn't see her eyes but stared anyway.

"But it looks terrible. One raw plank? Exposed? Alone?"

"You make it sound like an orphan. All right. The paint's in the garage, I'll find it."

"I'll take care of the paint. You go inside where it's cool. Out here, the air's too thick."

He couldn't even look at her without overheating. It was shame overtaking him, though, not desire, oh, that, too, but he couldn't bear her gaze on him. He hated scrutiny, especially hers. So he asked this insane, scary, but kind of awesome question:

"Could I cook dinner for you? Tonight. Remember? You said you might . . ."

"Oh. I must've been messed up. That wine. I don't usually drink."

"Oh."

"Or maybe it was because—I remembered my mom." She picked up her hair and let it fall. "And how," she paused, "*unfulfilling* her marriage was. She told me this at my father's funeral."

"That's terrible." But what did it mean, that she'd even said that? Would she come to dinner or not? He shouldn't be here now because he needed to work, needed the money. Their worlds, he saw, lay too far apart to connect, but he'd started a bridge. He'd continue construction unless, until, it collapsed.

"Marriage was terrible for her. I told you Nelson has left me, and that is true, but I didn't tell you this: I was glad. We weren't close, and I'm not talking about sex, but I wouldn't have had the guts to leave."

"Then think about dinner." He registered his internal mishmash—shame, fear, and anger. Why couldn't she come? He'd ask and ask until she'd accept or refuse or he wearied of asking. "I live at the old Palmetto Tourist Court on Boneyard."

"Thank you for the invitation. I'll see you this weekend at the show? And, someday, I may take you up on that dinner, when I'm ready." She gathered up her dress hem and fanned herself. "Hotter'n floogens?"

Her coded reference to Saturday's date pleased him. "How hot *is* floogens?"

"Who knows?" She got up and went inside, and returned with a hundred dollar bill.

He pushed it away. WTF?

"I needed to see you. I saw rot and fixed it. The end." He packed the tools, loaded them in Pearl, and drove away.

10

Laugh

Late in the afternoon, we packed Jack with wet sand. "Can you still see me?"

And then, another voice. "Lucille, right?"

The low sun silhouetted the dark, noodle-thin kid who tried to outrun me Sunday. He shaded his face with his hand. "Hey."

I shielded my eyes, too. "The runner returns to the scene of his defeat."

"Yeah, my bad, my eyes were on my feet instead of in front of me. Dumb." He kneeled and joined our sand-packing party.

"Hi." Mayzie stuck her sandy thumb in her mouth.

"I'm Renaldo. Guess what? I used to suck my thumb."

She pulled out her thumb and smiled. "I'm Mayzie."

His warm voice reminded me of Marco, except this guy was tall and skinny. Mayzie and Jack saw Marco every other weekend, and sometimes I went, too. He'd helped me measure phosphate pollution in the Detroit River for my science project. When I won first prize, we celebrated, the five of us, at Slow's Barbecue. That was last year.

"Can you still see me?" Jack again, from the sand.

"*A man in your line of work start worrying about how other people see him playing to other people instead of himself*," Mayzie said, "*he gonna get dead.*" Replaced thumb in mouth.

"*The Wire*!" Renaldo scooped wet sand and mounded it at

Jack's biceps, transforming him into a muscleman. "I'm jealous you could *memorize* that!"

Mayzie hooted. We pressed sand into Jack until he was a white tube with oversized arms and legs. Only his dark face, hair, and ten toes stuck up from the beach. Jack moved his head, cracking his sand skin.

"Run!" Renaldo shouted. "Sand monster's alive!"

Jack sprang up, danced a little jig, and Renaldo grabbed him. He pretend-threw Jack, and easily caught him three times.

He took one of Jack's hands, I took the other, and Mayzie's, and we four jumped waves, bigger than yesterday's because the tide was high; the breakers knocked us to the sand.

"Water's rough. Let's get out." I guided Mayzie and Jack.

"Nah. It's fun, isn't it?" Renaldo lifted and dangled Jack so his toes tickled the sea-froth.

Mayzie and Jack screamed—they liked the surf beating them down, but my calves stung with the force of that last wave, and here came another. It took me down. I fought to stay on my feet, and turned from the wave, but it lifted and swept me out, though I tried scrambling up, hollering and breathless. I surfaced but couldn't see the kids or even tall Renaldo. The water was murk. My feet finally found sand, but I struggled against a strong sideways current. Soon I made it to knee-high water. The lifeguard blew her whistle and kept blowing as she raced toward me. "What's going on?"

"I can't find my brother and sister. They were just now in the water." I pointed. She scanned the beach and the water with binoculars. "Dark? Yay high?" She used her palm to indicate height. "I've got them in my sights."

My stomach unclenched.

A minute later, the kids ran at me and collapsed, giggling, in the sand. Renaldo caught his breath. "We weren't paying attention—playing in the water—when the lifeguard blew her whistle, I realized the current was carrying us down the beach. We're fine. Honest."

Jack and Mayzie couldn't stop talking about wave-smackdowns.

"I'll take them home." My voice sounded cold. I didn't care.

"No!" Mayzie and Jack shouted. "More. More!"

"What's wrong? Don't you like salt water?" he asked. "Or, are you mad at me?"

"I'm so done with that ocean." He should've kept them here in this one spot; the ocean is unpredictable: One minute it's a friend, cradling us in salty arms, the next, it's trying to suck us out to sea. OK, nature was just being nature, guess I needed to get used to that.

"Are you scared? Go back in, you don't want to stay afraid, what's the fun in that?" Renaldo said. "I'll spot you. You'll love floating and body surfing." He grinned a wide-mouthed grin. I'd never seen whiter teeth.

I shook my head. "We need to head back." Even as those words came out of my mouth, I wondered, why? Nobody cared when we got home. On the other hand, who was he, besides Queen's grandson, and why was he so friendly?

The kids ran for the water.

"Water babies, both of them. Come out again. You're an athlete—you can handle water."

"Why are you so friendly?"

"Um. Let me see. My grandma taught me good manners? I like meeting kids near my age? And, what's wrong with friendly? I'm done with my chores and feel like company?" He caught Mayzie and Jack and sat them on the beach. "Turret time." He and the kids dug sand and dribbled water until tall spires rose.

"They'll be fine." He raised his eyes to me. "Let's walk out, maybe waist-deep."

"Will said knee deep."

"OK, knee deep."

The water surface seemed calm, but currents could drag people down. Still, everyone in the water dove, swam, or made their bodies into arrows, sometimes disappearing briefly into waves that hurled them to shore. I counted at least a dozen in the water, including one or two I'd seen at the Court, even Mrs. Pitts, the smoker. If, old as she was, she could swim, I could. I told Mayzie and Jack to stay on shore, and signaled to the lifeguard, pointing to my own chest, then to Mayzie and Jack. She gave me a thumb's up.

They flipped sand at each other, and though I knew somebody would start crying any minute, I giant-stepped with Renaldo into the water, waist-deep, with Will's "knees, knees" echoing in my head.

"Far enough," I told Renaldo, a head taller. Waves curled beyond where I tried, but failed, to stand still.

He placed his hand at my spine. I startled at the touch but let it pass.

"You can float. Lean on me." He opened both arms.

"OK. OK." I used all my strength to stay in one spot.

"You're nervous. I'm here, try, you'll get the idea."

I stiffened but leaned into his arm.

"Let the water float your legs up. Study the clouds."

I tipped back, my head on his shoulder, my legs in front of me. The water, soft like bathwater, buoyed my body, and I instantly craved the freedom of moving arms and legs the way Dad and I drifted, weightless, in my sea-dreams.

"You'll be a great swimmer once you lose your fear."

Fat chance.

The pale sky grew dense with clouds, temporarily blocking the sun.

Renaldo grinned and lifted both arms.

"See? Floating. Conquering fear."

A wave washed me. I went under and struggled up, spit and coughed.

"Gotcha."

He said it, and, for real, he did have my back. On shore, I saw that Mayzie and Jack had lost interest in the castle, and were staring at us from shore, but the breaking, salty waves had hooked me.

"Let's practice treading water." Water beads clung to his barely-there beard.

I lifted my legs and pumped them even though I didn't need to because I could touch. I tried butt kicks and high knees. The slow-motion made me giggle.

"Have you been to Cumberland Island?" I shouted over the sound of waves hitting the sand. "Is it great?"

"Bigger and wilder than here, even though Boneyard Island's mostly wildlife refuge. There's an inn everybody raves about and one of the Kennedys got married on the island, at a little African-American church, but the inn, that's not a place Queen or I would go."

"Why?"

"Caters to money, but there's maybe a campground. I've never been."

"Do you come to the beach every day?" We treaded water, and I was surprised at how long I stayed afloat. Every so often I touched bottom, and scoped out the kids.

"Two or three times a day. I love the ocean. Today I came because you were here."

"Us? Why?"

His eyes smiled but this mouth stayed serious. "Making sure y'all are doing OK. Will can be a butt. He can get grumpy."

I tried not to smile. I'd call Will moody, and it felt good to hear someone else thought the same. Once I started smiling, I couldn't stop, then the smile turned to laughter.

"The man's got a good heart, but pretends to hate the world, guess it's sandpit defense, that's what Trip said."

Oh. I started for shore.

"You OK? I say something wrong?" he yelled.

"Just tired, we're getting hungry, too . . . ." I turned back toward him. "And my dad . . ."

"Oh! I need to keep my big trap shut."

"S'OK. How would you know? Let's exchange numbers. We can stay in touch."

"How? Cell out here takes voodoo. It's ridiculous. Probably you'd find better service in Mongolia. Planets need to line up just right for signal."

"You, too? I figured the permanent people might get better service. That's wack, but we're taking off for Key West, hopefully tomorrow."

His eyes went big. "Key West. That must suck for you." He couldn't suppress a grin.

"Yeah, right. I've carried this dream around forever—to see the Keys, the Florida reef, the biggest coral reef in the continental United States."

He closed his eyes, raising his arms overhead, and moving his hips. "I've seen videos of coral, swaying. You're nearly there."

On shore, we joined Mayzie and Jack, me in hero position, the only yoga posture I like because folding my calves under my thighs and sitting still calmed me, especially when I imagined I was a bird asleep on a branch.

He knelt in the sand and studied me, the bird. I was usually the watcher not the watched, and so I closed my eyes and felt myself float into space.

"Cool," Renaldo said. "Show me again?"

I stood and dropped again, knees, then calves.

"That's it?"

I shut my eyes and placed my hands, palms up, on my thighs.

When I opened my eyes, he was still struggling to sit all the way down. "Ow. Ow."

"Takes practice. Sit on something—a pillow."

"A sand pillow?"

"How come you live with your grandma, not your mom?" I'd seen him and Queen walking to that sweet old cottage behind the Court.

"The short version—I don't have a father—my mom thinks it's better for me. Plus, she thinks Queen needs looking after."

"You have a father. You just don't know yours."

He didn't say anything.

"Queen seems so *able*, for an old person."

"Sure she does—but, between you and me, it's more that my mom doesn't want me with her. She's busy; she's a social worker. And Queen's too stubborn to have the cataract operation, so her vision's going, and she's forgetting a lot."

I knew hardly anyone old except my teachers. How would it feel to lose sight? To lose memory, even a little? Naomi forgot. Why? She wasn't nearly as old as Queen. The waves found us. Water spilled into our laps. OK, Naomi was not mother of the year, but she'd never send us away. Would she? My heart felt lighter and heavier at the same time. Naomi'd never once even considered sending us to somebody else. Of course, who would that somebody be? She had on purpose maintained no contact with Dad's family; Naomi's grandparents had raised her, and they were dead.

"Did you make trouble?"

"No. I've always lived with Queen. Mom wasn't cut out to rear kids. She's only, like 33, and I'm almost eighteen."

"I'm almost fourteen. Can't imagine . . .," then I remembered I already took care of kids.

"Living here's pretty dope. Will's used to me and he is no easy dude. When he first came, after Trip bought the Court? Hair trigger temper. Sheesh. I walked, like, on eggshells. And drunk? Dude pounded whiskey. Always effed-up. Sheriff Trip practically saved Will's life. Don't tell Will I blabbed. Trip still stops and checks me out, checks Will out, checks Queen out. Makes sure I 'toe the line,' whatever that means. We've even got police protection, the whole shooting match."

He shared all this with an ear-to-ear smile. Why? Did living on the island make him this happy? His grandmother? However he became his smiling self, I didn't question it, didn't want to: Happiness was contagious, so I helped myself and giggled.

The day now seemed cozy and restful, easy. Jack and Mayzie rolled over and over in shallow water, slathering each other with foamy spindrift while I talked with a real person almost the same age as me, someone I liked.

Jack came up and stood behind Renaldo, dripping sand on his bald head, asking him how come he was born without hair, and suggesting maybe he could draw a headful.

"What color?" Renaldo asked.

"Red?"

"Lemme think about it." Renaldo took Jack on his lap. "What else can we talk about? I know. Do your summer reading yet?"

"*Their Eyes Were Watching God*. Read it as soon as school let out. Zora made Janie's world mine; the heroine made me think of Naomi, my mom, but Janie at least found Tea Cake and *fulfillment* and then when I read on Wikipedia about Alice Walker locating Zora's grave, I thought how sad that Zora'd written and written and written about people, mostly poor, doing jobs nobody does these days—harvesting turpentine from pine trees, cutting sugar cane—forgotten until Alice told the world about Zora's work."

"We read that freshman year. I can't forget that first line: 'Ships at a distance have every man's wish on board.' How true is that. We've got Chimananda's '*America*.' Immigrant experience."

I nodded. "I'll download that from the library when I get someplace with decent wireless. Maybe Key West." Even mentioning the Court's winky wireless cracked us up, and we kept laughing, about things nobody else would understand except us, here and now, on this island, on this day.

These laughs were food I'd hungered for but hadn't known it. My insides fluttered, almost like wings that floated me, with no past or future, to the clouds.

"Almost outta here. Senior year for me!"

"Yeah? Then what?" My mind drifted.

"College. I hope, engineering school. Or if I can't afford it, I'm gonna join the Coast Guard, so I can bust drug-runner ships."

"Coast Guard does that? Scary."

"No way. We'll roll up in our big boat, and the smuggler dudes with their little boats? They'll stick their hands in the air so fast. Course we'd call in choppers."

"Sounds easy, but I bet it isn't. I'll be a scientist, maybe an oceanographer, so I can learn how the earth copes, that is, if the world stays sane and dry long enough, which it won't. Or maybe a doctor who specializes in infectious diseases. Funguses. With the world heating up-or 'hotting' up as Queen says—" we giggled again—"we'll need doctors. Everybody'll be sick."

"I know! Weather? Effing wack."

I rolled off my hips, got to my feet, and stomped the sand, howling with laughter I couldn't control even if I'd wanted to. I didn't know what drugs were like but laughing transported me, somewhere I'd never been. Spacey me.

"Queen and I laugh a ton, especially at Will, who's funny as hell even though he doesn't know it—sometimes he's a walking human *frown*." Renaldo furrowed his brow, stuck out his neck, and darted his eyes side to side. "He's done less of that with you guys around—guess he doesn't want to be a negative influence. Will's OK, though. He taught me carpentry. Nope. Can't complain about Will; by the way, we're cousins. He's related to Queen, I forget how. Around this island, natives are mixed breeds. Everybody's kin to everybody."

"Mongrels," I shouted. We laughed more, while Mayzie and Jack threw sand-mud at us. We could've stopped ourselves from laughing, but why? We got up and sank our feet in wet sand, and that turned silly. With our feet in ankle-deep sand, we fell over and crawled to drier sand. We rolled over on our backs, flapped our arms and legs, and dug our shoulders, hips and feet into sand, making angels, then sat up and piled damp sand over our feet. We slipped them out carefully so they didn't collapse.

"Frog houses," he said.

Frog houses? The idea of frogs inhabiting the sand-caves created by feet made no sense, and set us laughing again. We stood, brushing sand from our hands as though it did make sense, in our little alt-universe.

Mayzie and Jack stink-eyed us like we'd gone crazy and left them in charge of sanity. We finally controlled our laughter, but I hated calming down now that I'd drifted into happy.

Adults usually wanted kids to calm down, why? But now even the ocean had found peace, as the tide ebbed. I gathered our gear in the orange tote, and we trudged through the sand to the Court.

When Renaldo said goodbye, to all of us, at the end of Will's sidewalk, the simple words *good* and *bye* struck him and me as giggle-worthy. *What the hell*, Renaldo mouthed. I shrugged, doubled over, laughing. Jack and Mayzie trooped into Will's porch, but I watched Renaldo, in a trance, until he turned and waved, then disappeared among the live oaks behind the Court. At Will's door a tiny blue lizard darted behind a hibiscus.

On the porch, Will smiled, but only with his mouth. "I've got news."

"Huh?" I'm somewhere in the clouds, not inside my body on Will's porch. What was wrong with me? I smiled, secretly, to myself, until my roaming eyes landed on his *disaster relief.* Scraped raw and stained. With what? Blood? I inched closer. Will's fingers looked like they'd strangled sharp saw-palmetto fronds.

He moved a few tools around as though reorganizing, but his expression was blank; this was not about organizing. He jabbed a knife into the wood where it stuck. I'd never seen him do that; his knife is part of his hand. Now I figured he'd drop and do pushups, like he did Monday morning, for anxiety. He didn't.

Instead, he did this weird nice thing. Invited us for dinner.

He choked the words out, both hands flat on the worktable. "It'll be you guys, Trip, and me." He worked the knife from the table, and sliced a curl from the tableau of whatever he'd been carving. "And Naomi called from the resort by satellite phone. She'll be back Friday."

Mayzie chewed on a braid. Jack hopped foot-to-foot. I started a round of squats. We'd caught Will's anxious vibe.

"Call her back. We're due in Key West. Today's Wednesday, if she doesn't come soon, there's no going. It's 643 miles from Savannah, more than ten hours. School starts Tuesday, so we'd need to leave Key West Sunday to be home Monday—Labor Day. My birthday, my birthday, my birthday."

"How about next year?" Will asked. "Come work with the sea turtle guardians. There's an intern program at the turtle center, on the mainland."

"Next year! Next year, the Keys could be underwater, the coral, dead. Next year, this island could be swamped."

"This weekend," Mayzie said, her voice grave. "Saw it on TV. A storm's coming."

"A sub-tropical, no big deal," Will said. "Those weather people feed on a steady diet of panic—panic drives ratings."

I pulled Jack and Mayzie close. "Mom always comes back, like when she works overnight shifts."

But Mayzie shook her head. "That's a lie. She comes back after one day, not a bunch of days. Anyway, who cares about Key West? I'd rather stay here." She shuffled to Will's side. "With Will."

A questioning look crossed Will's face. A tiny smile.

11

Fish Eyes

Will patted Mayzie, trying to surface from confusion about Belva, the best he could do to comfort the kid. His clumsy attempts with people made him feel more animal than human, a harmless, wordless animal who knew only how to bark. This time he gave the three kids a sorta-smile and dropped his eyes to his ruined piece.

Lucille studied his work. She studied him. "What's going on?"

"Dinner." He registered her red face, and scrunched his.

She nodded. "I know. Guess my sunscreen washed off. You? Cook dinner for four?"

"Five. The sheriff's coming. I cook, I count. Don't argue with an invitation to eat. It's impolite and just plain dumb."

Jack commandeered Monk into his lap and the two boys, Monk and Jack, sat on the bare cement. Jack stroked Monk's fur, trapping the poor tomcat.

"Renaldo showed me how to float." Lucille grinned.

"You can't float?"

"Now I can."

"Thank heavens. God, you probably can't swim either. What kind of *in loco parentis* am I? I should've taught y'all the basics."

"What's *in loco parentis*?" Mayzie asked.

"Latin for crazy parent." Lucille's brows jumped up her forehead. "Sounds like."

"Do I look crazy?"

"Why didn't you order Naomi back? Tell her you're done with *in loco parentis*. Cumberland Island's not that far. A couple of hours. I looked on the map."

"And a boat ride," he added.

Her face distorted, but she shepherded the kids out the door. "We'll shower and change."

"Six sharp. I'm frying fish. Splash vinegar on your burn, there's probably some in your cottage." He went inside and lathered and rinsed his hands thoroughly in hot water. With his sharpest knife he chopped a head of cabbage and dumped it in a plastic bowl, set out a dish of crusty sugar, left by a tenant, a half-jar of mayo, also previously tenant-owned, and vinegar, enough to keep the coleslaw on the sour side. The kitchen came with no fancy processors, only a few pots and pans, but Will owned a twelve-inch iron skillet, an 1875 Griswold, of his grandmother's. He poured in oil and switched the biggest stove-eye to high.

Waiting for the oil to heat, he ran a glass of tap water and drank it down, maybe his first hydration today. Lucille even had him saying hydration. He liked her influence. He reached for the sack of cornmeal and shook some onto a platter. The oil crackled. He lowered the heat, unwrapped package of tiny silver porgies, dredged them in cornmeal, and laid each small, fleshy fish in the pan.

Mayzie and Jack showed up, damp and sweet-looking, soap-smelling.

"That was fast. Grab a spoon and glop mayo in the cabbage. Drizzle in a little vinegar." The fish bubbled—he lowered the heat and flipped and flipped and flipped and flipped. Oil splashed the floor. When he took his eyes from the skillet, Lucille had slipped inside, scrubbed and red-faced, her rope of red hair soaking, wearing her same track clothes, damp from her day at the beach. She smelled like vinegar; she'd heeded his remedy.

"How's Jack doing with the slaw, Lucky, will you check?" His thoughts strayed to swimming—thanks to Renaldo, at least she could float. It had not occurred to him that children vacationing at the beach wouldn't be able to swim.

"How's Will's secret sauce going, y'all? Lucille, step back, you don't want me sloshing oil on you." He lifted the golden fish slabs onto a plate.

"The oil's, er, mostly on the floor." She grabbed a roll of paper towels and swabbed the sheets around with her dirty shoe. "Are you *trying* to burn the place down?"

Behind her, a voice boomed. "Don't let my house go up in smoke like yours."

Trip stood in the doorway, rimmed in sunset. The kids stared. So did Will. In that moment, the grease caught fire. Trip took two giant steps, and slid the pan onto a cold burner.

"I've got this." Will poured salt from a box; it killed the flame. He switched off the stove.

"Crisis averted, man, good work." Trip grabbed Will's hand so tight it hurt.

"Loosen that grip, big guy. Lay off these hands, they're my livelihood."

"Mayzie, Jack, have you ever met a real-life sheriff? Take a good luck at that shiny bald head, that tattoo—a great blue heron. Trip's a sight, isn't he?"

Jack walked over and stood eye-level with Trip's thigh. "Where's your badge and gun?"

Mayzie tied her braids under her chin, asking, "How's a sheriff different from police?"

Trip gave each kid a separate look, a regular Officer Friendly, and dug in his pocket. He flipped open a thick laminated pouch. "ID. Gun's in my apartment downtown. We're policemen. As sheriff, I'm head policeman."

Jack inspected the ID. "That's your badge?"

"Real one's at my apartment. Today's my day off."

"Oh." Jack returned to Lucille and coleslaw.

"These kids came all the way from Detroit," Will glanced at Lucille, "to work as my apprentice wood carvers, cat handlers, and amateur naturalists. Experts in marsh life."

"That's a lie." Lucille stirred the slaw, dripping with mayo-overload.

"That one there," he pointed a spatula, "the one with the flame hair and long legs of a cross-country runner—"

"I do not like other people describing me." Her words jumped out of her mouth fast.

"How'd these folks come to know you so well that you'd cook dinner for them? Took you years to share your frying secrets with me."

"They're under my aegis for a few days."

"Eejis," Mayzie repeated. "What the?"

"Shhh! Authority. We are completely on our own because our mother traveled to Cumberland Island with someone she knew in high school, and she isn't coming back when she said she would so that we can start for Key West, which is my birthday gift, and also my treat for babysitting *all the time*, and my lifelong dream because the Keys will disappear soon; we stay alone at home when my mother works twelve-hour overnight shifts, but she is burned out, so she may not be going back, and we're not sure when—or even if—we're going home. We also nearly out of money, but bait-store Linda might give us jobs."

Will noted Trip's tongue lodged between his teeth, sizing up the scene: Will, the kids, the greasy floor—while palming his bare skull.

"How old will you be on your birthday, Lucille?" Trip smiled.

"Fourteen on Labor Day. Not even five days away if I start counting at midnight."

"Most kids your age can't carry such big responsibilities," he said. "How are you doing?"

"I am not most kids. We are fine."

Trip said nothing more.

Will broke the quiet. "Let's eat."

Everyone squeezed around the pine table, Will between Mayzie and Jack, opposite Trip and Lucille, who couldn't keep her eyes off Trip. Neither could Jack and Mayzie, the guy seemed like a real-life, dang superhero.

"Ahem. Earth to Lucille." Wait. Was Will jealous? "Please pass the fish."

"OK." Her eyes went from Trip's forearms to the fish platter. She gasped. "They have eyeballs."

Will wiped sweat and grease from his face with his bare arm. "OK, good stuff, people, and, yes, fish have eyes."

"I forgot something." Will dug his phone from his pocket and stood.

"Everybody on one side of the table, please?"

Mayzie and Jack slid off the bench, crawled under the table, and popped up behind Trip and Lucille.

"Smile? Pretty please?"

Lucille frowned and crossed her eyes, but finally clamped her teeth together, and smirked. Will snapped a photo and passed around his phone. Three startled-looking children and a tattooed giant.

Trip served himself two pieces of fish. "Are y'all Will's long-lost relations?"

The thought of being related to Will sent Jack and Mayzie into hysterics. Lucille watched Trip, slicing the fish top to bottom, sideways. He flipped the flesh, revealing the spine's tiny bones. Symmetrical. Perfect.

"Those bones held living muscle and tissue," Lucille said. "Wish I'd seen it alive."

Will knifed the other porgies and lifted a boneless slice onto Mayzie's plate, another on Jack's. "Nice outfit, Mayzie. Purple and orange—a sunset."

Mayzie shoveled chunks into her mouth. Tonight, she'd layered a purple top over an orange T-shirt.

"Choose one, Lucky. Fish play a noble role in the food chain, right?"

She pointed to the smallest. Will slid it onto her plate, head and all, probably a mistake, while she said, "Micro-plastics in the food chain can cross the blood-brain barrier and cause neurological damage."

A tear snaked from her eye down her cheek to her chin, where it hung until her skin absorbed it. How to handle a tear? Will hoped it stayed single.

"There's no plastic in cabbage, right? The porgy's already dead, why not avoid waste?"

She forked a morsel into her mouth, left it slightly open with the fish inside, then removed it with her fork and replaced it on the serving platter. She squirted the fish with lemon.

"The fish is crying lemon tears." She scooped slaw and ate bite after bite.

"You're a vegetarian? You eat fish sticks, right?"

"Only when necessary. I'm just not in the mood for fish."

"That's not the only problem, though, Trip, Lucille's upset about the glaciers melting, the planet heating up."

She shot Will a look. "I don't want to talk about that or anything else—not my mother, not my father, nothing."

"She's upset." Mayzie talked around a mouthful.

Will got up and ransacked cupboards, found mac and cheese, and rattled the box, but Lucille shook her head.

"Fake cheese. Chemical."

"You need food. We're celebrating."

"Celebrating what?" Jack and Mayzie asked. Lucille frowned.

"That you'll be around three more days, well, two whole days."

Lucille smiled, tears checked but threatening. She knew Will was lying but had game.

"She's worried about Mom," Mayzie announced.

"Is that so wrong? We're here with a stranger while she's off with this guy?"

Trip's eyes moved from Will to Jack to Mayzie to Lucille and re-started the rotation.

No breeze graced this cave, only the old A/C valiantly pumping lukewarm air. Will was grateful for the noise.

Lucille pulled her wet hair off her neck.

"You OK, Lucky?" Will asked. "Tell you who's lucky. Me. Getting to hang with you three." He finished eating and got up.

Trip cleared dishes. Plates, forks, and knives clattered in the sink. Trip took Lucille's plate, stooping to see her face. "You should eat," he said. "When's your mom due back?"

"Soon. Till then, they've got Uncle Will," Will said.

"Thanks, Uncle Will." Trip wouldn't take his eyes off Lucille. "You and your brother and sister staying alone in your cottage?"

She nodded.

Busybody. Will gritted his teeth, and noisily scraped the frying pan, banged it, and rubbed the scouring pad hard against the iron. Lucille turned toward him; he plunged his hands in the dirty water, setting off waves that washed over the sink and onto the floor.

"Jack and Mayzie, time for bed," Lucille said. "Nice to meet you, Sheriff. See you, Will." Polite. Docile. Very un-Lucille-like.

"It's not even all the way dark," Mayzie hollered from the door.

"One more thing? You guys need to move to a different cottage because yours is rented, since you'd planned to check out today."

"Move?" Lucille froze.

"Labor Day weekend—we're booked. Sorry. We've got just this one cottage left because the A/C busted." Will didn't talk money. He'd make it right. Wet bathing suits, food, she'd need to pack her mother's clothes, too. "I'll install a new A/C tomorrow—it's not rentable this way, so it's lucky, don't you think, we have a vacancy at all?" Odd for him to look on the bright side.

Lucille and the kids went outside; shrieks told him they were playing. Kids! One minute they cried, the next they laughed.

"What's going on, Will?" Trip asked.

"Mom's AWOL with an old flame. I don't mind watching them—the mother would've gone no matter what, I'm convinced—and Lucille claims she babysits at home while the mother works overnight shifts at the hospital. This girl, I kid you not, is more responsible than me. You don't need to sweat."

"I don't make the law, Will, I enforce the law."

Will ignored him and headed out. "What's all the commotion? Fun? I need me some."

"I get Will," Jack hollered. "We're playing Capture the Flag."

"Nah, Lucille's all by her lonesome, gotta help her out."

Trip burst from the door. "I'm with Mayzie and Jack."

"Yay," Mayzie yelled. "We get the sheriff."

Take the sheriff, little girl, Will thought, but beware of men who do their jobs too well. Will pulled his T-shirt up to his head, and shook his whole body.

"Let's goof it up, y'all." Trip, tough and operating by the book; Will, soft and excusing the wandering widow. Was he only postponing the inevitable? What stunt might the mother the pull in Key West? And why did Will give a rat's ass? Because Lucille's dad was a casualty of our uncivil society's killing fields?

"Mayzie, toss Trip that top shirt you're wearing over the other one."

She complied and Trip fit the frilly thing on his bald head.

The kids whooped.

"Ha ha ha HA." Will danced in place. "Go!"

Trip called time-out and imposed new rules. "Whoever loses a hat freezes." He joined Jack and Mayzie.

Will jogged past Lucille, warming up with high knees.

Renaldo loped over from the office, wearing a ball cap backward and carrying assorted hats. "Raided the lost and found." He sailed a sombrero toward Lucille. "I'm with Trip and them. Can't resist that fancy hat, Sheriff."

"What kind of loyalty is that?" Will asked. "Two against four?"

"You got Lucille—I've seen her blasting down the beach." Renaldo threw Mayzie a golfer's visor and Jack a kid-cowboy hat.

Lucille worked the sombrero over her ponytail, and took off, yelling, "Boundaries?"

"Wing it," Trip hollered, frills fluttering.

Will ran to Mayzie and tickled her, tapped her golf visor, and made faces at Jack, pushing his hat over his eyes; both froze. Lucille sped well past the Court, doubled back, snatched Trip's headgear, and took a running leap for Will's head.

She stopped, panting, waving Will's shirt, yelling, "Success."

"Wait. I'm on *your* team!" he yelled.

"Maybe." She eyed him. "Or maybe it's everybody for themselves."

At least she was winded. Everyone chased Lucille, double

speed, but she flew past, danced a quick victory jig in the shells, and ambled toward Renaldo, who bowed low as he presented her his cap.

Everybody for themselves. The girl did know the score.

While the kids argued over rules and winners and losers, Trip motioned Will behind the office, in the shadows, lecturing him, breathlessly, about the kids, and running a day care at his motel.

Will shoved him. Trip pushed back. Will lost his balance, waited a moment, got to his feet, and landed a solid punch to Trip's jaw. Trip stayed down a few seconds.

"Satisfied?" Trip worked his lower jaw side-to-side.

Lucille and the kids stared at them on their way to Cottage Ten. Renaldo stood in the middle of the parking lot, glaring holes in his two bosses, and finally jogged over.

"Y'all OK?"

Trip, palms up, shrugged, and called to the general population, which included Mrs. Pitts and Grandpa Webb. "We do this from time to time—a sign of brotherly love."

Mrs. Pitts slammed her screen door, then Will figured she probably lit up. If he and Trip couldn't behave decently, why should she?

Trip bought two Cokes. On Will's porch, he flopped in the wicker armchair, a sign he planned to linger. He kept the conversation going, the downside of working for a friend and living at your workplace, while Will leaned on his hands over the relief, *Out There.* At least the name still suited the sorry piece.

"This babysitting? It's no big deal." Will swallowed a mouthful of Coke, beat on his chest, and waited for the burp. It resonated. *Good one,* an unseen voice said from one of the Court's porches. He lowered his voice. "This girl's competent. She said so herself: She stays with her sibs all the time when her mother works nights."

"She's underage." Trip stretched his long legs and crossed them at his ankles.

"Girl's fourteen next week. Remember what we were doing at fourteen."

"That's how come they need supervision."

"You aren't drinking?"

Will lifted the Coke. "I certainly am. Thank you."

"Back to the kids—who are these people? I'd be derelict if I didn't serve the parents some kind of notice."

Any official action would snarl them in red tape. Will would hate that. Lucille knew how to notify the father of her siblings, but hadn't. Was the girl reluctant for a reason? She didn't want him to drive down and cause a fuss? Was he a problem? Was she protecting her mother?

"Trip, if you are so inclined, you will find the woman in question with her paramour at the Grassfield Inn." Let Trip go after them. The kids were scared on their own, though Lucille pretended otherwise, and this way, Lucille wouldn't need to take blame if someone—the mother or the little kids' father or even Tom—decided to place blame.

"They could go to jail," Trip said.

Will gripped the edges of his workbench, and felt like shooting himself into the air the way Jack had, on that first day. What, he'd regressed? He was five?

"OK. OK. Unlikely, unlikely, don't panic, but could happen, depends on juvenile court. Who's this companion?"

"Tom Barnes, the developer. Who would press charges, Trip? Who really cares?"

Trip leaned his forearms on his knees. "The state cares. Thing is, what goes on at home? Could be a disaster waiting to happen. What if Mom's sick or has drug problems? Kids could get hurt. What'd you notice while the mother was here? How about after? Bruises? They got money? Enough to eat?"

He hadn't followed his earlier impulse, typical Will, to track their food supply. He thought about the leftover coleslaw and made a mental note to give it to them tomorrow, but Lucille was the only one who'd eaten any. He'd need to do better. But Trip should lay off. The troubled family didn't need more grief. "This girl's got the mind of a mature thirty-year-old, not an immature one like me. She's even got MY back, lecturing me on the planet's fate, and how I need to appreciate what I've got."

Trip fell silent. "That right there, that she's got the mind of a thirty-year-old, is weird and worth investigating." The Court lay still and, except for the roar of bug noise and an occasional whoop from a cottage, tranquil.

"FYI, Jack and Mayzie's father lives in Detroit, but Lucille lost hers. Guess how."

"That so?" Surprise edged his voice; he rose and walked to the door, paused, and said, "I take it you think it's . . ."

"Time to GFOT." Will hadn't used the old soldier saw—*Get the F*** Outta There*—in years.

"I'll try but can't promise." Trip shook his head, gleaming under the yellow bug light.

"Do better than try. Let's leave this family be—for the moment." Trip couldn't, Will knew that, not if the mother didn't respectably show herself soon.

12

Time, Water

Thursday morning, Renaldo and Will moved our duffels. I lifted Dad's ashes from the shelf, hugging the lidded jar, a classical shape like I'd seen in the Detroit Institute of Arts, narrow foot, wide shoulder. Foot. Shoulder. Like a person. It was a person. The weight—was that Dad or the jar? Could ashes weigh as much as five pounds of flour?

Even smaller than Ten, Cottage Twelve's beat-up countertop separated its dollhouse kitchen from one big room with a sofa, a chair, a TV, and a partitioned-off bedroom. One double bed. Talk about close. And the shower was a wooden closet behind the cottage. A place fit for hobbits, not five-foot-seven me.

Heat forced us kids outside for the rest of that day—we body-surfed, catching only tail ends of big breakers, swelling and spitting: Sometimes the ocean felt warm, soft, and inviting but you couldn't trust ocean, driven by invisible fields and forces. By late afternoon, we stumbled home tired, and more sunburned; the sounds of tide-and-ocean jabber couldn't untangle my belly-knots. At least the new-old cottage was cool and dry. Will must've installed the new A/C while we were out—there was coleslaw in our fridge. Ugh.

I trashed it and splurged on supper. At least the girl on the phone, maybe it was Patty, of Patty's Pizza, cared whether we wanted pepperoni or cheese or peppers or large or small. I ordered both:

large meat for the kids, small veggie for me. Too late I remembered tailpipe pollution—ten miles for pizza delivery. My bad. Mayzie and Jack bought Cokes. After the pizza, twenty-five dollars, and the dollar-a-mile delivery charge, ten plus tip of five dollars, we had twenty dollars left of Naomi's seventy-five. I'd saved food receipts: bologna, cheese, bread, M&Ms, cookies, peanut butter, jelly, eggs, Vienna sausages, fish sticks. No one knew about my own stash: ninety-some dollars I'd earned babysitting for neighbors' kids, cats, dogs, and a little pig kept by a dude in our building.

We drank Cokes. We blasted the A/C. The kids tuned in a cop show. None of the TV cops looked like macho Trip. I worked a wedge from the veggie pizza and transported the flimsy paper plate to the porch, biting off a chunk—they'd rushed it from the oven and the dough in the middle was raw. I scraped off the peppers and spinach with my teeth and crumpled the dough and plate, same consistency. Steamy air. Fat and wet, like the pizza. I poked my head inside, where Jack and Mayzie sprawled, legs entwined on the sofa, mouths smeared with sauce, the TV blaring gunfire. They'd knocked over a Coke. Brown liquid sprayed the wall. Puddled the floor.

For sure, we'd forfeit the $150 security deposit. I shut the door. Laughter bubbled from other porches—cigarette smoke drifted from Mrs. Pitts's place.

Queen knocked at the screen door: "Flame girl, it's the hatching."

Inside, I pried Mayzie and Jack, carbed and comatose, from the sofa. They needed to see.

On the dark beach, we sank our feet in the creamy spindrift scribbling the dark sand, the tide nearly all the way out. It happened so gradually when I watched and so fast when I didn't. Time seemed like water—shapeshifting and sneaky. You never knew what either one was up to.

The moon gave off weak light, like day had almost but not quite drained. We followed Queen, wobbly in rubber boots, carrying a clipboard yards up the beach, to the nest I'd passed when I circumnavigated the island Sunday. People in shorts and windbreakers milled around or squatted near the site, some with red-cellophaned flashlights. Someone had placed two-by-fours like a temporary corral so the turtles could follow the path to the water, but turtles weren't cows or pigs. Would herding work?

Mayzie strutted in her PJs along the walk. "It's a runway. Like a beauty contest."

"These babies need safe passage from the devil, the land, where human ignorance can kill," Queen said, "down to the deep blue sea, their true home."

True home. Jack pulled on my arm. "I'm tired." He climbed up my back.

"They'll spend the next ten years in the Sargasso Sea—a big patch of seaweed in the ocean," Queen said, "where they hide from predators and grow."

Renaldo split from the knot of people and took Queen's arm, guiding her to the nest. Jack slid down my back and plastered himself to my calf. I half-dragged him up the beach, where people stared at the nest like a movie screen. Mayzie flopped on her belly, chin in her palms, and gaped at the sand, forcing people to step over her. "I don't see nothin'."

Renaldo held a flashlight while Queen rubber-banded red cellophane over the end, but in the moonlight, I didn't need the red-tinted light. Renaldo spouted turtle facts I already knew, but his voice made my insides bloom.

He started on coastal overpopulation scaring turtles from nest sites, fishing nets and lines snaring them, and how the seaweed beds—

"Are dying," I finished. "No good news. "I've seen TV specials."

"Except this—," he pointed. "You gotta hope. We're wack without hope."

That word tickled me. He played the flashlight over the nest, the sand full of tiny cracks.

"Everything in nature's in danger all the time except invasive species, and they ARE danger." I glued my eyes to the sand. A live birth, a dream come true, not only the birth, but witnessing it with people like Queen.

"Mothers often lay eggs on the same beaches where they were born."

"Yep." I didn't feel like talking.

"You know near 'bout everything." Queen offered more: The turtle babies use the earth's magnetic field like a compass, along with ocean currents, to locate feeding grounds and guide themselves home. And nest.

This jolted me. "I was—*sort of*—born here."

Queen said *incredible*, and other stuff that made my thoughts race—watching turtles hatch, maybe even Naomi going AWOL, because, if she'd been around, Naomi would be sucking my energy—was meant to be. Thinking this felt disloyal but true. Why should I lie to myself? She'd never mothered.

"I meant conceived." I figured out how sperm met eggs years ago. "My mom and dad made me. Here."

"You're home. Like these turtles will be in about twenty years. They'll swim back to shallower waters to finish maturing."

Finish maturing. When does maturing happen? The raw pizza. Will. Naomi. Were they done? Me, I felt mature. Was I? How would I know when I was done?

People started jabbering. I dropped my eyes to the fracturing sand.

"More than a hundred, I bet," I whispered to Mayzie. "Loggerhead mothers laid these almost two months ago. They lay different clutches, mate with different males and the eggs come from different fathers."

"Where are *their* parents?" Mayzie asked.

"Could be around here or off Africa, almost anywhere," Queen said. "These babies are on their own; if they needed parents to mind them, the species would've died out long ago."

"They'll be lonely." Mayzie snuffled. "Can't we keep them till they get big?"

Queen tapped her shoulder. "Girl, nature works better without humans butting in."

Humans butted in all the time! Polluting, uprooting, shooting nature in the heart—my mind flooded with underwater images of trawl nets, sharks, the floating Pacific garbage dumps.

Will jogged up the beach, panting. "What'd I miss?" He knelt in the sand and elbowed my arm. "Out after dark without telling me? You're all grounded."

"Quit it." I grinned.

He rose and turned to Queen. "Glad you notified the resident smarty pants—this one knows everything."

She clapped Will's shoulder. "These turtles timed the hatch for you."

I gaped as he swept the tiny old thing into a hug that lifted her off her feet. Oh, yeah, Renaldo said they're all related.

"You doing all right?" Queen asked, her voice muffled in his shirt.

He set her down. "As all right as ever."

"Heard the sheriff busted your jaw. What was that all about?"

"You heard wrong. I'm the one busted his jaw, but Trip's a tank."

Queen shook her head. "You two will never grow up."

Beach chatter died. The lumpy sand broke and dark shapes no bigger than my palm slipped out, two or three inches long. The pit churned with flailing flippers. Babies struggled from the sand, waddled drunkenly, guided, more or less, by the two-by-fours. Murmurs, squeals, and cries of, "Adorable," or "this one's going the wrong way," rippled.

Mayzie gasped. "They're too tiny to survive!"

Queen walked along with her clipboard, reminding people to count. "Four nests to go—one went in last Saturday."

That nest for sure wouldn't hatch before the storm. "Can't they relocate a nest?"

Queen shook her head. "We're not sure what'll happen, but if we move the nest, we think the babies will die." She circulated and recorded. "How many?" she asked me.

God. I forgot to count. Running my eyes over the still-lumpy nest, I panicked: What if one overslept and missed its chance to swim away? Something awful could happen once the humans pulled the stakes and dismantled their freedom highway.

A few minutes later, the litter had vanished into the water. Queen probed the empty nest with knobby knuckles. My hands met Renaldo's as we separately fingered the sand, gently, breathing deeply, studying the pit as if we could draw out any left-behinds with our minds. So much in life was mostly invisible; animals we'd never heard of, may never hear of. I dipped my nose to the sand; I saw movement.

"Look."

Queen stared. "Phooey. Can't see like I used to."

"A baby." Upside down and struggling, half buried. "Can't we help?"

"She's right—got a straggler." Renaldo shook his head.

"Won't do to interfere. Just won't do. Baby needs to memorize this sand. If it's a she, she'll need it in her DNA."

The baby paddled air with flippers as big as its tiny body. I leaned closer. A cloud veiled the moon and darkened the beach. Willing the baby to live, I closed my eyes. A moment later, I opened them and the turtle righted itself and rested. Maybe exhausted by its ordeal, maybe saying goodbye, at the edge of the pit.

Between the devil and the deep blue sea, its *true home*.

I pulled Jack and Mayzie close. The small sandy smear scuttled into the world. Alone.

That night we read *Horton Hatches the Egg* twice; I left Mayzie and Jack snoring and shut the door to my room, and made my bed on the couch. I slipped on Naomi's robe and switched off the lamp.

The iPad buzzed. I let it buzz, shocked that WiFi worked. Marco.

"I can't reach Naomi." His big smile dominated the screen.

"Marco, you won't believe what we saw." I threw my legs over the sofa-back and rested upside down, my head on the floor. "At least a hundred hatchlings. Turtles."

"*Lo dice en serio?*"

"I'm *not* kidding." I told the hatch start to finish, even about how mothers mate with different males, and how I was conceived at Boneyard Beach, so I was a turtle homing in on my birthplace, not technically. Then Marco told me about *another* glacier melting.

This thought hit me: I was the one stuck between the devil and the deep blue sea—Naomi was the devil and Marco would be the deep blue sea.

"Put Naomi on."

"She's at the beach." Now I knew kids lied, too.

"Have her give me a buzz, WiFi or cell, either one. Probably she doesn't want to talk, but try to get her to call me. OK?"

Would Naomi would go back to Detroit at all, if she had no job? We had enough savings for how long? Was this Tom a permanent addition? Questions, no answers.

"I'll try, but, honestly, Marco, cell service hardly exists and WiFi here is beyond winky—Will, the motel manager, calls it a dead zone."

As I listened to Marco's voice, warm and sincere, I asked myself where I'd been when she took off. Asleep. I'd eaten the fancy dinner Sunday night—linen tablecloths and napkins at the table overlooking sailboats and yachts. Tom had even seduced us.

I'd *enabled* her. My stomach turned over.

"You'll be home in a few days. While I've got you, how's Naomi doing?"

"You get adults better than I do. Guess she's OK."

"The older I get, the more complicated people become, but I shouldn't be discussing this with you, Lucille."

"Yesterday, Queen's grandson showed me how to float and then we started laughing our heads off—could NOT stop. I don't remember doing that ever."

He laughed. "Is he cute, this guy?"

I ignored that. Cute. Like he's a teddy bear? "You worried about Jack and Mayzie?"

"Not worried, no, I miss them. Are you getting any free time?"

The heat started in my toes, traveled up my spine to my hair, buzzing. Love buzz.

"People here are super nice. Tonight at the turtle hatch, I came back to our cottage feeling like I was part of this *totally random family*. Silly, huh? People will leave, sure, but Will and Queen and Renaldo and Trip, the sheriff—even the store clerk—"

"Hold on, you know the *sheriff*?"

"He's strange but OK. Will warned us"—I remembered it was illegal to stay alone without an adult. I shut up.

"What? Warned you about what?"

"Oh, that he might lecture us about staying in school or drugs or alcohol, or those e-cigarettes and vaping, that crazy stuff."

"You're too smart for that."

"For sure."

"Got enough money? Do you have a credit card?

"Yep. We're good. Will cooked dinner last night and invited us. Fish. I couldn't eat it because of all the overfishing in the ocean. I tried not to bring that up because I talk enough about depressing subjects. But I did."

"This Will, who is he?"

"Manager." OK, I needed to shut up. "Gotta go, talk later."

"Do right by me, Lucille, OK? Talk me up. I'm hoping she changes her mind. About us." I could not promise. Hated to cut Marco short, but if he knew we'd been alone all week, he'd zip down and whisk us back to Detroit before school started, and I was desperate to bury Dad and see Key West.

"Bye, Marco." I hung up.

Now my insides itched, like poison ivy had inflamed my heart and lungs and belly organs. The lie was poison. I'd kept the lie going. When grownups asked questions that made me squirm, I should tell the truth. Was I wrong? Or should I make lying a habit, like adults do?

13

Market

Barely eight o'clock, and the old slave market in Pinesboro, complete with the standard Confederate general, jumped with life. Three city blocks long, under one roof, swallows drunkenly swooped and dove, above fifty-some merchants transacting business. The air stewed with smells of overripe everything, including humans. Smoke from fried fruit pies greased the air. Flies attacked fresh-picked peaches. People sat on upturned wood crates, shelling peas with raw red fingers ending in dirty nails like Will's. Every kind of body roamed the market—young men and women wearing hijabs or braids or ponytails or buzz cuts—they fussed over tables of jams, cakes, kebabs, halal, falafel, or homemade remedies. Some toted bags of tomatoes, peaches and zucchinis or clutched oblong striped watermelons under an arm. Sunburned tourists carrying tall lattes pushed children in strollers or tried to chase toddlers without spilling coffee.

Will trailed his unpaid child labor—if he did OK today, he'd tip them. A twenty? A five? He had no idea what was a lot and what was a little to these kids, but the thought lifted him out of himself and quickened his steps. He traversed the center aisle to the end—the arts and crafts section, with painters, blacksmiths, candlemakers, potters, weavers, and makers of art he'd never imagined. He stopped at a display of antique books. The artist had removed pages, and created tiny scenes between covers, containing odd, found objects, photos or newspaper clippings, around a theme—one about Bhopal, after a chemical spill in the 1980s, another about nuclear disaster. Still another dark box showed children levitating above the cares of the world, represented by a mad mob below shaking fists at happy children, trying to pull them down to ugly earth with a net. Real art.

Lucille's eyes lingered on the images, too. The artist was an older black dude.

"You understand what I'm saying?" he asked.

"Yeah, this one in particular, 'Childhood'," Will said. "I'll be back if I make money."

Lucille elbowed Will, pointing at the artist's titles. She was right.

The man cocked his head and offered his hand. "Always the question, my friend, of the almighty green. I'm Sid Turner."

"Will Altman. Good to make your acquaintance." Will had had no idea what he'd stumbled into with his hobby. Original work was complex beyond anything he'd imagined. And the deeper he dug, the more the work demanded. Satisfying. Frustrating.

At the check-in table, Belva wore her "Market Manager" badge—Belva Johnson—her married name.

"Here I am." Will mustered a cheerful voice. "I could use a corner space. Galleries are buying work for fall and the holidays."

"Will, glad you made it." She smiled. "Who knows better than I, the manager, that the holiday buying season is here?"

She turned, checked in a potter, and consulted her phone.

"You're right. This is your project. And you're doing a fantastic job." Will's claustrophobia descended, his chest tightened, and for a moment, he rocked on the balls of his feet, and, with effort, inhaled, and exhaled.

She glanced up from her phone, furrowed her brow, and shook her head. "Will, you're not on the list. You never registered, and we're full. I'm so sorry. That stinks. I know you were counting on today's sales."

"Can't you squeeze me in? Somewhere?" Begging.

Her creased slacks, her bangs, today, pulled from her face,

her endearing fat braid twisted at her neck, pearls in her earlobes, somehow had pushed her out of reach.

She cut her eyes at him, stood on tiptoe, and whispered, "Will Altman, I thought this might happen. You're just not an 'in advance' kind of guy, are you? We're going to fix that, but today, honest, I've got nothing. I'm super, super sorry."

"But I *need* this show. I've got new work I'm excited about—even a tiny corner would work." He finger-combed his beard, his hair, and couldn't stop. He flexed his jaws. Clenched and unclenched his fists. He stared above Belva's head, and there was Lucille, trying to control Mayzie's fried-pie intake and Jack's shadow boxing, and, now, mouthing, "No," and pressing her palms down, as though trying to conduct Will's screwy symphony.

He leaned down to Belva's ear. "But what about—Sunday?"

"Unfortunately, this is business. I should've registered you."

OK, so she had to maintain standards, yet his mind played scenarios—no, the husband couldn't be back, not after what she'd confided when he'd fixed her porch; maybe someone else had her attention. Maybe she'd lost interest.

Adrift in the people-tide moving past, he couldn't stay in place without being jostled. The market hadn't even started and he was fried. Worries about the kids and their mother's return or non-return, the possibility that Trip might go off the rails and arrest Naomi, had stymied sleep the past two nights running.

He stared at nothing, unfocused and muddled.

"Will? Will."

Belva was saying his name. "I'll register you for next weekend. The buyers will be back. If there's anything else you need—or any solution you can think of, please call or text, but we're limited to fifty exhibitor spots. I'm sorry you went to the trouble to pack and drive over, but I'm happy to see you."

She squeezed his hand, and headed off, speaking into a walkie talkie. For a second, he considered stopping her and telling her this: *I might be in love with you*.

Instead, he walked toward Lucille, massaging his neck; he'd slept on it wrong. He caught Lucille's eye and motioned her over.

"Stay with Pearl, will you? Don't let anybody tow her. I've got to make an arrangement." Studying the strange crowd, the blurred faces, he turned zookeeper again, observing this human race to which he did not belong.

14

Wave

So cool how Will named his truck Pearl. Opal would also have been nice. I threw one leg over the tailgate and landed on my tail in the bed. I scrambled up.

"Hon! Hon!" A lady with a name tag dangling at her chest waved her arms. "Tell your daddy to move his truck."

"Hello! He's not my daddy." I jammed my hands into my hipbones.

"Whoever he is, he can't park here. Find him, Hon."

The woman moved on. Across the street, Will was talking to the manager again, but getting nowhere, judging by her face—kind smile, but her head wagged no, no. He bombed across the street between Jack and Mayzie, each holding a hand.

"We're on the *lam* like on TV," Mayzie said, breathless, as he hustled them into the cab. Jack bammed his fist on the back window to get my attention. I looked. He made a gun with his fingers.

Stop, I mouthed.

Will hung halfway out of the window and backed into traffic. "Stay down, Lucky."

I dropped to the scratched rusted metal, feeling trapped in a hillbilly TV episode. Soon we crept past check-in, puttered three more blocks, and stopped.

Will dropped the tailgate. He pulled and I pushed crates to the edge. "You see Belva, holler."

Jack and Mayzie hopped out and scanned the street and sidewalk. "Did you bring your gun?" Jack asked.

"*Yeah, you ain't no suit-wearin' businessman, you just a gangsta.*" Mayzie.

"Shut up," I told them. "Behave."

Will sent them to distract Belva. "Monopolize her attention so she won't notice me."

They had no idea what monopolize meant but nodded as if they did.

"Ask questions. She won't mind." A moment later, he called, "Be careful."

A traffic volunteer motioned them across. Mayzie was a running blur, in her lime-green halter top over a red T-shirt and red shorts. People passing stared at Will, setting his sculptures, one by one, on the sidewalk. He ignored the looks because he didn't see them—his eyes focused on nothing. We lowered a crate to the concrete.

"You're illegal? Don't get Jack and Mayzie to do your dirty work—I'm certainly not going to."

He smiled for the first time since we got here, and straightened, pointing at the crate.

"You just did. And to answer your question, let's just say I'm headed for that fertile ground between legal and illegal." He tipped each crate, braced it against his thigh, and let it rest, bent his knees until an edge touched the sidewalk. I jumped down and grabbed one side, taking hardly any weight. "Easy, let her down easy. We don't want to crack these babies." He glanced at me. "Especially not Mortimer."

We safely lowered the crate. "Mortimer's here?" My heart puffed.

A cooler remained in the truckbed. Maybe he brought beer. I hoped he'd brought water.

"What's in here? I'm thirsty."

Will's grin covered half his face. "Lunch. Carrots. Celery sticks. Egg salad. Do you eat egg salad? Wait. You're not vegan—are you?"

I shook my head. I hadn't seen Will eat lunch all week, except that half of a PB&J on Monday. Today he made ours.

"And grapes. Seedless green. You like grapes?"

"We love grapes more than anything in the world!" I imagined Will, up early, boiling eggs and smashing them, opening his fridge door, spooning pickles from a jar and mixing in mayo. He cared what we ate.

"I don't think they're organic. You get hungry, help yourself. The cooler'll be under my chair. I figured y'all wouldn't have had time to think about food.

"You go and have fun—there's wonderful art here. I've got this."

"You do not have this." The sun felt like a big dog panting hot breath. The sun could burn up the world. Someday it would. I pried the lid off a crate with Will's screwdriver, and he emptied twelve bubble-wrapped bundles. As we unveiled them, I grilled him for intel, trying to catch him off guard.

"Do you think Trip will do anything about us because we're—um—alone?"

Will cut the tape securing bubble wrap around *The Wave*, and positioned it on the pedestal. I fingered its convoluted pathways. With no start and no finish, it whooshed into space, curving into a sharp crest that hung over nothing, and towered, wildly, nearly as tall as the display crates, though not as tall as me. Something grabbed at my insides, forcing me to stare at *The Wave*. Good art demanded attention. This must be good art.

"Never mind Trip. He's a fuss budget. I think everything's cool." Will folded the bubble wrap. "Always stopping by to see if I'm OK."

"Some people might like that." I didn't understand Will but worried about him, weird even for me, a worrier. I didn't blame Trip. I felt like the guardian of the whole world. Maybe that's how Trip saw things since he became sheriff. Maybe that was why he might keep his eyes on us. Maybe that was OK.

"Are you and Trip best friends?"

Will stashed the bubble wrap inside an empty crate. "We grew up together, joined the army around the same time, served in different zones. He got into deep—um, stuff—in Fallujah."

The sun blasted my eyes and purple gyrations splashed my vision. *Fallujah, Fallujah, Fallujah.* I shut my eyes, but the vibrations continued inside my eyelids. That word sent me cockeyed. *Fallujah.* When the officers in gold-trimmed uniforms rang the doorbell that day nine years ago, they said that word, and after that nothing stayed the same, not Naomi, not me. We packed and moved to Detroit from Fort Benning, Georgia, six months after a social worker threatened to "remove me from the home." I'd started searching neighbors' trash cans for food, they said, and one called Children and Family Services. I mothered my mother, in bed.

Will's voice broke my thoughts.

"Lucille." He was yelling.

"What! I'm right in front of you."

"No. You went someplace in your head, you don't gotta hide it from me because I do it, too. You go see your Dad?"

I couldn't speak. It was wonderful of him to say—most adults figured they'd upset me if they asked about my father, but they really meant they'd upset themselves.

"It's normal to check out like that, but I am not normal." He winked—another adult signal: He'd said all he would. He flipped four more crates, turning them into pedestals, positioned his six sculptures on top, and then propped the flat relief, the one he'd struggled with Tuesday, against a parking meter.

The Wave stood alone.

I kneeled on the sidewalk and inspected the relief. *Out There.* The lines rolled like grasses, no, waves, or even worms, deep-cut grooves rubbing and rolling over each other, natural, but chaotic, like the earth. Wednesday, when he'd carved it—I bet he had an artistic vision that tapped his unconscious. I read about Picasso and Van Gogh and how they painted the unconscious mind; I'd fallen into trances, once or twice, when I ran or concentrated super hard.

Mortimer went on a five-foot-tall pedestal. I placed him there because he was tiny: People needed to see those sad, round eyes up close. I grabbed a pen and paper from my tote bag and printed a title: *Wake up, World.*

Will fussed with the setup. While he did, I asked him

questions. I've done this with grownups before—caught them working and they automatically told the truth because they were too distracted to think up a lie.

"How'd you carve those wave lines so realistically? I feel like I'm choking on water when I look at them, either that, or looking at the guts of the earth, roots and stuff."

"For real, Lucky, those lines carved themselves."

"Yeah, like Trip automatically asking about our story."

Will edged along the sidewalk from pedestal to pedestal, adjusted, repositioned, stood back, arms folded, observing. "Oh, that, once he realized the situation . . ."

My vision cracked again. "What do you mean?"

"Look, he'll keep his eye on you but you're a pro and the kids are in good hands. Heck, at the Court, you've got me, Queen, Renaldo, and even Trip will cruise by to make sure everything's fine. It's all good. Instant family."

Instant family. I clutched Mortimer, chewed my lip, and watched a river of shoppers split around Will's jumble of pedestals. *The Wave* reached into space, caught in action, ready to crash. All Will's sculptures were rickety like Will was testing the limits of wood and gravity. But Will seemed like he was the one about to break. I'd seen that in his face with Belva. Will had broken on the inside like Naomi. She'd once told me about a new mother who bled on the inside. To death. No one knew, not even the doctors, not until it was too late.

Will tucked in his shirttail—a white button-down. He climbed into his tall canvas chair, placed his big sneakers on its footrest, and slid his sunglasses from his head to his nose. Jack and Mayzie ran across the street dodging cars. Will jumped from his chair, darted into the street, and yanked them to the sidewalk.

"I got Belva coffee, Will," Mayzie yelled, panting. "Guess what? She never even mentioned you, but she wants me back 'cause she's got a job for *me*! Later!"

She bounded back across the street, paused in the middle, stopping traffic, and hollered, "She fussed at Jack for spilling coffee on her laptop."

Jack's face contorted. "Like one drop. Pterodactyl did it. Like one drop." Jack opened his palm and there was the wood scrap of a dinosaur, with the wingspan of a fly. Will stayed nose to nose with Jack like he was breathing Jack in, he touched Jack's cheek, a sprig of his hair, and placed his hands on Jack's shoulders. Jack wiggled away. Maybe Will was smiling behind his beard, but, if so, it was a tiny smile.

The town baked. I huddled in shade behind Will and his chair and dug into the cooler. I wolfed half an egg salad sandwich. Tiny, sweet bits of pickle tickled my tongue. By chewing my last bite thirty times I made it last. I unwrapped a half for Jack, came out from my hiding place, and handed him chilled water. An old lady hobbled toward Will, cane poking the sidewalk.

"I'm Cecelia Bauknight. We've never met, but you're a friend of my great nephew's. Trip has talked about you." She touched *The Wave*, which tensed me up, but the lady was gentle and asked Will tons of questions to which he gave two-word answers like "sycamore snag," or "three hundred."

Will's tongue didn't seem to work, so I took over. "I'm Lucille, Will's assistant. Images shape the ideas behind his work, and free his imagination, which takes over."

Cecelia stared at me. So did Will. The sun's tiny shade patterns danced on the sidewalk. The great aunt—what *was* a *great* aunt?—was buying *The Wave*.

"Can you deliver the piece today?" she asked. They arranged time and place. She lived someplace with the cool name of *Sunbow*. What was a sunbow? Everybody here named everything. Trucks. Houses.

A policeman wearing shorts wheeled a bike from the street onto the sidewalk. Beside him? Belva. The cop wrote Will a ticket and ripped it from his handheld ticket-writer.

"Oh, I'm sure Will is happy to move—no need for a ticket, for heaven's sake," Belva pleaded, glancing from the officer to Will and back to the officer.

"You're obstructing pedestrian traffic on a public thoroughfare." He gave Will the ticket.

I hoped Will wouldn't do something stupid like punch the officer the way he socked his *best friend* in the jaw.

"A public sidewalk belongs to the public." Will cut his eyes at Belva.

"A shame, Will. I only wish there was something I could *do*." The ticket looked like it hurt her worse than him.

I had no sympathy for her. She could have bent rules and found him a tiny, tiny space—I saw spots where he could've displayed his pieces. I frowned.

"And where's your retail license?" the policeman demanded.

"Retail license?"

"Included in your fee," Belva explained. "Will, if only you'd registered. I meant to remind you Wednesday, but forgot."

Will faced the policeman. "I'm not in the market proper—I don't owe a fee. You have no right to interfere with my entrepreneurial effort, and, besides, haven't you ever heard of looking the other way, and furthermore," he paused for breath, "I am a . . ."

The officer interrupted, "I don't care about any of that. Pay the fine or appear in court."

"This is public property. I pay taxes. What damn code have I violated?"

Will's hands curled into fists. I stepped between Will and the cop, facing the cop, and held up my palms. "We'll pack right away, Officer."

I wove in and out of the crowd, found, and mobilized Mayzie. Girl was swapping *Wire* stories with a woman manning a table of fried pies. How many had Mayzie eaten?

"Gotta go. Will's in trouble."

"Figures." Mayzie called to her new friend, "*It's all in the game.*"

"*Keep my name out of it*," the woman said.

At Will's sidewalk display, the policeman watched Will pack. Will clenched his jaws and jutted his chin. Usually even when he tried to be mean, like when he kicked us out of his workshop, he couldn't manage, but probably he could get mean. If he had to. Soldiers would need meanness.

Everyone pitched in except Belva, who waved and returned

to the main market. Will stared after her, his shoulders slumping. Even with the sun lighting the street, it looked like someone had switched his off button.

Poor, crippled Cecelia insisted on helping pack: she wrapped sculptures in bubble plastic. "This one's mine." She handed Will a hundred dollar bill for *The Wave.* "I'll give you the other two hundred when you deliver, would that be all right with you? Do you know Sunbow?"

Will stared at the hundred and nodded.

It took a couple of minutes, but Will finally squared his shoulders and sauntered off without smiling, walking backwards, past the still-waiting policeman. As he passed me, he whispered, "Don't want to appear but just so compliant."

A sudden, joyful laugh escaped my mouth.

15

Sunbow

"You mind keeping an eye on those three this afternoon?" Will asked Queen. "I've got a delivery to Sunbow."

Queen squinted at the office computer screen. "These news people, yammering about a storm dawdling in the Atlantic." She tilted her head. "Sunbow! That's some high cotton. Sure, I'll put them on my radar, but that girl's always got those chicks in her sights. Why are you home early? What went wrong?"

"Nothing a whole new life wouldn't fix, but here's the good news." Will skipped his run-in with the law and narrated the story of the three-hundred-dollar sculpture sale.

"Bully for you! You've got the good life, see?"

He dismissed her wise-woman words. The other two hundred will disappear fast, between the fine and next week's market entry fee—and he owes fifty dollars for the gas nozzle.

"Make them tell you where they're going."

"Renaldo will be only too happy to tail that redhead."

Renaldo and Lucille? She was something, never mind those sloppy track clothes. That hair. That *charge* she carried. Will scrunched his face. "What? What have they been up to?"

"Phooey. Grandma'd be last to know. You're not so old you can't remember how teenagers keep secrets."

"But Lucille's too smart. . ."

"To act like a kid with hormones like every other girl her age?

She's nearly fourteen. Looks older, acts older, but don't let that fool you, she's hungry for love, attention, all that good stuff, you've seen how she mothers those children. I came up that way myself, mothering at an early age, it was normal back in those days. I recognize it. She's downright sweaty with . . ."

Whoa. Who wanted to hear what she was sweaty with? He was missing cues and needed to open his eyes and his mind. First Belva. Now Lucille. If only this were a problem glasses could fix. He'd noticed big grins on their faces when Renaldo and Lucille crossed paths, even briefly, but hadn't processed their now-obvious joy as love in the making.

He guided Pearl into Cecelia's parking spot on Sunbow Hummock, Boneyard's western edge; the sun low and syrupy, still packed plenty of heat. Everyone knew the place, its own little island. Over centuries, sediment and vegetation built hundreds of hummocks. Cecelia's in-laws, Trip's people, once owned the whole island. They'd grown cotton till the bottom dropped out of the market and they eventually had to actually pay workers; at some point the family sold a few lots to working folks from inland towns like Jesup and Waycross. They gave Queen's forebears the acre where Queen and Renaldo live, at the Court. Since the 1970s, the federal government had owned 1,326 acres, the national wildlife refuge. Only a few in-holders like Will, with *Loblolly*, still hung on. What would happen when Cecelia died? Trip could inherit; Boneyard could sprout gated communities, courtesy of someone like Tom Barnes.

At the house, someone had planted the lawn with citronella torches, flaming tongues lapping torpid air. The white clapboard two-story, peeled and pocked, offered few signs of life, but voices from the creek side of the house carried, even in the dense, motionless air. Will pounded the tarnished knocker and soon the salt-spoiled door swung wide. Here was brown Cecelia, her smile activating dozens of lines in her face. She could be a thousand years old; the wrinkles didn't date her, it was her sphinxlike manner, and coiled oyster-colored braids that gave her a timeless air.

"You managed to find the place without a hassle?" She put her hands at his neck—he froze—and pulled him to her height, into her citronella-and-lighter-fluid smell. So she'd lit the torches. She kissed one cheek, then the other.

"I can hardly find your face in that beard."

This affection unnerved but thawed him. His own grandparents, on his mom's side, died, one after the other, when he was in high school. He missed them—he'd inherited his love of woodcarving from Grandad and his fish frying skills from Gran. Mute, he pointed to his bubble-wrapped burden, flipped open his knife, and sawed the tape. The plastic dropped.

She studied the piece. "So natural. Crude. And I mean that in a good way."

For a moment, he was quiet, but felt compelled to throw out words. "Honestly, the shape was halfway there. I take my cues from nature and try not to mess up what she's already started."

He shut up. It was bad luck to talk much about art—too mysterious, and he feared losing whatever inside him had sparked the creation. He changed the subject.

"You're so close to the native shell rings, just across the creek, am I right?"

"Yes. And I'm sorry we haven't met before—I've only come here in the coldest winter months for these last fifty years. It's time to change that. I've never seen those shell formations. Of course, my husband occasionally spoke of them, but he's been dead ten years."

"They don't look like much, but when I visit the site, I shiver. That says something."

"That's one reason," she said, ushering him, still carrying the sculpture, from the house to the deck, "we donated our land to the wildlife refuge. We hoped all the set-aside land would protect archaeological sites."

"My family owned some of that land, too, before the Depression. We held onto fifty acres, barely, and I'm hanging onto those if it kills me."

"I'll wager my husband's family bought your parcel, included in our gift that became the wildlife refuge back in the 1970s, if that makes you feel better."

It did.

"We take these ancient sites for granted because the history is buried," she said. "But when you live, really live in a place, you can imagine life that long ago—five millennia, maybe more. I hope they never build one of those 'interpretive' centers. Better to let archaeologists quietly uncover evidence and shed what light on civilization and science they can."

Cecelia spoke Will's mind. So few people did.

"I hope you won't mind if I show you off to my friends."

He wrinkled his nose. She laughed.

"Don't look so dour. Your work makes people want a piece of you, whatever in you has generated your fine art. When they buy a sculpture, they're buying a piece of the artist."

That notion deviled him. "Do I look like I'm for sale?" But she had called him an artist. She was a collector. Maybe they shared something.

"Why didn't you bring those spunky kids? I love the redhead's talk about your ideas."

"I have no idea how she fabricated that spiel."

"It sounded authentic."

He shook his head, not because it wasn't true, but because he didn't know where she got the notion and why she'd spilled it this afternoon.

Out back, a dock cut into Chicken Creek, and ballooned into a deck. People murmured. Ice clinked in crystal. Torches lined the rails. At a bar, two stylish young women in white shirts and black pants mixed drinks. The gray-green creek, and likewise muted marsh grasses clashed with carnival colors leaking from dark clouds. Distant lightning.

Cecelia pushed Will gently onto the deck, shuffling beside him, propelling herself by cane and handrail. The crowd shushed.

"Everyone, my discovery, my great-nephew's artist-friend, Will Altman."

He cringed. Show and tell? His parents might have known these people, but no one acted like they recognized him or his name. A blunt-nosed man in khakis and a polo shirt pulled over his belly stepped forward and gripped Will's hand, a big grin on his face. "Dick."

An easygoing, a winner-of-sales-awards type.

"She and I only just met this morning. I'm a friend of her nephew's."

"If she says you're an artist, then you are. Let's see the thing."

Will thrust the sculpture forward; the reddening light torched its crest.

Dick rubbed the fragile top curl. "Wood's got a contradictory softness. You can't cut but so much with the grain, cut across the grain and you get a complex pattern. Tell me your experience." Dick dug his wallet from a back pocket, licked his thumb, and peeled off a card.

"My grandad taught me to whittle, shop class taught more, framed houses in high school, and even reproduced historical carvings. Lately, I've stumbled into sculpture."

"No formal art training?"

"None."

"I've done hobby time with wood tools, but I'm mostly a dealer. I've got gallery contacts from Miami to New York, even across the pond."

Dick looked like too much of a redneck to be an art dealer.

A few guests closed in and admired *The Wave* while Cecelia introduced Will. After the oohs and aahs, most retreated into private conversation. The crowd was well-heeled, at total ease with money and luck, which so often mated; the old bitterness rose in Will's throat, the "not good enough" refrain, but he reminded himself that today he'd gotten lucky. Sold a sculpture.

Even so, the tide slapping the deck's pylons, vibrating the floor, shook loose his worries about how he'd earn enough of a grubstake to finish *Loblolly*. A black mood reared as dark descended, so he focused on the marsh. At times like these, only the mallet and chisel and gouge could sweeten his mood—the chipping of pathways, the crossing of grain transported him.

The Wave grew heavy in his arms and his heart sank with that weight. Who was to say if the work was any good? Even if it was good, could he repeat this success?

Dick disappeared and returned in five minutes with two shot

glasses of amber liquid. "I don't like this martini craze, how about join me in a toast to a new partnership?"

Partnership? Will stared at the lit and dazzling substance in cut-glass tumblers, and then studied Dick's face. The prospect of Dick representing Will's work scared him. If Will had talent, he should be home carving, not schmoozing. And Lucille? Where was she? A good kid, but he was uneasy. Queen was forgetful, never mind her keen observations about human nature.

Somehow the notion now hit Will that babysitting, even as lame a job as he'd done, had triggered instincts that bred worry, broke his concentration, even as he was—possibly—at success's doorstep. He worried about those children *all the time.*

Dick handed him a glass. Will lifted his palm. "I gotta scoot."

"Don't make me drink alone. It's not often I find art I really cotton to, art that's authentic and honest, what we might have called man's work in an earlier era. It sprang from your hands. It's unselfconscious."

Will shifted *The Wave* from one arm to the other. Finally, he held it in both arms, unable to let go, like it was ballast and without it he would drift away. The salt-scented wood in his arms reminded him who and where he was.

"To Will." Dick proffered a full shot glass.

"To art." He set down *The Wave*, took the glass, and gulped the fiery drink.

"How'd that go down? Straight from Scotland."

Will's throat burned and so did his empty belly. He'd never eaten his own egg salad, and he'd never tasted good whiskey.

"One more? For the road?"

"It's been a long road." Will could handle this. He kept no alcohol at the Court, so he couldn't get at it, and he couldn't afford drinks in a bar or bottles of booze.

"I'm honored."

"You're honored?" Dick laughed. "I'll buy more of your work." He left and returned with two more shots. "What should we drink to this time? Prosperity?"

Will's insides smoldered. "I'm all for prosperity."

"Let's talk business another time, but let me say this: I'm someone who understands that art is a commodity: Once you convince people they've got to have the latest—in your case, primitive-style carvings—the pieces will sell."

"Glad to hear it. I've had trouble selling my work."

"No shame in that. You needed to be discovered. And Cecelia has discovered you."

Cecelia made her way toward them by cane. "I need one more moment with you, Will."

She took Will's arm. "Let's talk over here."

Away from the crowd and stinky torches, she said, "Trip has told me you served, too. How have you fared since your return? In my generation, we called it *soldier's heart*. All our boys had it but never discussed it. Trip's had a rough time."

This stunned Will. The liquor had overheated him, melted his edges, the razor sharp ones, and, maybe, just maybe made him feel part of the human race. Trip had never said word one. Too busy advising Will. But what should they do? Start a support group? The trauma right this minute felt far away, all those overseas hours, 9,760 times two, lay buried in the same way "civilization" had buried or bulldozed native shell rings out of existence. Maybe there was no need to feel like an outsider. Will need not think about those hours at all, not when this world was showing him its good side, when these art patrons were treating him so well and seemed to trust him enough to ask his thoughts about the sheriff, his best friend, the one Will thought had his shit so together. Had Will healed? Had the movie ended? The film in his head where the plot was the ne'er do well, the alien no one understood or gave a damn about?

Here was Will, enjoying drinks among friends.

"Will?" Cecelia was saying. "Will? Are you OK?"

He heard her voice and observed her lips move, but could not grasp her words. Other voices flowed in a river of white noise. Will pointed northwest. He wanted to talk about the fire at *Loblolly* but was drunk—with euphoria. People glowed. The creek twisted below the deck, a gilded ribbon.

"I'm still so angry about that policeman issuing you a ticket. I'll talk to Trip."

He shook his head. Her comment reminded him of Belva, who now seemed reachable.

Will cast his eyes on the water, beyond which lay his once-upon-a-home, just across the creek, a mile, maybe two. Maybe he should be glad the bankers wouldn't lend. Rebuilding the home wouldn't resurrect his parents. Maybe he should sell.

Nothing stayed the same. The seas would rule. How could they not?

Even before Lucille arrived and hammered him with information, he knew, but her harping on global warming reminded him that inundation loomed.

He pointed across the creek. "Burned. Trying to rebuild." His arm stayed aloft, finger pointed, imagining the last loan officer who'd turned him down, a pleasant woman with sympathetic brown eyes and bitten nails. He dated her once. The loan would work out now, with Dick representing him. He'd shown his sculptures all summer, with little or no response, good or bad. People walked past and smiled, but rarely stopped and bought.

Cecelia was saying, her face to the sky, "I'm a traveling ancient ruin, guarding my few remaining assets. This was my husband's place, but I don't belong here. I have no children, no grandchildren to ground me, but," she fixed her eyes on Will, "if I had roots, if I had a home-place, I'd move heaven and earth to preserve it. We can leave home, but home won't leave us—it's in our blood, our brains."

Will chewed on her words and eyed his empty glass. He shifted the sculpture, just couldn't let his creation go, he felt like kissing it, and why not? Cecelia and Will took the few steps back to Dick, and Will helped her to a nearby chair.

Will thrust *The Wave* at Dick, ready for the solitary sojourn along the walkway over the mud, to Pearl, maybe one more drink in his hand. At last, success. It's taken years.

Dick set down the sculpture and touched Will's arm.

"One more thing," Dick said.

"What?" Will was sure Dick had changed his mind.

"Don't look worried, son. I'd like to visit your studio, see your work. Next week?"

"I work on my porch when the weather's nice, and inside when it rains."

"I've got warehouse space I'm rehabbing near the old slave market. You interested?"

"Maybe. I'd hoped to finish my workshop over home, across the marsh, but I've considered selling, so, sure, I'd think about a studio in Pinesboro." Maybe Trip and Will could share a space, if Trip was serious about woodturning.

Dick summoned another young bartender. "Good plan. You don't want to work all by your lonesome. You need company. Other artists."

The barman poured them fresh shots. Dick lifted his glass. Will hoisted his.

"Here's to a partnership." Dick downed the shot.

Dick could really hold his liquor. He'd probably started drinking before Will even got here, yet seemed sober. Dick grabbed Will's free hand and they shook.

"Will," Cecelia called, from her chair. "Dick can promote you and your work. If you're like Trip, you don't want to accept help, but think what it might mean for your art, for you."

Will waited for the deck to stop moving; it never did. The water below churned.

"Yes, ma'am, but . . ."

"Your work can make me money," Dick said. "I am talking real money, Will, not that piddly-ass art fair change. This piece? I'll turn around and sell this for a thousand bucks, easy."

Dick threw back his head and laughed a loud, ebullient laugh.

Will caught Dick's mood, and pumped the man's hand, smiling until his face hurt. For the first time in forever, a new path. He nodded to Cecelia, Dick, and wove down the walkway over the fire-tipped grasses. At the truck, he couldn't find keys, maybe a pocket? No. Maybe he was over the legal limit. For sure, he was over the limit. Fuzzy headed. He got in. Keys in the ignition.

He threw Pearl in gear and crept along the back-island road, praying he wouldn't steer Pearl into the creek. Was the tide low or high? Either way he'd be fucked—sinking in mud or drowning in sea.

Just this once. Tomorrow would be a new day. "I'm an artist," he crowed out the window. He struggled to stay on the blacktop, rearing up at him. The light tricked him, or maybe it was his brain, haywire, hyper-aware of being inside his own head, the ringing in his ears, a roar, turning roadside shrubs and moss-draped oaks into threats. And why was it taking forever to drive these few miles? He jerked his head left-right, and jumped when he saw black plastic in the road. He'd forgotten those improvised explosives at dusk, the worst time of day, and for a moment, he was gone.

The marsh reeked of sulfur.

The road took him across the bridge and to the giant palmetto sign, blinking and buzzing. The big blue wave. Crash. The green fronds. Flash.

The Voyager. Oh. He stepped out, gripped Pearl's door, steadying himself.

A voice called, "Jack, Mayzie, fried chicken, come and get it." Whose voice? Children squealed. He'd lost his radar. Kids. Right. He closed his eyes and reopened them. Inhaled and exhaled. Smoke.

Where was Lucky? Running? Not in the dark. He'd check later. He found his own screen door, shut and latched it, and collapsed into the ramshackle wicker to rest and listen. Voices faded in and faded out. Mrs. Pitts's smoker voice. Talking. Who? Was she smoking? Of course.

Footsteps scattered shells. People wandered. All normal. No worries.

"Jack. Mayzie. Lucille." That voice. Right. That was—who? What was her name?

From somewhere Mrs. Pitts said, "Out back. At Queen's." Will should check things out.

More footsteps. Somebody banging on a door, muffled by distance maybe Queen's place. "Come on in," a faraway quaver said. "I've got your kids."

Minutes of quiet under the neon buzz. He'd forgotten to set the timer for the turtle-lights. He dropped his head back.

16

Drop

I trotted across the dune and down the beach, cataloguing my thoughts. I kept to the high tide line, checking the four remaining nests, chanting *om*, sending light and love to hatchlings asleep in their tough little shells. If I had x-ray vision, I'd see for sure whether they were okay in these birth pits. Wishing them well, I jogged down the wide, low-tide beach, running straight at the water, staring at the flatlined horizon, a pink smudge, soon my feet pounded wet sand, then yards and yards of shallow water, me sloshing shin-deep in warm water, panting.

Behind me, footsteps splashed, and the late day sun made extra-tall shadows of legs longer than mine. Our shadows crossed.

Renaldo called my name. The horizon drew me until the land fell away, one minute, sand underfoot, the next, current swept me out, my chest tight, tighter. I tipped my head back, sucking air, sucking air, sucking air, legs pedaling water; I couldn't even scream.

"Dropoff! Tread water." He yelled.

I pushed. Pushed and pushed away water, and bicycled my legs to fight tide taking me to sea. An arm slid across my chest, dragging me a few feet to where we touched bottom. He let go. We walked and walked.

On shore, my knees buckled, my legs jellied, *don't collapse, don't collapse*. I gasped for air. Why had my strength failed? I sank to the hard, low-tide beach, and cut my eyes at Renaldo. He squinted at the horizon, kneeling beside me, his hand on my forearm.

"You didn't panic. You *can* swim, right?"

"Not much."

"You need practice."

I gulped more air. "Too late. We're leaving. I've packed, fingers crossed Naomi really comes back, but for all I know—," this was the first time I'd spoken my fear out loud,"—she won't." My heart flipped and flopped. Then what?

He studied me. "Sorry I never mentioned that dropoff, at this end, seems like the land goes on forever at low tide—until it stops."

My ears, full of ocean, distorted his voice and mine, too, inside my skull. Was I the only one who could hear myself speak? Renaldo scooted closer, and rosy, sunset-red drops stuck to his sleek skin like tiny lenses magnifying pores, refracting light, and turning his body neon.

"Seriously." His mouth touched my ears. His breath tickled. "I can teach you. Stick around."

I rested inside Boneyard time. Why had I fought it, all week? It felt normal.

Maybe he read something in my face because he shut up about the swim lessons.

"Let your scare settle."

"Know what makes sunsets? Dust. Pollution."

"Sure. Good and bad always mixes. You wanted Key West but got Boneyard Beach and me. That's good. Right?"

The words stirred the week's stew of new: a turtle laid eggs; a clutch hatched; I rubbed dirt and shells from a five-thousand year old civilization; Will shot a rattler, and showed us how to carve; I lost myself and ran to the end of earth. And here I was with a stranger who felt like a friend, with tide snatching sand out from under us while I wondered when Naomi would remember us and who she would be when she did. I felt like an orphan. Jack and Mayzie at least had a still-alive father. I shut my eyes and tried to imagine her, Mom, Naomi, but she was more of a ghost to me than Dad.

17

Wild

Something had ahold of Will's arm—he flung it off.

"Altman. Altman."

Will struggled to crack open his eyes. Trip. Will got to his feet, groggy, lurching. "What time is it? When did it start getting dark so early?" He regained his balance.

"Way past dark, Bro."

He backed into the chair and let his head fall, big mistake. It pounded.

"Your man Renaldo, that one's a keeper, perfect understudy for your job, which you are about to lose. I had to bust your doorlatch to get in the porch."

Will's brain roused itself to semi-conscious thought, put together date-time-event, and why he was about to get fired, too much to absorb in a few seconds, especially when—oh, yeah, he was still half-lit.

"You can afford to shut the door on your only home? Because if you lose this job, you lose your cottage. I can read your mind, don't say a word and don't bother getting up." The sheriff palmed his skull. He looked like he wanted to draw a six-shooter, which he never carried.

Will stayed slouched listening to Trip's loud, controlled inhales and exhales. Or was that the sea?

"At least make yourself at home while you lecture."

Trip flopped in the mate to Will's chair.

"Got so fried at the market—" had Will even unloaded Pearl?— "Drove home, sat down, conked out."

"Your little stunt on the sidewalk. Heard all about it. That how come you passed out drunk?"

"Here's what happened." Will tried raising his head, woozy and swimmy with booze. He grabbed it with two hands as though he could subdue the enemy. "Even though it's none of your business, and, despite the fact that you think you're my guardian . . ."

"Conscience. Alcoholics can't drink. You can't drink. None of God's alcoholic children can drink. Show up at AA, it's the only way to stay sober."

"This was a one-off. A celebration. What was I celebrating? Glad you asked."

"Sure, like the others, like the DUI was a one-off."

"I, Will Altman, have an art dealer."

"Sounds illegal, like somebody who traffics in stolen art."

"OK, play dumb. This guy hawks art—gives the artist half, I think, but we didn't discuss terms." Could Dick really sell a sculpture like *The Wave* for a grand, like he claimed? And, if he did, would Will get an additional seven hundred, above the three hundred Mrs. B. already paid?

Even drunk, he got the math. Oh, wait. Dick's percentage.

"You see why I was tempted by the sauce? How could I say no?"

"Repeat: N-O. You smell like a distillery. Let's get you showered."

Will was pickled but couldn't smell himself. "Sorry my odor offends, but, as a successful artist, I'll soon be in a position to change my ways . . . oh, forgot the most important news." He dropped his hands from his head to his lap, but the head refused to stay up without a prop. He slid lower in the chair. His gut was also roiling. He laid his arm across his belly.

"Back to my benefactor. His name is Dick."

"Aunt Cece's boyfriend? He's OK. Pretty successful businessman, a come-here."

Will spoke slowly. "I'd never have met this dealer without your aunt's purchase of my most ambitious piece to date, which Lucille, my personal art critic, convinced me to title, *The Wave.* That little girl is a genius. It's only because of her that I even took that piece to the market." Will rattled off as much of his visit to Sunbow as he recalled, bits and pieces, about the flowing whiskey and Dick's constant refills. "And he promised to buy whatever work I produce."

"Too good to be true, maybe, but, say it is. So what, so you're an artistic prodigy? Nobody could be happier for you than me, but that won't cure your boozing—nothing but determination will stop that—you can't work under the influence."

Will broke a sweat. He'd just dropped the best news of his life, and Trip delivered a sermon? Let it go, said Will's better self. Trip was loaded with bull, and he itched to knock it out of him, but remembered Cecelia's comment about Trip's pain.

"Right. I can't work drunk. Yes, Aunt Cece is an interesting lady, full of insights. She confided a few tidbits."

"What? She tattled about childhood antics, like me peeing off the roof?"

"You and I did that together, numbnuts. No. You've got *soldier's heart.* Same as me. That's old school for trauma." Will was right proud of simply spitting the words. In the dark, though, he couldn't make out Trip's expression.

Silence. "What about your underage guests? Your long lost cousins? They might've drowned before their mother got back. You knew she was back?"

Vaguely, Will recalled hearing what could have been Naomi's voice.

They slumped lower in the chairs. Will had nearly passed out again, but Trip's words, unusually low and confidential-sounding, compared to his customary in-your-face delivery, jarred him.

"Aunt Cece was right, Will. I've done time with booze, pills. You remember Shawn? One of my men? His father called yesterday."

Trip always lost sleep over those calls, but Will had never noticed any irrational, erratic ways associated with any drug, and Trip had never mentioned such. Had Will not paid attention?

Two men from Trip's platoon, now three, had offed themselves.

They sat in the dark, tuning in sounds of the dog-day cicadas, katydids, crickets, and horned toads scrambling around in dead leaves.

"Lord help us."

Which one said that, Trip or Will, Will couldn't say, they'd been friends that long.

"Give up the drink. For me."

"I did. Tonight was just—a one shot."

"Guarantee you had more than one."

"Yes."

"Wonder about that storm," Trip said.

"Heck, the weather's so wild and wooly and unpredictable, Lucille schooled me."

"Where is Lucille now? And her sibs?" Trip asked. "As I said, Naomi is back."

Why didn't Will know where they were? Because he'd gotten wasted.

"I chatted the woman up and gave her the lowdown on Children and Family Services guidelines for a few minutes," Trip said. "She slurred her words and I noticed a little drool. The kid covers. That's how it usually plays out."

"Plays out? What are you saying?"

"I see this, in my line of work. Plus, benzos are a class of drugs—I get why she'd do it, she's hardworking, if she's a nurse with three kids, and who doesn't suffer anxiety? Yoga's my drug, but I once self-medicated."

"Wait. What are benzos?"

Trip went on to describe the whole gamut—Valium, Xanax, stuff like that, he said, have side effects galore—memory problems, mood changes, slurring, confusion, dry mouth and/or increased salivation, hence drool.

Will said nothing. And Will considered himself the weak member of the herd—turned out the whole herd was still fighting.

"Said she grew up in Jesup," Trip said. "They—she and her husband—used to come here, they were married here; he died in Fallujah, 2004. I decided against pursuing a charge."

But if she was seriously, dangerously medicated, maybe Trip *should* make a big deal of her leaving. It was abandonment, no matter how Lucille tried to explain it, no matter how many times she told Will how much she knew about kids.

"If Naomi's got a drug problem, shouldn't we do something?" Will asked. "If she's messed up, she and the kids are in trouble. Maybe she's swiping them?"

"Why? That's what makes these drugs dangerous. Like alcohol, they're easy to get. She could even be doing something like Adderall to stay awake on her shift, then coming down with tranquilizers."

"If this is true," Will said, slowly, "the family could implode. Eventually."

"Yes."

"Then we need get her help."

"Easier said than done. We'll all go down if that storm rubs us the wrong way—I'm filing a request with Mother Nature for a fast blow-by-maybe a day of rain."

Will didn't care about the storm, there was nothing he could do about that, but the children? Somebody had to do something.

18

Lunatics, Love

Spine-to-spine, soaking, Renaldo and I leaned into each other's backbones, electrifying me inside and out. Moonlight bled through scudding clouds.

"Are you worried about your mom?" he asked.

I'd refused to name the prescription-drug problems. But the tiny blue Xanax tablets and Ambien and assorted unknowns in her robe pocket shook me awake.

He wiggled his spine. Our bones were talking. His said he understood, and mine messaged that I was grateful.

"Kids need mothers. I've got Queen, but a grandmother's not a mother. I worry about Queen; sometimes I feel like her parent."

"Mine's messed up over my Dad, keeps trying to find him in men? I guess?"

"My mother keeps crazy social-worker hours."

"Social workers butt into people's business. One tried to take me away from my mother when I was five." I pushed my heels into sand, using Renaldo's back as leverage.

"You might have been in danger." He turned. Without his support, I fell, laughing; I lay on my side and propped my head on my folded arm.

He kneeled and faced me. "Your mom wants a mate. It's a biological urge."

"She's had plenty. She could marry Jack and Mayzie's dad. He asked. Some animals mate for life."

"Swans," he said.

"Wolves."

"Beavers." A grin exploded his face. His teeth shone, a mouth of dazzle, and I grinned, too, like yesterday, and now his mouth came at mine, but stopped. I squeezed my eyes shut and sensed his close-but-not-touching mouth, and soon we were eating each other's lips, mine raw with sunburn.

We pulled apart. I'd never kissed or been kissed unless I counted the sleepover last year when boys showed up and a preppie kid from biology lunged at me, aimed for my mouth, but missed. His beery slobber-lips landed on my nose.

We kneeled, and Renaldo squeezed me, his arms wrapped me, burying my face in the skin of his neck, flooding me until I warmed all over, and, though he held me, we drifted among clouds. Was that his heartbeat or mine? His skin or mine? I couldn't isolate a single thought from the scramble that was my brain, with his arms binding me like wire strands. Tomorrow, I'd be gone, but this minute, he transported me from the sting of sand and my own hollow insides.

All week, I'd felt buried in my shell except with Will.

I opened my eyes. He was staring past me.

He jumped to his feet. "Some lunatic's got a light on the beach—light confuses turtles."

"Turtles are out?" I got up and turned. The light blinded me, too.

"Could be. What an idiot, with signs everywhere." He loped toward the beam, shielding his eyes with his forearms, shouting, "Kill it. Kill the light. Sea turtles nest here."

God. Naomi staggered, beam bouncing. She pounced on Renaldo first, but he easily evaded her, took the light, and switched it off, then she came at me, but I dropped to the sand.

Naomi bent low, clamped my arms with her hands, fingernails gashing me. Why fight her? She was strong—when she wanted to be.

On my feet, I brushed sand from myself. "OK. OK. I'm up." I shivered, without Renaldo as windbreak.

He stepped between us. Naomi elbowed him, her fingers grabbing and gripping my shoulders. I wriggled free. Renaldo held her forearms and pulled them down, hard. She couldn't move her arms. She kicked at him, lost her balance, and wobbled in the sand until she fell and dropped the flashlight, throwing us into half-darkness.

I helped her to her feet. "This is Queen's grandson—Renaldo—Jack and Mayzie are at their place, eating a home-cooked dinner."

We backed away and left her to her wildness. I counted to five silently to make sure she wouldn't bite, and took one arm, Renaldo took the other, and she allowed us to walk her to the Court. He let her go; her free arm reached around my waist, but the anger Naomi had sloughed off had entered my body, powering new energy. I'd halfway gotten used to life without her this week, but she'd come roaring back, and I'd need to pick up whatever pieces she'd broken and strewn, in herself, in me, in Jack or Mayzie. Where was Tom?

"Let's go home." Her voice dragged.

Home was the Court. My brain switched gears—what now? I should pretend I was a normal girl in a normal family? And the adult world wasn't full of lies—Naomi said she'd come home Wednesday; secrets—Naomi wouldn't talk about Dad or drugs; and idiotic behavior—Naomi treated me like I was the one who had misbehaved.

If I were a loggerhead, I'd crawl to the water and sink to the ocean floor, where I could rest for a few hours without surfacing.

Naomi disappeared into Cottage Twelve. Renaldo and I touched hands, a goodbye. Inside, she didn't even glance up when I shut the door, reclining on the pleather sofa, forearm over her forehead. Where was her meditation app?

She sat and straightened her spine. Saliva formed at one corner of her mouth. Uh oh. The blue tablets? It was hard to keep all that information straight. What did what and when?

"Why'd you go nuts out there?" I sat beside her.

"What happened in here? It looks like a battle zone."

A moment later, she patted my knee. "I don't care about the mess." She stood, swayed slightly, and folded a greasy pizza box.

I crushed two more, crossed the room to the kitchenette, found a trash bag, and hunted paper plates, one had become wedged behind a sofa cushion, and another lay on top of the TV. From the porch, in the sweet, soft humidity, I retrieved my ant-covered plate, and crammed it into the bag. Ants marched up my arm. I tried blowing them off, but they ignored my breath and soldiered on.

"How many pizzas did you guys eat?" Naomi asked.

"Two." I rolled a greasy plate into a tube, and told the ants, shaking them into the bag, that I was sorry. I squeezed dirty napkins into tight balls. OK, so my birthday trip was dead. Fine. We had fun here *because* she went AWOL; if she hadn't, there would've been no trip to the five-thousand-year-old shell rings, no working in Will's world, no Mortimer, no goofy games, no funny/sad trip to the market, watching Will try to connect with customers and his girlfriend. No Renaldo.

She read my mind. "Why were you on the beach with that boy?"

I ignored her. "I hope you pay Will for his trouble. He was super busy but watched over us, took us places, even cooked dinner." At first, I'd thought I could take better care of Will than he could of us, but Will turned out to be strange but incredibly *decent*. "I should be grilling you. Even the sheriff wondered where you'd gone."

"Oh, yes, Officer Whatsit stopped me in the parking lot and gave me a talking-to. I've forgotten what he said."

As she spoke, I consulted my oracle, the jar on the mantel. Dad. "It's Trip's job to look after people. You could've died. We could've died. People die." The jar sweated in the hot room.

"Please don't do this. Being mad at Trip doesn't help. I'm sorry." But I wasn't.

Her syllables ran into more syllables. She made it to the counter, fascinated by the black door of the microwave on the fridge-top. I followed her across the room and passed a hand in front of our faces; we stared at our reflections in the black door.

"Don't check out. I don't care how low your chi is or how much you need to 'go inward,' or how badly you need Xanax or Valium or Ambien." Or whatever. I hated how I felt inside, filled with steel wool prickling me all over. I hated her at this moment, and tried to remember that when she was herself, she was really something.

I'd kept one memory secret but alive, from our first day here. Between tides, Naomi'd borrowed a net—a seine—from the office. While the little kids napped, we waded in the creek.

"Pluff mud." She'd inhaled through her nose. "I'd forgotten how sweet decomposition smells." Never minding the mud-water, she bunched the net, clenched it between her teeth, and swung her right arm in a wide arc, opened her mouth, caught it and tossed that end to where I was stationed opposite the tidepool. Together we dragged the seine through the pool. She gathered it like a sack and pulled it to the bank where we unwrapped our gifts. She named all we saw—shrimps, pale and small and pink, with thready feet, and antennae as long as they were, clams and mussels. And silver, lemony fish. I'd never seen her so peaceful and dirty, with mud striping our legs. We were sea creatures, alive together. We cooked and ate the few shrimp we caught; that haunted me. They needed to grow.

She said nothing. I reached under the sink for Mr. Clean. Across the room, I sprayed the mold already growing on the sea-foam green wall, the fuzzy patch had incubated in a medium of Coke. I sponged the stain. Naomi headed back for the pleather—she'd need to sleep there, we kids had the only bedroom. I felt her eyes bore into my back as I scrubbed the wall, and wiped the stain's woolly surface; the scrubber bruised the paint. "Where's Tom?"

"Tom is history." She said this carefully and slowly, possibly trying to sound normal.

"The resort. How was that?"

"Nice, not super fancy. You'd love the fresh shrimp and red snapper at supper. But you don't eat red snapper, Luce."

The more she talked, the more she wanted to talk, but how drugged she sounded! Her *s's* and soft *c's* turned to *sh's*. I ran a glass of tap water and handed it to her. "Drink this: You're acting weird. Maybe you're dehydrated."

I scoured while she told me she couldn't relax because he was too polite, and she felt inferior, having grown up with millworker grandparents; she worked at the mill, too, till she went to nursing school.

"Besides, he ran into another woman last night. He apologized, oh, he's polite. 'Great seeing you again. I've settled the bill,' he said. 'Take care.' I packed, and got the late ferry."

No wonder she'd hit the Xanax.

Pine-scented liquid dripped down the wall. I tuned her out and concentrated on the stain. It seemed permanent. Scratching the spot away only wrecked the paint.

"Wish you'd called."

"No service—Tom had service, but . . . I didn't want to use his phone . . ."

"We wondered. We waited."

"In my bright, shiny memory, he was young, smart, kind, but he wasn't that boy."

I was tired. I needed to put her down first, but not before I asked my big question:

"Why'd you bring Dad unless it was to bury him for good? And move on?"

She dropped her head on the sofa-back and threw her forearm across her eyes. "Turn down the lights, and please, please don't interrogate me. If you want the ashes gone, flush them. Toss them in a parking lot, in the ocean, the sand. Check my robe pocket, will you, to see if I've got something? Preferably Ambien."

I switched my setting to numb; I automatically refilled the bucket and sprayed more cleanser, once, twice, three times until the chemical pooled at the baseboard and filled the room with its acid smell. I ironed the wall with the sponge, top to bottom, right to left. I turned back to Naomi, but she'd melted into the sofa. Xanax and Ambien. I saw the description in my mind because I'd read it many times: "Potential for abuse/addiction and side effects: mental confusion, impaired coordination, dizziness, drowsiness."

In burst Mayzie and Jack. Jack scrunched into the space between the sofa seat and the back, behind her, while Mayzie tried to keep from falling off her lap. "We ate fried chicken."

Mayzie shoved a bag into Naomi's face.

That chicken smelled heavenly. Salivating, I took it from Mayzie.

"Get cleaned up—run outside and shower. Let Naomi sleep."

Mayzie tried prying one of Naomi's eyes open with her pointer finger.

I tore them away, herded them outside, and into the shower. In bed we read *Horton*. We'd read it all week but I'd never seen Will as *our* Horton. The thought of Will as an elephant stuck in my head, theirs, too, after I said so. We couldn't stop laughing, despite my fears, and we tickled each other silly before bed, worth the hour it took to quiet down because they asked nothing about tomorrow, whether or when we'd leave or where we were going.

Back in the main room, Naomi, drowsy, wanted them again. I ignored her. At the wall, I dipped and squeezed the sponge and gave it one last scrub. The brown Coke streaks stayed.

"Found Xanax in your robe while you were gone." Enabling.

"Thanks. I'll save it for morning; maybe I can get a refill. I bought y'all turtle T-shirts."

"Nice." A T-shirt? Never mind, I told myself, keep her calm, don't react, and get her in bed. "Thank you."

"What is Xanax?"

"Tranquilizer. You know how tense I get."

Squats were my Xanax. I stashed the cleaning supplies under the sink and approached her, studying her eyes, staring beyond me, at the door, the porch. What did she see in that distance? She smelled of lavender. I kneeled and laid my head in her lap.

Her fingers lightly traced the dried blood on my bicep. My breath burned down to my belly; my heart, so full an hour ago in the dark with Renaldo, the ocean lapping, lapping.

Now my insides were on fire.

She started, in a thin, wobbly voice. "When they rang the bell . . ."

I'd heard this bedtime story. She'd installed her grief in me, but I'd stopped listening.

The words came anyway.

"The officer knelt and you played with his medals. They were shiny, and hung with colorful ribbons. I couldn't save any of us. None of my skills as a nurse, a wife, a mother—nothing could fix our unit."

I looked up. Her eyes were open and red but tearless. I found her robe and covered her, found the Ambien, and gave her that, too, but left the Xanax. She pushed the capsule to the back of her tongue and swallowed it with the rest of her water. I took a pillow from the kids' bed and lifted her legs until she lay prone, her head on the pillow.

The little cottage passed for clean, or would, once we moved out. I switched the lights off and carried Queen's grease-soaked paper bag to the front porch. All that drama left me starving, and the chicken tasted like love. Naomi's love was messy with hurt, but this bag of chicken was pure Queen saying, *Hey, I fried you some chicken because I thought you might be hungry.*

We'd been so starved for so long.

In the rocking chair, I gnawed a leg while life-scenes with Naomi returned in fitful flashes: moody silences spliced with foggy stares into nowhere, spurts of twirling, dancing, hugging. Manic. Maybe going from wife-to-mother-to-widow *could* make you crazy. But *I* had come out of that OK, sort of; maybe those turtle babies, alone, would do fine.

Will's cottage was dark. I wouldn't wake him, though I wanted to hear about the trip to Sunbow: Was the house magical like its name? Had he gotten his three hundred dollars? I missed Will already, the way he forgot he was an adult and played capture the flag; he showed us all he knew and all he was. I also needed a favor.

19

Home Ground

6:08 a.m. Sunrise, low tide. That's what chart on the fridge said. I dressed, ate a banana, and loaded Dad's urn in my backpack. Around it, I stuffed the last can of Vienna sausages, a sleeve of Saltines, and my water bottle. Hefting the pack, and my duffel, I giant-stepped outside, my feet landing noiselessly in the shells. I stashed the duffel in the Voyager, let myself onto Will's porch, and stowed his Flexcut in my pocket. The door to his cottage stood wide open, but the inside was dark and silent. I wanted Will to lead me across the mud and into the forest, and scatter Dad's ashes. I waited in the doorway, listening for getting-up sounds. What I heard was nothing. I hated to wake Will. If I left now, I'd be back before he got up. Monk watched, from the wicker chair, but didn't meow.

"Tell Will not to worry," I whispered. "I'll take good care of his Flexcut."

A familiar "last time" vibe chilled me—last time with wood tools, last scents of these shavings, limp with humidity that tickled my nose. I hated last times. At least I had Mortimer, a respectable souvenir whose sight and smell would forever bring back the island and Will. Naomi might "get" my urge, but telling her would make my pilgrimage all about her, and boy could she create commotion, contaminating the trip with her own needs, greater than I'd known.

My mother needed help. The thought gripped me like the flu. My life was about to get worse, now, when I'd started to dream that maybe I could *want* something, even though I didn't yet know what there was to *want*. A home. A life, not without my mother and brother and sister, but a life of my own.

I was a runner for a reason. I had to go. Now. I'd never get another chance to properly scatter Dad's ashes. I slipped out of Will's screen door, sticky with humidity, as always, and closed it all the way shut, maybe for good.

The Court, so demented-looking seven nights ago, with its leering windows and cockeyed porches, felt like home. I'd never lived where people called me by name, where I was just me. Down here, Will, Linda, Queen, Mrs. Pitts, Renaldo, knew me. Maybe even the Grandpa whose ears sprouted hair.

Seashells crunched. Oh no. Here they were, barefoot in PJs, Superman and a plump tangerine in a nightshirt. *Shh.* Bribing them with Cokes, I sent them back to the cottage, knowing Naomi slept late. "You did not see me. I trust your *Wire* experience to guide you, Mayzie. Keep it quiet?"

She screwed up her crying face, but didn't. Maybe my tone—less bossy than pleading—equalized us. Tapping Jack's shoulder, she whispered, "*No way of running down them or their stories.*"

"You got Will's gun?" Jack asked, big-eyed, open-mouthed.

I shook my head and tiptoed away. At Mrs. Pitts's cottage, I smelled smoke, and hoped she couldn't see through the mesh. No luck. "Where you off to so early?"

"Nosing around," I stage whispered. "We're leaving soon, wanted to say goodbye."

Another somebody I'd never know.

Passing Queen's sturdy, simple cottage, hidden inside its live oak, temple-like canopy, I prayed Renaldo would appear, imagining him asleep, his perfect cheekbone resting on joined palms, tapered fingers. The thought dizzied me, and briefly sent me floating. In a flash, the door opened and not Renaldo but Queen popped out and threw up her palm. She disappeared inside. Minutes later, she stood in waders beside me, shouldering her own backpack on her tiny frame. My spirits muddied and sank, briefly, then lifted. She would slow me, for sure, but she also knew the way.

Queen motioned me forward. "You lighting out? I'm coming along."

"OK, but hurry, a storm's coming and my mother will be angry if I'm not back soon."

"My herb supply is low; we won't be long."

I couldn't turn back, but my Spidey senses prickled—Boneyard Time could and did often stretch minutes into hours.

The patch of live oaks and pines behind Queen's cottage opened on the creek. The sun had stained the sky. Pink clouds bubbled like soapsuds. We women—I'd graduated to woman this week, for whatever *that* was worth—descended into the creek's bed, wove among the grasses, placing our feet on the grass roots that stabilized the mud. Once across, I scrabbled up the bank, hoisting my gangly self, clutching fronds and smashing my chest into mud and roots.

Up top, I braced my quads, planted my feet in a runner's lunge, and pulled Queen. Those fragile hands. Knuckles so crooked I was afraid to squeeze, but I levered her up. Not one complaint, only pained, clouded eyes. She found a stick and took a different forest path, wilder than Will's, one with no steps, no boardwalk, no historically-inaccurate text panel. I reached for Will's knife, and every so often, cut a branch to mark my return path.

Yards later I glanced back and saw vines and fanned-out fronds hiding the path. I'd dulled Will's blade for nothing; my cuts were useless. I pocketed the Flexcut.

Trees rose up and the ground swelled underfoot, shell shards poking from chocolate dirt, and again the idea that something was trying to surface nagged me. I stared harder and deeper at the shells, squatted two or three times, fingering dirt or a shell, hoping to feel what the dead natives had, eons ago: the weight of a fishing net in water; the texture of clay, coiled or rolled; the heat of fire. Women grew children inside their bellies, cooked, tanned hides, formed pots. What else could the place show me? How to live my own life? Help my mother? Find home?

Dad's weight grew heavier as we tromped—*tromp* was how you walked in this place, overgrown with brilliant greens, deep grays, and mottled browns; thorns grabbed at my skin and mosquitoes attacked. Sweat pooled between the pack and my spine, and ran to my waist; I badly wanted to quit but I was no quitter. Queen kept and kept after her mission and I wanted her to finish. Though I'd felt trapped, at first, by her, I knew we might never see each other again, and that she could somehow help me.

A sudden stop in a clearing. Between clouds, the sun glared. Ten o'clock? She emptied the pockets of her man-britches, worked thick gloves over crooked fingers, and unlatched her clippers. She snipped perfumed, bright-berried branches, stopped and crushed the leaves in her gloved palm.

"Spicebush. Old time people use this to cure what ails you—even bad moods. It calms the nervous system. I was a science teacher; this is no crackpot, fool remedy. It works." Old school Xanax? Queen stared at me. Maybe I needed the cure, scared and tired, obsessing about what might be going on at the Court, whether Naomi was even awake. Should I have left Mayzie and Jack alone with Naomi? Not after last night. I needed to lay Dad to rest and cross back over the creek before the tide rolled back in.

I'd never met anyone like Queen, with old-fashioned ways, but she reminded me of Naomi back before Jack and Mayzie. Naomi had her own way of coping with stomachaches: half-teaspoon of soda in water, not herbal, but still. For coughs, she'd rub my chest with smelly ointment and cover it with a warm towel. Or dose me with a tablespoon of whiskey. Why did her unscientific ways work? They probably didn't but I always felt better.

Queen slipped back into the brush until she was invisible, rattling and cracking branches; I followed her noisy progress and landed in a patch of vines armed with barbs. They latched onto my legs. I yelled. She staggered out of the thicket and clipped me free. No wonder Queen wore head-to-toe clothes.

"Wild blackberries." Something had picked the bushes clean. She plodded back to her herbs but in a minute busted out with an armload of white-flowered branches with gray-green leaves. "Here you go. Rabbit tobacco."

We'd be here all day. Naomi would be out of her mind. Dad's urn pulled at my spine and my mind, and I imagined ashes burning the pack, burning to be laid to rest. We hadn't kept up with Dad's family, though his mother had sent card after card. They finally stopped coming after we pulled up stakes again and again and again.

I wanted my errand accomplished. No way I could walk us out of here alone. I checked my phone, not for service, but time. Dead.

Queen filled her arms with rabbit tobacco and spicebush and I carried her pack on one shoulder and mine on the other while she found a spot under a pine oozing sap. It had to be noon, at least, but I couldn't see the sun for the clouds. If it was noon, high tide wouldn't let us across.

Among the pine needles, Queen seemed at ease; the sharp scent momentarily soothed me. I kneeled and pawed inside her pack and found a paper bag, a water bottle, and a gun. God. Did everybody down here carry? The rattler memory hissed.

Dad had suffered TBI, traumatic brain injury. The books all said trauma can affect children of the traumatized. The sight of the gun dried my mouth, shallowed my breath, and then I remembered Queen's poor eyesight. My heart clocked in at panic speed. The gun was heavy.

What if the thing was loaded? But if I checked, could the gun accidentally go off?

"Get yourself something to eat." Queen settled and worked her hand inside the pack, around herb stalks, and removed a tiny can with a pop top. Contents: stinky and brown. She smeared this on a cracker with a plastic knife.

"Rattlesnake liver." She passed the offering under my nose. The smell gagged me, but I was hungry enough to chew. Ugh. Sure, the name was a joke, I got that, but she *ate* like this was serious food.

"How's that going down the old gullet? It's a delicacy."

This could be anything squished into a can, like those Vienna sausages we'd gobbled this week. I insisted she have a Vienna and she did. I drank half my water and saved the rest for the return trip. My eyes wandered, searching someplace for Dad, and wondering how I'd mark the grave because I saw no stones, only shells, but didn't want to dig shells. What if I disturbed the ancestors—and the calcium concentration—that kept this history alive?

Down here, nature stayed busy. Pine branches needled the sky. The tree canopy sculpted itself into shelter. I loved this up-close nature, but we needed to get out. The kids would be flying high on caffeine, shouting and throwing fake punches, which would drive Naomi deeper into Xanax. I wiggled the stainless jar out from my pack and cradled it. Queen watched but said nothing, asked nothing.

Queen had probably forgotten that I'd told her my mom and dad married here. Besides, I wanted to mark the moment. "This is Dad. He and my mom married and honeymooned on this island in the year 2000." I made my voice loud. "I was *conceived* here."

"You homed in on your sacred ground, the perfect resting spot for your father." Queen's talk comforted me, the way she mixed old-time sayings and wisdom with science. "This ancient civilization is no burial site, but was a true home for the first people. I see by your face and your honest eyes that this is your home ground."

Home ground.

"Old-time people also call rabbit tobacco *Life Everlasting*. Some people believe, like me, that the herb is *more* than medicine."

I waited for the more.

"The plant's a messenger between the living and the dead, when the dead wish to share."

How could I believe that? I didn't attend church. There was no God. But I wanted to seriously consider her words. "How would I hear him?"

"Listen to your thoughts, your memories. Here's the important part: This plant—take some home—never dies." She clipped a short branch, maybe six inches, and stashed it in my pack. "Root it in water."

The plant gave off a strange smell, and the flowers freely shed white fluff; the idea that this herb connected a spirit world with the world of the living? Silly, but I'd have tried anything to reach Dad. Maybe even seances and other paranormal experiences. People who believed that lived in a dream world, but if I could, I'd live there, too. If I mentioned those to Naomi, she'd say, "We'll walk on water after that. Just forget. That's all you can do." That hadn't worked for her or me.

I opened the lid and scooped a handful of crushed bones, not light and airy like wood ashes or shavings, but weighty, worthy. I stood and flung him to the treetops. Specks fell, in the leaf litter, the pine needle carpet, among buried bones, shells and souls, animal and human. A soft breeze blew the mixture back in my face: ashes in my hair, ashes in my eyes and lashes, my mouth, and down my track jersey. On the ground, the ashes looked nothing like ashes.

Queen dusted her own face, spit, and sang. Her voice strengthened until it ruffled the leaves and needles and became forest noise. *I am a poor, wayfaring stranger, traveling through this world below; there is no sickness, no toil or danger, in that bright land, to which I go . . .*

Her voice trapped and suspended Dad in time and space. This place surely would live inside me forever the way Dad lived in my muscle and blood and skin and bones. Six handfuls and six verses later, the urn, as Naomi has always called it, was empty. Without Dad's weight, the container seemed flimsy. I filled it with dirt so it wouldn't topple, and screwed its base into the forest's soft soil until I'd buried the lower third.

Dad's spot, where Life Everlasting thrived. I chose shell bits from the surface and formed an outline of a turtle to mark the grave. Even if I didn't come back till I grew all the way up, he would live in the forest until the ocean claimed *Orcoosa*. I raised my eyes to the canopy, the cloud-clotted sky, smelled the fertile earth, and heard wings beating the air—a heron passing overhead. This was my home ground.

20

Checkout

Will's forty-pound head flopped back to the pillow. He pressed his palms to his eyes. Dry mouth. Fuzzy tongue. He rubbed his eyes with his fists but that only tore his head apart. Angling his torso, he checked the window, offering a view of Naomi's rear as she pushed and pulled canvas suitcases in and out of the Voyager. Her halting, irregular footsteps rattled the shells as she made trip after trip from van to cottage to van.

Skilsaw sounds ripped the air. Right. Storm. Renaldo, boarding windows.

Five minutes later, Will shouldered open the office's humidity-swollen door, booted up, and checked the weather. Psychedelic blues and greens surrounded a smear of white, chaos churning a hundred miles from Jacksonville, wind whispering, swirling, sinking, rising, and sucking up water, becoming the tropical depression due to smack the coast tonight. Driving rains and high tides could push storm surge miles into marshes.

The screen testified to Lucille's dire prophecy, the sidebar to every report: warmer water intensified storms. They lingered longer. Packed stronger winds. More and more pavement, fewer and fewer wetlands made for faster sea level rise, twenty inches over the next hundred years but that number was fluid, too, and changed with each new calculation. Will tried to fathom the hundred years: He'd lived almost thirty, Queen, seventy-three. When Will was her age, the seas would be—who knows how high? Today's estimates were worthless. Renaldo poked his head in the door. "Need more plywood, boss."

Will nodded. "You got those windows?"

"Yeah."

Ninety minutes and a trip to Pinesboro later, it was nearly noon. The radio forecast storm-strength wind speeds, rain. Pearl alone occupied the inbound lane; outbound cars and trucks puttered past. Though the eye of the storm was slated to hit fifty miles south, the dark, broody ocean fretted. Will cut the radio, hating the endless repetition.

Instead, he devoured the lonely vista ahead: the sea's puckered surface, whitecaps, vague horizon, no boundary between heaven and earth, both shadowy, threatening. In the desert, the sand rose and fell the same way, in waves, drifts, beyond and beyond, the wind making corrugated billows like sand surf; the ocean was desert, too, millions of years ago. This shoreline once lay sixty miles west and the ocean was out to reclaim its territory.

But not today. He swung by Boneyard Bait for canned everything—tuna, soup, beans, cat food—they'd sold out of bottled water and the best storm food—pork and beans.

"You sitting out the storm?" Will noticed but did not comment on Linda's dental affliction, which made her grin goofy and cockeyed. Endearing.

"No, hell no. Going to town. You?"

"We've never evacuated, but if we do, I can't wait to chow down on those Southern Baptist shelter meals. I hear they really throw down during a disaster."

"Get out, you." She tried not to smile, which really crippled her mouth. "I'm closing. You're it. Here, take these sparklers, we won't need *those* till next Memorial Day." She rang him up and locked the door behind them.

Linda's talk of town had dropped Will back into Belva's flowery bed. The sensations tightened his chest, squeezing him breathless, great, maybe his heart muscle wouldn't jump around so much. He packed the groceries in the cab and slid the sparklers under the seat, thinking that if anybody had a storm plan Belva would, and that plan would be perfect. Heck, she probably chaired the local Red Cross Disaster Relief committee.

At the Court, he unloaded plywood sheets, then, bags in both arms, nearly collided with Naomi, licking her lips. Dry mouth? Will tried to recall Trip's observations. Before he had time to open his mouth, she asked, "Where is Lucille? I dread the I-95 traffic. We've got to go." The whites of her eyes were rimmed in pink, but he was sure his redeyes beat hers as hungover as he was. He couldn't gauge the size of the pupils and wouldn't know dilated from pin-sized or which meant what.

"She can't be running—she's been gone too long and Mayzie and Jack haven't seen her."

Will jogged toward Queen's, where Renaldo had set up sawhorses and measured and sliced plywood. Jack and Mayzie lifted one end of a half-sheet, and together they pushed it toward Renaldo. When they saw Will, they dropped their end.

"Will, Will!" Mayzie bombed over and grabbed his leg. "Renaldo's making window covers for when waves crash into the cottages. Is it true? That's what he said." Thumb in mouth.

"Lucille left before we got up," Mayzie said.

He squatted and stared into her eyes. He'd never before noticed those amber streaks.

"Help." Jack struggled to pick up the end of a plywood sheet. "Too heavy."

"I knew we should've started prepping yesterday." Renaldo grabbed the kids' end and settled it on the sawhorses.

"Naw, we're fine." Will kept his eyes on Mayzie's face. "This storm isn't even a hurricane. Maze, where'd she go? Who'd she go with? Did she go somewhere with somebody?"

She nodded.

"Good girl. Who?"

Mayzie glanced at Renaldo and Jack and shook her head.

Will dug his fingers into her arms. "Who? Who'd she go with?"

"Ow. Quit it!"

Will dropped her arms.

"Queen."

He lifted her and squeezed her tight. "My best girl, Mayzie!" He set her back down.

"Ready to hammer these in place, boss, then I'd like to . . ." Renaldo's face paled.

"You and Queen are storm-ready, right?"

"Ready as ever." He jutted his chin toward their sturdy house, under which he'd shoved and tied down his kayak; he'd strapped foam coolers and a surfboard to a brick foundation pillar.

"Haven't seen Queen this morning. Where do you think those two went and why? Collecting trash?" Renaldo answered his own question. "Nah."

"Watch the office," Will told him. "Guests are checking out."

Renaldo unplugged the saw and walked the few feet to Will, keeping his voice low. "I've got a good case of the creeps. I'd sure like to lay eyes on those two ladies."

"Where'd they go? And why today? Think where you'd go if you were Queen. I took Lucille and them to Orcoosa their third day here. They could be there, or maybe on the beach checking turtle nests. You finish up here."

On the beach, two people soaked in the sea, another three or four took in stray sun rays, ignoring the offshore turmoil. Will wished he could. On his way back, wind filling his ears, he shut his eyes for a moment against the stinging sand, embedding grit in his beard, hair, even his mouth. Whipping around, back to the wind, he studied the tide's wrack line, iridescent and thick, seaweed hemming the strand, glittering with plastic-bottles, bags, caps, a single flip flop, more driftwood than usual, and the scattered bones of trees, white and twisted, ripped from the sea by the spinning subtropical.

Symbols of catastrophe lay everywhere. Maybe he needed to check out, go AWOL, let the chips fall. He was not and never had been a brave man. Back at the Court, Renaldo slipped notices about the storm and the Court closing under wiper blades. Only the Lambs—Lucille's family—hadn't settled up. Reservations for Labor Day weekend had been canceled. The island regulars needed to leave, not Will, but Renaldo and Queen, Mrs. Bauknight and Dick, all the 47-some year-rounders, beach or creekside.

The 120-mile Georgia coast rarely suffered storm slammers for a good reason: Its shoreline curved inward and the miles of marsh formed a buffer. More than a dozen barrier islands like this one protected the mainland but nothing shielded Boneyard. If the storm messed with the island, they'd evacuate, a first in his three years as manager, maybe first ever. In the office, he backed up the computer, pocketed the jump drive, and inventoried the supply closet: bottled water, flashlights, AA batteries, a regular old radio, stale granola bars. Outside, he tested the generator, spitting blue smoke. God, it was dying. He shut it down.

Outside, three families trotted to and from cottages with duffels, trash bags, piles of wet towels. Mrs. Pitts smoked at her steps. She offered Will a drag. He inhaled, coughed and pounded his chest, and took another. The nicotine tasted great. His mind swam, nothing was real, like he was watching himself. That animal-in-the-zoo business, but today he was animal and zookeeper.

"That storm in '79. David?" Mrs. Pitts blew sideways smoke. "You weren't even born when David hit Dominica, killed a couple thousand people; here, waves went eight feet higher than normal. Six-foot storm surge on top of that."

Will dragged again. "My mother used to talk about David like he was a *person*."

"A monster." Mrs. Pitts looked like she wanted her cigarette.

Will sucked a long, final pull. He hadn't bought a pack in two years, but could use one, that and a few drinks, never mind his brain-fog from last night's detour from Sobriety Road. He handed her the smoke.

"Been awhile."

"A lifetime, thirty-odd years. Never thought I'd see it again."

"I was talking about the smoke. Don't worry. This is no big-bad David."

She stabbed the cigarette in the shells, and turned to go inside.

He stopped her for some dang reason and quick-hugged her. "Next year."

"Lord willing and the creek don't rise." She spoke into his chest. She pulled away and went inside for her only load; she traveled solo and she traveled light. He wanted to marry Mrs. Pitts at that moment. Why? This wild, unpredictable day would break his heart and there was not a damn thing he could do to stop it.

Now what? Will asked the sky. Come on, give it up, what you got? Despite the deceptive shimmer, the wind had come up, massaging the few clouds moving in, making the trees behind the Court shift and creak like uneasy old men. Three sunburned kids wearing shell necklaces tossed parking-lot shells in the air while their parents urged them to finish gallons of ice cream or melting popsicles. The Webbs from Waycross. They came every year. Grandpa had changed out of his bikini-style swim trunks into shorts and a sport shirt.

"Later, Grandpa." Will reached for his hand in passing and shook. "Take care of the fam till next year."

"You do same. Saw how those kids got next to you—did right good for a bachelor."

So, the geezer had noticed him, noticed the kids, noticed him with the kids.

Naomi exited Cottage Twelve carrying a plastic bag. Somehow this set Will stewing.

"Is Lucille with you? I'm ready to hit the road."

"I have not seen Lucille."

Naomi blanched.

"Last night, I went off the deep end. Lucille . . . blowing off steam, getting even? Not her. I'd hoped . . . I thought, figured . . . Key West. She's around. Run."

Words jumping on words.

"Hold on." Will flattened his voice, trying to think up new platitudes, but out came phrases that only stoked fear. "No one's seen her. Renaldo's searched. Lifeguards haven't seen her. Maybe Trip can help. He'll stop by after yoga, any minute."

Fifteen minutes later, Trip jogged up. He looked at Naomi, and dipped his head.

"Ma'am."

Will filled him in.

"Where might she go?" Trip asked.

"She's obsessed with sea turtle nests but I checked the beach. I did take the kids to Orcoosa, Monday."

"Man, you did go native. I'll check that out. Do those two—Lucille and Queen—even know each other?"

Naomi's eyes wandered from Will to Trip, her face losing its last remnant of composure. "You can even drive there. I. Can. Find. Her." Everything about her wobbled—her head nodded, a flower on a weak stem; she couldn't seem to decide where to place her feet. Her wet hair showed she'd showered, but her shirt tag showed. She'd put it on inside out.

Will nodded, openly looking her up and down. "She and Queen bonded over recycling."

Trip radioed the dispatcher.

"Make sure it's somebody who knows the lay of the land, not some newbie," Will said.

Naomi repeated her intention to search; at least, Will thought that was what she said.

"No," Trip yelped. "Wait. Let my people check things out."

"The tide's too high anyway," Will said.

"I've been," Naomi repeated. "You can drive there."

"I remember. I worked here back then."

Her face registered his words: an eyebrow twitch, a half-smile.

"You stay. Jack and Mayzie need you. If we evacuate, we'll need your help."

She shook her head and used her sleeve to wipe her mouth. "Robert's urn. Gone."

21

Wormhole

By the time the wind ramped up, Renaldo had screwed plywood on most windows. Will stepped outside, motioned the kid into the office, and plugged in his cell, an automatic but useless response. Renaldo loaded Folger's in the coffeemaker. "Just in case. You never know who'll be around, stranded or too hard-headed to evacuate." Will reminded Renaldo about the spare thermoses, gallons of water, and boxes of granola bars that lived in the supply closet. Poor kid. Frantic with worry, he covered it by staying busy.

"Why tell *me*? Where are you going?" Renaldo asked. "We've *got* to find my grandma."

Will wished he'd bummed Mrs. Pitts's whole pack. "Let's assume we're staying put." He waited for the boy to acknowledge that he'd attend to the outlined tasks, waited, but the kid only cleared his throat, once, twice, three times.

Will coughed and cleared his own windpipe, was this communication? The strange language of calamity? The back-and-forth throat noises, plus Renaldo's shaved head, bald as an egg, his innocent eyes, open wide to the world, and his outsized Adam's apple all made the boy seem as fragile as a newborn. They all were fragile. And Will was so sorry, the way humans sense sorrow without deeply registering that sorrow while urgent tasks needed attention. Will observed his insight, if that's what this thought was, and it felt like a new stake for him. Could this become normal? Was that good?

The landline buzzed. Trip. The detective he'd sent to Orcoosa found nobody—nothing but fresh cuts in a stand of rabbit tobacco.

"What the hell? Rabbit tobacco?" Will cut his eyes at Renaldo.

"Queen can smell that stuff yards and yards away—she's been dying to collect her herbs. I should've taken her." Fear overflowed his eyes.

"Anything else?" Will slid deeper down the hole.

Trip hung up.

Monk slinked around Will's legs, rubbing his shins. "Monk dude, I got too much to do." But he stooped and scratched the cat between his ears until his motor revved. He scooped him up, cooing and sweet-talking, then placed him gently back on the floor.

Renaldo waited.

"What?" Will barked.

"Wind's kicking up in Jax. Storm's moving, and it's fifty miles away." He went on telling Will about the storm, it's flying, fifty or sixty miles an hour, maybe hurricane? Rain to swamping the coast?

Will knew Renaldo needed to say what Will already knew, aloud. The kid needed to absorb the information.

"If it stalls." Will thought, no, it won't, we'll be OK. "We'll only get leftovers."

"But it's now a category one, at least. Don't forget surge." Renaldo wouldn't let up. He grabbed Will's biceps. "We've got to find them. Queen's old. Her eyesight stinks—she's got cataracts forming."

Did the entire world need to explode in one day? How had Will not noticed? The coffeemaker spit weak brown liquid into its stained carafe, filling the office with the distinctive smell, even though they were plenty jittery without caffeine.

"She always leaves before I get up, so I figured no big deal. But she didn't come back." Will pressed his lips together to keep useless words inside his big mouth.

"I should've taken Queen myself," Renaldo repeated, "but I need all the work I can get around here, and, honestly? I didn't want to walk her over there because of her arthritis."

Will heaved a loud sigh. "She's a survivor. They're probably waiting for the creek to empty; they've seen the storm clouds. Please don't play, 'What if?' OK? Organize the supply closet to calm yourself. But if you remember an old-time notion she might have about storms, or a special spot, anywhere she might visit, call Trip."

Renaldo stayed rooted.

"Get this place in shape." Will waved his arm around the office. Nothing needed doing. A moment. Two.

"Suppose you're seventy-three, you can't see well, you can't drive. Where would you go if you had a young, able companion?"

Took Will half a second. "*Loblolly*. Queen needed to get back to her old place? Tabby Town? That's worth investigating. One more thing, make sure Monk's OK? The commotion's bound to confuse the guy."

22

Crumbles

Clouds moved in. Queen pushed us through thicket after thicket, with rotten logs crumbling underfoot. This path hadn't been walked in forever, but Queen marched along like she traveled it every day. Only a new hitch in her step told me the lady was tired, otherwise she seemed oblivious to nature's traps and snares; whatever she was thinking must've pleased her because she smiled like she liked life better out here.

I'd grown numb to flesh wounds on my legs, and hardly registered bug bites or briars or even welts from stinging nettles. But I wasn't numb to fear. We trudged on, and the ocean's muscly, scary soul, the wind's shifty nature, and the sky's fluky cloud maneuvers played with my mind. Nothing stayed the same here except the sucking mud. Rich and smelly and alive.

Right now, I wanted out.

My insides, whatever made me, me, seemed lost. Day after day, I'd wondered about Naomi without us, and Naomi with us. I'd waited, waited, waited. Finally I acted. Look where I landed—stranded again, this time with Queen. I'd been stranded all week, by Naomi, who'd been stranded by my dad. Even Will had been stranded, by his mom, who died, and probably by his war memories. Life really was about luck. Or no luck. I couldn't wait to grow up and run my own life. I'd never strand my own self—if I stopped letting Naomi use me.

We stepped farther into a shallow bowl of trees and bushes. Orcoosa got darker. This place looked nothing like where we went with Will, near the creek and marsh—the sky had opened on the marsh side of the boardwalk, sunlit forest grew on the other side.

"We've got to get out of here, it's getting darker." Could she even hear my panic? Did she remember I was here? I hurried to catch her up.

"Dark's nothing to fear," Queen called to the wilderness, her old friend, like she wasn't lost (which she was) or addled (which she was) or even hungry (which she must be.)

She'd at least heard me, about the dark. Still she wandered. Where? I tried telling myself that spending a night in the marsh beat going back to the Court and suffering fourteen-hours of highway to Detroit, not Key West, a lie, but when you were scared you needed to lie, if only to yourself. To keep going. *Be brave. Handle that gun if you need to.*

Queen must navigate by instinct, a homing signal, like in animals. She or her subconscious knew the way even if the sky told me it was past time to get out — soon, it would be impossible to see a thing, for instance, a thing like a rattler.

This was the perfect time to cross back to the beach side; the tide would be ebbing, but no, Queen forked onto a skinny, squeeze-through path, her bouquet of rabbit tobacco sprouting from her pack.

Ahead, Spanish moss made a mountain of a giant oak, wider than it was tall, like the one beside her cottage at the Court. Inside the thick drape was a fairy fort. The tree's branches, solid and thick, spread from a wide, flat lap big enough for a family—of hobbits. I wanted to crawl into that hobbit hole.

Queen jabbed the moss, swinging in a sudden, stiff breeze, with her stick. The trees around us whined. "Native women wore skirts made out of Spanish moss."

Did I care? Not today. She prodded the foliage carpeting one of the tree's fat legs. "These resurrection ferns live on air. Air! This old tree nurses a lot of life, that's why they call it a live oak. In a minute, we'll cross Mud Creek. We're in the wildlife refuge. Silly notion. You can't cut off clumps of land and call it wilderness. Forests take centuries to grow, re-seed, and re-adjust to weather. Animals, too."

She kept talking. I stopped listening. She stared straight at me, and saw, what?

"Sometimes it takes all you got just to survive—these old oaks know." She craned and studied the treetops, while I launched my own mind into the leaf-filtered gray sky that soon would blacken. Thank God, I'd packed my Maglite. I'd never been so jaw-clenching scared, not even when Naomi checked out after Dad died, me only five. Fear choked my mind. When Naomi left us overnight, I slept fitfully, but never admitted my fear. This week my fear-tumor had spread, but Will had stayed steady and sturdy, if weird, and I'd kept calm. Once fear grabbed me, I feared the fear would cripple me, and drive Naomi off some kind of deep end. *Hold your head high. Feel your bravery. Remember the gun.* The thought of needing the gun scared me more.

Outside the hobbit hole, Queen pressed one palm against a pine trunk and leaned into it. "My old knees—they're seizing up. That big blow's coming. My joints know." She hummed snatches of "Wayfaring Stranger."

Her vibrating voice returned me to the here and now. I wished I hadn't made Jack and Mayzie promise not to rat me out. We reached another random creek, draining. Surely any creek—this one dribbled brown water—would lead to the creek we'd crossed. But the brochure in the Court's office had pictured tons of twisty tributaries, inside an ocean of grasses; we could be anywhere in that picture.

"Where I'm heading is yonder—." She pointed to open land across the creek bed. She started down the bank.

"Wait! I'll go first." I jumped with both feet. I couldn't budge.

"That mud's got ahold of you now. You'll need learn to keep out of life's mud. Take those shoes off."

Crouching, I plunged both hands in mud, and felt for my laces.

"Wiggle those feet. Create air."

I loosened both sets of laces, extracted my right foot from

its shoe, and stood one-legged, hopping without hopping since I couldn't move, which meant bending my knees as if I *were* hopping, and pulling until I freed the submerged shoe. I maneuvered closer to the grass and smoothed a clump into a mat.

"Good girl."

Soon I was barefoot on the grass; I threw my mud-shoes and socks to the opposite side.

Queen sat at the edge and inched down on her bottom. She stepped to the grass and then across.

Squeezing roots and handfuls of grass, I got myself up. Belly down, I reached for Queen's hands, pulling the sleeves of her once-pressed, once-white shirt, smudged and torn.

"Are you OK?"

She nodded but I wondered. I wiped my shoes and worked my feet into my muddy socks and shoes. She drank half her water and I drained mine. I hadn't hydrated since lunch, but hoped—now against hope—we'd make it back before dark. I hallucinated Queen's fried chicken but knew even if we reached the Court, she wouldn't be frying any chicken.

We walked into a clearing of sprung-wire fences, missing posts, half-hidden among thigh-high flowering grasses; their seeded tops swayed and clicked, bending low in the wind. Slapping weeds with her stick, Queen paced off four corners. Walls of crumbling concrete, or something like it, mixed with shells, sat here and there like mini-monuments.

"Our tabby house," Queen said. "Built, lived-in, decayed, all in my lifetime. The Feds moved us off when they bought the land for the wildlife refuge." Queen walked to the middle of the wall-less, roofless house and sank. "Let's rest our behinds."

My blood stopped flowing. I registered her voice coming from the grass. She spoke of a shrub necklace that once ringed a house, chickens poking beaks into grass. Another community chased off like the Orcoosa natives by society's whim or fickle seas and storms. I scratched loose a crumb of this tabby stuff and rubbed it in my palm until it became dust. The sea would flood this so-called "refuge."

Home wasn't a house. If houses with foundations couldn't keep people together in space and time, what could? Would boards and beams or bricks and mortar make me feel like I belonged? To someone or something?

Queen smiled, lips-sealed, and sent high-pitched animal cries into the air. Maybe she sang of women and children, tomatoes and sunflowers, squirrels and fish, and all of life everlasting in this once-upon-a community. The wind moaned, grasses rattled their seeds, and all of it made music. At least someone had gone home.

23

Ions, Intel

Will smelled storm, and hoped, but doubted its charged, ionized air would calm anybody.

Renaldo drilled one screw in each corner of plywood, top and bottom, and both sides. Worried as this kid must be, he'd kept the extension cord plugged in, preserving the battery's charge. His energy and do-right nature lifted, a hair, Will's mood. He reset his wandering mind to the season's twelfth named storm, Louis, which he'd nicknamed Loser. He hoped Loser behaved and departed fast so that even if they lost juice, as they would, the left-behinds might pool suddenly-sodden freezer contents—burgers, steaks, fish—and party with however many summer and year-rounders stupid enough to stay.

The jumble of equipment—sawhorses, plywood, sandbags, and yards of cord running to the office, people coming and going—created an undercurrent of panic. The Webbs deflated their inner tube, squished it into the pickup bed, and slammed the tailgate. Will stashed their wet towels in one corner and stepped out of the way. Grandpa gave Will his two-fingered salute and revved the F-150's engine. The truck lumbered out of the lot. Lifting his hand, Will hollered, "Godspeed, man, see you next year."

A blue Prius rolled into the chaos. Belva scrambled out, her braid flogging her spine, shirttail flying, beat-up Keds spraying shells.

Renaldo stalled in his work and watched from his ladder.

"Are you evacuating?" Belva shouted, to no one in particular. She gripped Will's forearm; he caught her sweaty scent and felt the pressure of her fingers.

"Why? What's the latest?" She'd know everything Will didn't but needed to.

"Of course, they've stopped ferry service to the islands." She stopped and scrubbed her face with her hands, inhaled, and rushed the rest: harbors had closed, people were towing pleasure boats inland, and the Coast Guard? Unsurprisingly, they had prepared. "Saw Captain Guerrero on the noon news. Louis should bear down on Jax Beach tonight, that's what he said—'bear down'—, and lose strength once it reaches land. We'll get bands of rain and wind up here.

"It's now a hurricane. Category one or maybe two. Are you evacuating?"

Will stared past her to the sign's dancing neon palmettos. Note to self: unplug.

"I'm offering help, Will." Her tone commanded and received his attention.

She'd brewed a storm inside him, as someone who did what needed to be done under pressure. Was he? He hadn't been tested in years.

"Guests have gone, mostly. Renaldo's boarded windows. I'm set to weather the storm in the office. The generator's ready. I need to stick around." He leaned toward her until his lips grazed her ear. "Besides, I can always escape at the last minute in Renaldo's kayak."

"Cross in a kayak? Are you clueless or is it a death wish? It'll be hell out here. Hurricane fatalities are caused by—"

"Lighten up. I'm *joking*. The generator's working. If we're ordered out, we'll go . . ."

"Get out now—you're welcome, all of you, at my place." She threw him a half-pleading, half-hysterical look.

With Lucille and Queen missing, the hurricane's stakes had shot sky high. Will gave Belva the lowdown on those two and the down low on Naomi. "I'm headed to Orcoosa to find them, and when I do, OK if I bring them to your house? I mean, if Nelson's still gone."

"He is." Belva stated this scrap of significant intelligence firmly, just as Naomi stumbled from Cottage Twelve with a half-open first-aid bag, spilling bandages and cold packs and space blankets, pill containers and tubes of who knew what.

Mumbling, stooping, she stuffed contents back inside, stood and tried to uncap a plastic bottle. She looked up. "Headache."

"Her, too?" Will asked Belva. He giant-stepped to Naomi and punched the foil with a fingernail. Aspirin. He emptied two in her hand. She downed them with water.

"I'm going to those shell rings." Naomi looked up. Her eyes looked like they registered nothing, yet she'd spoken complete sentence. Maybe something was wearing off or kicking in.

He observed her for signs Trip had described—excessive salivation or dry mouth, fatigue. For sure, fatigue. Red rims around, and blue bags under, her eyes. Gray skin. Flip flops. She kneeled and obsessed over the bag's contents, but made no progress.

Trip pulled up in the Explorer. "State troopers want everybody off Boneyard. This means you, Altman. State roads, U.S. Highways—all closing. Remember who owns the place. Me. Get out. I've got search and rescue volunteers working, but they'll get out before the storm hits."

"10-4, Sheriff. Remember Aunt Cece." Will returned to Belva.

"Aunt Cece and Dick boarded the last plane from Savannah to New York," Trip hollered and drove away.

Will blinked himself back to reality.

"Why are you here?" Will asked Belva. A rogue sunbeam lit her eyes.

"I came for you. And the others."

He tore his eyes from Belva's to Naomi, and back to Belva, who took two steps and sank to the shells with Naomi.

"I'm inventorying the supplies," Naomi explained. "I'm a nurse."

"Belva, meet Naomi, Lucille's mom," Will said.

"Please, shelter at my home. Let's pack the kit. OK, bandages, adhesive tape . . . "

Naomi shoved the contents back into the bag.

Will marveled at Belva's calm as she handed Naomi the shiny silver space blanket. "Don't forget this."

Renaldo descended the ladder, stashed the screw-filled apron and drill in Will's toolbox, and leaned the ladder horizontally against the office. Will helped the boy store the Skilsaw, extension cords, sawhorses, and extra plywood in the office, Jack and Mayzie dogging his steps.

"I heard the word 'evacuate,'" Renaldo said.

Will nodded and walked Renaldo to Belva. "Belva knows everybody in town and could out-organize the Red Cross. This is Renaldo, the handiest of men and Queen's grandson. Please put him to work. He can do everything.

"Renaldo, will you go to Belva's for the duration, with Jack and Mayzie and their mom?"

He nodded. The two kids ditched Renaldo and Will for Naomi. Jack ran circles around his mother, shells spewing under his shoes. Mayzie took her mother's arm. "It's OK, Mom, let's go with Belva. She's nice. Will can find them. It's not your fault."

At this, Naomi rose, clutching the bag to her chest. Will expected the woman to melt down, but she only seemed flummoxed. He recognized the expression and thought he knew what it meant. Out. Of. It.

"Mayzie! Jack! Time to go," Will called. "Miss Belva needs you two. Hop in the Voyager and your mom'll drive y'all over. Renaldo's going, too." He steered the scene, hoping to get them gone before Naomi could object. She pawed the first-aid supplies again. Mayzie took the bag. "It's OK, Mom. I've got it." Mayzie walked Naomi to the van. She and Jack climbed in the back seats. Naomi stood at the driver's side door.

Will needed to dump her before she insinuated herself into the business of finding her daughter for whom he was responsible. He'd shown Lucille Orcoosa—what the hell for?—and given her the happy idea of revisiting. Orcoosa was part-home turf for Will; even that first day, he'd wanted Lucille to feel its vibe the way he did. The visit hadn't gone as planned, but so what? It inspired the girl to lay her father to rest. He prayed, silently, first time, maybe ever, that he and Lucille would laugh later today about both adventures.

The Court's hatches, battened; windows, boarded. Cottages empty, except Will's. His eyes lingered, as he calculated possible losses. Sculptures and tools. His so-called life.

Belva saw his mental survey and started for his porch. "Won't take a sec. We can fit a few sculptures in my trunk; we have space for all but the biggest tools."

They carried six small pieces and wedged them into the Prius's narrow hatch. He filled a canvas sack with the tools still scattered on the workbench, and stashed it in the car; their hands brushed an accidental goodbye.

"Will," Naomi said, as they passed the Voyager.

For the moment, Will ignored this wild card and her bizarre behaviors.

Jack suddenly screamed, "Pterodactyl!"

Naomi grabbed him as he leaped from the Voyager and ran past. "What?"

"I made him. I losed him."

Will knelt beside Jack. "We'll make another one—you remember how." This satisfied Jack, though Will knew—he'd learned *something* this week—that pterodactyl wasn't what was eating him. Will dreaded the night ahead, too, and couldn't wait for tomorrow. Messy mayhem should be his strength—the army trained him to stare disaster in the face—but chaos, where no one can practice for what actually happens, bred emotional outbreaks that tripped him up. Chaos was contagious and killed efficiency.

Will's longing for the wormhole intensified.

Jack climbed back into the Voyager. Naomi picked her way across the shells toward Cottage Twelve, calling, "Toothbrushes? I need Lucille."

Mayzie scrambled from the van, caught her mother's hand, they walked to the cottage, and emerged a moment later with toothbrushes, toothpaste, and shampoo, Naomi in shades.

As Mayzie passed, Will said, "*Anybody asks you if you in this game, you tell 'em you in it for life, a'ight?*" He'd watched a few *Wire* reruns on the computer.

She nodded, eyes and nose scrunched, close to tears. Still, she repeated her lines: "*No loose talk, no second thoughts, and no snitching.*"

He squeezed her shoulders. "Good girl." She grinned, maybe experimentally, but kept the grin, and found a spot in the Voyager.

Naomi took the first-aid kit and wobbled to where Will stood with Belva.

Clouds piled. Air died. Atmosphere bided its time, building heat and power to fuel the storm. Altman, he told himself, don't let your imagination run but so crazy, not yet. Focus.

Beach stragglers found parked cars and drove off, slick, half-naked bodies crammed one-by-one into a van. They scratched off in a spray of sand and a blare of drumbeats. Perfect storm soundtrack.

Renaldo hung close to Belva, too. The woman exuded competence. Point person and defacto leader. She peeled off a pre-written sticky note—her address—and held it out for Naomi, who shifted her gaze from Will to Belva. The note wafted to the shells.

Naomi tossed Renaldo her keys. "You drive. I'm going to find my child."

Belva cut her eyes at Will but addressed Naomi: "Will knows the territory. He'll find them before the storm hits. Nobody needs or wants amateurs out there—you'll only slow him."

Naomi's skin was sallow, and who knew what her eyes looked like now because of the sunglasses. Her shoulders hunched and she seemed sweatier than even this humidity warranted.

Belva sucked in air. "You don't look well." Belva and Will exchanged glances.

"Naomi is a nurse," Will stupidly offered, àpropos of nothing.

"That's great," Belva said. "Do you need medications? We'll find an open drugstore. I'm sure you have the prescription number. Please come. We may need to shelter others; we could use your skills."

Will cupped Naomi's shoulder and pointed her toward the Voyager, where Jack and Mayzie motioned through the open door.

"Take your hands away. You do not have permission to touch me."

"Please get in the van. We can't—." Belva's calm manner, though, did nothing to dissolve Naomi's woozy but determined focus.

"Lucille's angry. Mayzie and Jack," she called to the little kids, "I need to go with Will."

They nodded in synced slow motion, but their faces told Will that all they saw was grownups going haywire.

"Let's go then, before the rain. Call my landline, your cell won't work." Belva gave Naomi another sticky note with the address and the number. "If you change your mind, Will can drive you. Renaldo, follow the Prius."

Will gave Belva a weak peace sign, for lack of words. You couldn't go wrong with a peace sign. Everybody liked peace.

"Renaldo, you go on, I'll finish." Still, the boy hesitated. He appeared reedlike—thin and breakable. "Go ahead. You'll like Miss Belva."

"But I know Tabby Town better than anybody."

"Not better than me. You forget how much older I am. Miss Belva will lose power, and she'll need help distracting Jack and Mayzie. Please."

The boy's voice grew fierce. "Queen's all I've got. And, Lucille . . ."

"Just go. Please."

Renaldo headed to his cottage. Five minutes later he stood at the Voyager in sneakers, T-shirt, and shorts, carrying a plastic bag; he climbed in the driver's seat.

All of them—Will, Belva, Renaldo, Naomi, Jack, and Mayzie—hung by a thread.

Moments clocked by. Wind alternately died and gusted. Hang on, Will told himself, OK, so you only got that bronze star because Monk died, but you can do this. You pulled him out, already dead. But you need to go this mission alone, otherwise it'll be hell, making sure nobody trips and falls into eddying creeks or cracks bones. Will could make tracks alone. Fast. Alone. He did better alone. Loss, he saw, was inescapable. Renaldo's lanky frame, sticking-out ears, and skinny arm hanging out the Voyager's window told him that.

Will trotted over. "Man-to-man, look after Belva and these kids?"

The kid swallowed and nodded. "You'll find them and get out quick?"

"You know me, man, too chicken to tarry, too stupid to quit. And, take care of Monk?"

Will glanced at the idling Prius, and called, "OK if he brings Monk?"

Belva gave Will a thumbs up. Will scooped Monk, swaddled him in a towel, and handed him to Mayzie. "My little man'll calm down in a minute." Not a chance. He'd howl all night. From outside the van, Naomi hugged Mayzie, then Jack. "Be good. Mind your manners." Jack wedged himself between Naomi's head and Mayzie's body and grabbed Naomi around the waist.

"Where's Lucille?" Jack moaned.

"I'll find her," Naomi said.

God damn her. She was not traveling with him. He wanted to shove her in the van, lock and slam the door. Instead, he turned his back and silently screamed at the sky. Lucille and Queen could somehow make it back to the Court; someone needed to stay on site. He got Trip on the office phone, but Trip had no spare deputies. "I'll dispatch a patrol car to check on things every couple of hours but you get the fuck out, idiot. You're welcome at my apartment. Can't promise food, but it's shelter."

"I'll be at Belva's," Will lied. "Who's searching?"

"Two deputies. If need be, state troopers. For God's sake, don't let the mother go and don't you go. Nobody goes out in the thick of things, you hear? Search and rescue resume *after* danger's passed. We do not *lose* lives trying to *save* lives."

That depended on whose life you were saving, didn't it?

He tried again. "Naomi, we've got a great search team. Sheriff Trip's on his game. You go with the kids, and I'll be along once I doublecheck windows and doors and sandbags."

She drew out her no, and said, “I can help you.” For a moment at least she didn’t sound like a woman who’d missed or taken one too many doses.

Renaldo had forgotten the window on the marsh side of the office. Will grabbed his apron and the still-charged screwdriver and re-positioned the ladder. He concentrated on not pulverizing his thumb. This simple job. Solid and easy.

Listening to the shells crackle as the Voyager and Prius crept from the lot, Will drove the screws in, clean and swift, eyeing only the screwdriver. He secured the plywood over the glass, the most important job in the world. Monk said, and Will repeated, to quiet his insides: *Awareness is a matter of life and death. The homeland of the moment.* He put away the tools and ladder. “Ready when you are.” Naomi’s voice could’ve busted a jaw or made you weep.

24

Shelter

Queen lowered herself, knees then bottom, and slumped against a tabby pillar.

"My ancestor, Still Waters, was here thousands of years ago. They were big women, like you, big-busted, black-headed, not red-headed or blonde like Europeans, and strong. They dug clay and made pottery, tanned hides, and sharpened antlers into spears, and, wove fishing nets. All that, while they made and reared babies." Words poured from her mouth, a river of words she couldn't stop—worried though I was, the images the words painted fizzed my insides, and the ancient people, these women worker bees who still lived in her heart, spoke through Queen, as we walked where they walked, lost our feet in mud like they had; I even felt a child's weight—but, no, that was my backpack.

Queen's talk inspired me. I'd make myself into something big—I owed them that, those ancients. Women did the work of the world.

She read my mind. "Lucy, women bear burdens. Your mother knows, and one of these days, you will, too." I thought of Naomi as undependable and scattered because you never knew what she'd do. She'd always used me, and so I forgot how constantly and tirelessly she worked. Volunteered for extra shifts in labor and delivery, even stayed past her shift with single mothers, scared and alone.

I cut my eyes at the sky and counted to 300 while, above,

a cloud-roof formed. I listened, worried, and fought the heavy, charged air, filling with storm. Queen didn't notice. Was Queen crazy or at peace? She acted like she'd seen everything; her calm was weirdly contagious.

A breeze whispered. We had so little food and water—how could I get Queen up and out of here? Throw her over my shoulder? Even if I could, I couldn't find the route.

All the while, Queen sang and sang about Still Waters, and kept asking the spirits if they were weary. I shut my eyes and crossed my legs yoga-style, counting and holding breaths. Duh. No. I jerked myself from the grass and shook off Queen's delusional peace. We needed to get out.

A weird wind billowed the now-black woolly sky, but Queen had forgotten the storm, and paid no attention to the hissing air, or the dips and twists we'd need to navigate back to our creek, whichever one it was, and the Court.

Lightning bolts froze distant old oaks into monuments and made creek grasses into upside-down icicles. Thunder rocked the earth. Bracing my mud-caked feet, I placed my hands under Queen's armpits and lifted. Light-but-dead weight. My efforts broke her Tabby Town spell.

"You hightail your heinie back without me, I'll be along directly. You'll see the big oak, high enough off the ground, inside the shell ring. Spirits will protect you. You won't float away. These trees know me and you. We're the same, those trees and us—muscle and blood and skin and bones. Trees are half-human."

I could find the oak, but no way I'd leave Queen. Lightning halved the sky. After that garish bolt, the world grayed.

"Take a pill or something," I shouted over the rumbling thunder. "Don't you have a remedy? That Life Everlasting? Chew it or smoke it or whatever."

She sat, untroubled. "Go on, we'll meet at the old oak."

I offered her my hands and stood my ground. Finally she gripped both, teetering on legs wrecked, from a lifetime—of what? But at seventy-three, couldn't just using legs grind them to nothing? She was squeezing the life out of my hands; where did she find muscle for that grip? I felt her finger bones, her swollen knuckles. She tried but failed to rise.

"I'm not going without you." I stole frantic glances at the sky. "I'm as stubborn as you are. You decide: go or stay. Here we're in the open but we need shelter."

She surveyed the sky and the wind-whipped grasses. "Reckon this'll do me, no need to cause worriment; maybe you'll bring me back another day."

I choked on silent sobs, half-dragging Queen, and maneuvered us back to a creek, swelling with tide; rain came sheeting down. I went first this time, piling on more and more grass, covering the foot-eating mud. I helped her down the bank and pushed her up the other side, then scrambled my own self up.

No choice but to trust Queen's instincts, sharp earlier in the day, but addled now. We stepped through the soaked forest in near-dark, moss drooling from trees and slapping our faces as we used the last daylight, me praying the creek would stay behind us without twisting and turning and suddenly appearing. The storm would bloat the creeks, never mind Queen's protective spirits. Storm surge was real.

Queen warbled about the wayfaring stranger, verse after verse, reminding me of Dad. I lifted and lowered one foot then the other, touching earth that was totally in love with my feet, soft swollen ground dying to steal my muddy runners, steal me. I tightened my death grip on Queen's elbow. We hobbled along in rain falling hard and fast. Could rattlesnakes swim? Did alligators hole up in rain or did they roam? Questions and no answers. We kept going. Walking a wooded path maybe a foot wide in the deepest dark of my life—Detroit was never, ever dark, a weird pink always glowed in the sky, besides streetlights and lit-up apartment complexes and other city fixtures.

Cold and colder. How could rain make my teeth chatter in August?

Hours or minutes later—caught in time—no sense of its passing—the oak loomed, a dizzying sight, reminding me of the time I sipped whisky from one of Naomi's boyfriend's bottles. I moved the moss aside, and eased Queen into the tree's shallow, lumpy bowl. The thick canopy and its moss coverlet had kept the inside practically dry. I propped our packs together, secure between two thick limbs.

Queen pawed inside her pack, and settled, lizard-like against a limb. The night got weirder when she showed me a hand-carved pipe. She tore soggy leaves from the rabbit tobacco and stuffed them in the bowl. "Lighter's in my pack."

Like they'd catch. I dug out my Maglite anyway and found her lighter. After many tries, a flame flickered for a teeninesy second of psychological warmth, then died. My teeth wouldn't stop rattling. Queen shivered uncontrollably, groaning, her body's attempt to warm itself. I felt in my pack for the ibuprofen I carried for monthly cramps.

We hadn't hydrated in hours. I wet my tongue with the last drop in my own bottle and made Queen drink hers with the ibuprofen while I rubbed her arms and legs, under her shirtsleeves, under her pants' legs, hoping to stop chills and ease sore muscles, trying to forget my own rubbery limbs. We half-sat, half-lay inside the tree's curved fork, blind but not deaf to the storm's bluster.

Rain finally seeped inside the dense canopy, and I uncapped my water bottle and wedged it into a gap. The wind grew louder and cried like a person, like many, many people, marching, snapping branches, crashing trees, the wet woods halfway muting the violent noises. Rain beat leaves. Trees dropped into other trees and shook the earth. Could our tree stand up to this attack? If it's as old as Queen said, it's seen worse. I kept her arm inside mine to keep myself from jumping out of my own skin.

"Tree's been here 350 years." She patted my hand. "You know that, BooWoo."

Uh oh. Who was BooWoo?

Water lapped at the trunk; even our solid tree swayed its gi-normous appendages. Above, a bough cracked and toppled, and got stuck halfway.

Even inside our sanctuary, the wind shoved the tree and I felt its muscles move yet stay strong. I covered Queen with myself—her body, so fragile—and wrapped my arms partway around the tree. Queen trembled even though I'd pinned her. If I had a rope I'd tie us to the tree and pray it didn't go down; people did that, I read, in the Sea Island Hurricane of 1893. Water splashed below.

Nothing had ever gripped and shaken me until all my cells were dancing and jumping. Did people feel the most alive when they might die? Does fear jazz blood cells? Did Dad's blood cells gyrate in the heat of battle? He and I shared the same blood. But nature and war were two different monsters.

The night dragged. Boneyard Time stopped, started, slowed, stretched, and snapped, until I wondered where my mind was. Time couldn't go backward, could it? Were we trapped in a parallel universe? Was I reliving a riot or living it in "real time?"

That cracked limb finally dropped. And missed us.

25

Old Pal, Enemy

Naomi fiddled with the radio. The storm bore down. Pearl's headlights pushed against rain-walls. Sudden brightness flared, forming lariats of lightning big enough to rope the planet.

Phrases burst from radio static: *high winds, storm surge, stay off roads*. Will glanced at Naomi, ransacking her purse. Her phone lit up. Thunder. She dropped the phone and plugged her ears, and spoke words Will couldn't decipher, as though she'd grabbed, randomly, chewed, and spit them. He couldn't stop the truck on the highway, not with the rain knifing down. He made his voice loud and calm. "We're OK. Don't panic."

She stared at the phone and put it away.

He hung a left, taking the turn in first gear. Quitting asphalt meant mud, the Forest Service road. He'd forgotten—preoccupied with Naomi—to pack a chainsaw. *Won't be your last screw-up tonight, Altman, this is no-win territory. Do what you need to do then GFOT.*

He'd park at *Loblolly*, and they'd hoof it from there—the only way to cover ground. He switched the wipers to blast-off, and strained to see beyond the thick downpour. Pearl's tires skidded, she fishtailed, and Naomi bounced; her head hit the ceiling at every mudhole.

"Buckle up? Please?"

She complied. His mind inventoried supplies he'd packed. Water. Protein bars. Blankets. Check. The chainsaw was a stupid oversight. Even ER vehicles would need to stop, cut, and drag trees off the service road. *Soon, you'll be at Loblolly,* he told himself, *maybe you'll soak up a smidgen of mojo from the place, chant an incantation, anything to stave off fear.*

A thick branch banged the windshield. He shifted into park, set the emergency, jumped out and shoved the limb aside. Windshield. Cracked. Through the fracture, the road got even harder to read. He might as well shut his eyes and drive, for all the good his rods and cones were doing him. Finally, Pearl's twin beams found *Loblolly's* crumpled roof and lit the bright blue tarp on the foundation he and Trip started last Sunday, not a week, but a lifetime ago.

He parked in the clearing, hoping to protect the truck from blowdowns.

"Time to get dirty." He reached in the glove box for his headlamp, adjusted the elastic, and positioned the beam so it shot from his forehead.

Naomi froze in her seat. Confusion marked her face.

"Shut that off." Her eyes darted. Will's diagnosis was simpler and possibly unrelated to drugs—panic?

"Why'd you bring us *here*?" She plucked foam pooching from the torn upholstery.

"Why can't we go pick them up?"

"No road leads to the shell formation—we'll need to hike."

Behind Pearl, they faced off.

"You OK?" he shouted.

"You brought her here—she'd never have come on her own." She wobbled on her feet, yoga pants already sopping. "If only Robert were here."

Wait. Robert. Her husband? Ashes.

She removed a tiny round tin from her pocket, a doll-sized water bottle, and popped a pill so fast he couldn't've stopped her.

"What'd you just take?"

She ignored him. "You said they'd be here. Lucille's the one who keeps me going, keeps us all going. Even when she was a little bitty thing, she'd say, 'Mom, time for breakfast.'"

She paused. "Whatever that pill was, it was the last one."

He was stuck.

"Lucille, Mayzie, Jack." She yelled the family roll. "Robert!" Her voice died in the rain.

Will grabbed her shoulders: "That girl's got a solid mind in emergencies." He hoped.

The downpour soaked up Naomi's weepy wails and blended the sounds into a sorrowful hymn that haunted Will's bones. Was this drug-induced or normal? How would he know? These circumstances would drive anybody mad, and yet, he indulged his dark urge. "Stop. You wanted to be here. Use your eyes. Stay out of my way."

When the weeping subsided, he pulled a black trash bag and an old pair of waders from behind the seat. He plunged his fist into the bottom and both sides to make openings. She sat sideways in the driver's seat while he slipped boots on her feet and tugged the bag over her head.

He hoped the big waders wouldn't slow her, but no way she'd make it in flip flops. He shrugged into his parka, tightened the hood, and they slogged off.

"We're gambling they're somewhere around here—the shell rings are not far."

The storm din enforced silence, but after awhile, when the width of the path allowed, he turned and shouted, "You've just taken something. Should I worry?"

"A prescription that calms me. You could work faster without me. But what if *you* get hurt? I *am* a nurse. I'm not good enough for you, but I'm *good enough* for basic first aid."

Complete sentences. Maybe she would prove useful, but it'd taken her *how* many tries to pack the first-aid supplies? Had whatever she'd taken kicked in?

She tripped. He gave her a hand up. "Don't get too calm to keep up because I'll leave you here. Alone. I swear." He was lying.

Somewhere a tree hit the ground, which received it with barely a thud, and he pictured an army of trees toppling one by one or all at once. He steadied his breath. They inched forward and his jitters reared up. Stop. Wait. Focus. He turned and there she was in his spotlight, a ghost. She lagged, splashed with mud, a drippy draggy smear drifting in the understory. Rain had shellacked her hair to her head.

His beam paled her into a phantom. Why couldn't she have done that one simple parent thing: Look after your own kids? His mind made hay with that thought. But, they'd been his this week. Maybe he could adopt them.

She finally caught up with him. He touched her shoulder. As she passed, he shucked his parka. Her pallor, her shuffling walk—those boots—alarmed him.

"Wear this."

She stopped and he dragged the trash bag over her head. He took the bag and zipped her into his jacket, hooded her head, and shouldered the first-aid bag.

They plowed through the rain curtain until a creek's roar stopped them. Chicken Creek. Will's thoughts roamed as big and wild as the water, rising fast. The tide theoretically was out at six, but the rain had already swelled the creeks.

He turned sideways to the creek. God, what if she stumbled and fell in? She moved slowly, all good, but she was clumsy; Will's radar said to stay creek-side. When he took her arm, she pulled away, but he tightened his grip.

Rain turned to white frozen pellets fired from the sky. Hail.

The plastic bag was stewing him in his own juices. Water lapped his boot tops, and reached halfway up Naomi's waders; if they took on water, she'd be a goner. Again, he grabbed her hand. Again, she resisted. Again, he squeezed harder. He did not let go.

He'd faced worse, but over there, he'd shut down his senses completely to survive—and pretended he could do the job of living. Now, he struggled to stay present. *Help me, Monk.* His legs registered the gentle rise of the native shell rings, up and up they climbed, while his headlamp probed the darkness, revealing, bit by bit, the wilds of Orcoosa. A sopping deer, white tail up, startled among the shivering maples and sycamores. The rain subsided briefly, and Will scanned the surroundings, turning 360 degrees, yelling and yelling, hoping to hear someone yelling back.

Branches hung, compound-fractured, mid-air; vines roped their legs, trying to take them down. A tree could drop any second. He eyed everything suspiciously through the veil of water. He'd thought of trees as friendly, but tonight they were out to get him. *Your turf*, he reminded himself. He could find these two. They belonged to him.

At the top of the shell ring, Will did another 360, played the beam around the woods, but saw only trees coming alive in the wind. Animal paths snaked, and here was the missing rabbit tobacco—the new-cut swath.

"They were here, Naomi, they were here."

She caught up and stumbled, mumbling words drowned by the rain. Will prayed she wouldn't pass out. He aimed the headlamp at the clipped stalks and pointed. "Queen clipped this herb." He doubted she heard or comprehended his words over the rain, alternately slacking and intensifying, but showing no sign of letting up. He revolved, again, slowly, and lit the surroundings. "We need rest."

A yelp puckered his flesh. He wheeled, spotlighting Naomi on her knees in mud, hugging a muddy container, rocking convulsively. Her wails carried, even over the storm-drone. Will watched, frozen. For a moment, he couldn't imagine what ripped that animal sound out of her.

"Robert." Endlessly, she cried his name. *Robert, Robert.*

And so the daughter had, at last, buried her father. Though Will had never seen the urn, there it was, had to be. On closer inspection, Will saw that Lucille had placed the urn inside a circle of shells. An odd feeling hit him, not peace, but satisfaction for Lucille. Hope rose in his chest that the two women were nearby. And safe.

Wind. Rain. Both loud, both heavy. Will pulled at Naomi's torso, trying to raise the dead weight of her from the mud. She collapsed in his arms, spilling sorrow and talking gibberish; the harder he worked to get her upright—he needed to warm her in his arms, for comfort and to stave off hypothermia—the heavier she became. Maybe dehydrated. On his knees, he drew back, trying to get in her face, but couldn't see in the downpour. He prayed she wouldn't die from whatever gripped her now. Had grief had taken hold? Was this a seizure? She shook him off. He rocked back on his haunches, leaned forward, pulled at her shoulders, and tried lifting her again.

Sobbing and mud-bound, she slipped from his grasp. On all fours, she clawed mud, and with handfuls, tried to refill the urn. He reached around and wrested the urn from her hands. He rolled it aside. She shuddered so fiercely that he placed both his hands on hers and crawled on top of her. She bucked twice then surrendered. Will feared he, or the fit, had injured or even killed, Naomi, and he raised himself. He located her pulse at her wrist. Passed out. He stayed on top, tense with his effort to warm her. He vowed to stay awake, sheltering her inside his own body—a human cave. He'd never witnessed such shameless grief. She mourned, he knew, far more than the missing Robert and Lucille, though those were sorrows aplenty. He didn't care so much now about her weird and dangerous behaviors, whether pharmaceutically-fueled or exacerbated, what she was taking or why. Her raw gut-reaction to life's terrible tricks submerged him in envy. If he could purge, empty himself of the long and loud screams that had set up shop inside, oh, he'd ranted, but his sly, sarcastic screeds had built bigger and stronger defenses that made him feel smaller and smaller. Finally, Will, too, slept. Until a deafening quiet woke him.

26

Taste of Time

Dawn. Boneyard Time. Wimp-winds flung water from the leaves, a green flurry: The forest was crying. Water soaked my skin down to my bones; my clothes, even my body, felt like wet rags. I lifted one foot, dropped it and repeated with foot number two. I tried out my arms the same way, and tapped Queen's bony shoulder, hoping the woman hadn't rusted, that her mind worked, and mostly that she remembered the way home.

At my touch, she struggled to sit. I braced my feet in the lap of the tree and steadied her.

"I'll get the fire going," she said. "But it's wet." A moment later, she called me Mama. The lady was out of her head. Maybe deep in dream, since she'd mostly seemed sane. But, I'd been thinking about space and time and parallel universes. Had I lost *my* mind?

Thirst and cold and hunger had invaded my body and my brain. Cold, as in hypothermia. That's what had scrambled Queen's brain, and maybe mine. Also dehydration. I pawed Queen's pack for the last of the nasty-tasting spread, swiped the can with a finger and swabbed two soggy crackers. I forced mine down, upended my water, half-filled with rain, wet my tongue, and gagged. I handed Queen her cracker and the water. She ate and drank.

Rain had watered down my strength, which had ebbed like the tide.

This terrible quiet—the storm had silenced the forest.

Eventually, we'd get out of here. Eventually, we'd warm up. Eventually, we'd eat. How long was eventually?

Light struggled inside our leafy, mossy roof. I grabbed a branch, and stood. Stomach-sick, woozy, I waited for my insides to settle, and mentally sent messages into my stalky, weak legs. I leaned over and shifted Queen to sitting, shouldered both packs, and slid the few feet to the sloppy ground. Bracing one leg behind me, I reached for her forearms, and gently pulled her forward on her bottom. Her breath rasped. I grabbed her calves.

I will catch this bony creature. She slid-fell into my arms. We landed in mud, me on the bottom, hanging onto each other. I pushed her aside and squatted, tucked my hands under her shoulders, sat her, then stood her up. Walking as one, we sloshed into the world through ankle-deep water.

Trees, uprooted, had snapped in half. Every few feet, we faced a fresh-downed tree or mossy old log, and walked around or over. Where were we? Queen was in no shape to say. One minute I was her mother, the next, a cousin. With both arms around her, I led her down nearly impassable trails that yesterday were ribbons curving into labyrinths curving into animal tracks.

Twenty-four hours ago, she knew where these paths led.

Should we walk? Stay in place? *Hug a tree*, I'd once heard a forest ranger say. We'd done that all night. I tricked my mind into believing that we were going somewhere. Thankfully, the rain was over, though random drops still patted leaves, like they were saying, *there, there.*

Afterwhile, we rested in a paste of leaf litter. Under my backside, the strange land stirred and vibrated; I smelled the soaking dirt, and imagined zillions of microscopic bugs marching, marching under spiky cabbage palms, beaten ferns, and tangled, horned vines.

My eyes adjusted so the forest no longer came at me collaged in green and brown and gray, but in distinct shapes, remnants of paths showing themselves.

It was me. I'd gotten better at seeing. Every leaf. Individual water drops, hanging from single pine needles. Soon a dark shape—with eyes—stared. I squeezed my eyes shut and re-opened them.

Boar. Major snout. Tusks. Hair. He blended not-quite-completely in nature. He sniffed. I'd never seen animals in the wild up close unless I counted trash-can coyotes in Detroit. But this big thing could crush us. He stood only five yards away. Maybe less.

We stayed still, Queen, the boar, and me. The forest infiltrated my skin like a spy, its smells filling my nose and air inflating lungs; my tongue tasted leaves, moss, and pinestraw.

I was eating the forest, biting off chunks of time, if time had a taste and smell.

It tasted like dirt. It tasted like rain. I could touch time. The marsh and mud felt like forever.

My eyes roamed beyond the boar to the mist wrapping the pines, splintered but standing. I bit my lip and tasted blood to make sure I existed. Fully awake, and hearing the tiniest of sounds, I swore I heard ants under logs and smelled them, too. Restless leaves scraped each other. Pine needles dropped water beads. I leaned over and pressed my ear to the ground.

It hummed. Was there a name for the noise of the earth?

Queen sensed and smelled the boar, her ESP worked even if her eyes didn't. She touched my arm. The boar cocked his head, grunted, and looked straight at us. His animal-ness pumped into my heart and lungs. I inhaled him, absorbing him in the way he seemed to absorb us. He dug his snout into dirt, leaves.

"We need to keep moving. He's not going anywhere," I whispered, worried for Queen. She needed fluids. I maneuvered Queen to her feet, and hobbled her away, glancing over my shoulder. The boar grunted once and trotted off.

We plodded. The sky lightened, silvered, and shined the forest. I tripped on a root. Queen offered a freezing hand as we headed uphill. I hoped this was Orcoosa, and we'd find the boardwalk.

We reached a clearing. Weed trees sprouted at another ruin. A house. In the middle of everything, a mud-splattered truck. After a day and night of forest, the clearing gave us sky; it also scared the daylights out of me.

M time in the forest had turned me nocturnal.

Oh. Pearl. The sight of Will's truck buckled my legs. I dropped to my knees. Will, from the alt-universe, had I dreamed the whole week? Where was *he*?

Distant sounds—chainsaws screaming the way I longed to scream, if I had a voice.

I forced my feet to the driver's side—Will wasn't the type to bother locking—opened the door, and blasted the horn three times, but nature absorbed and muted the sounds.

Up close, the burned house. *Mudhole*, Will's once-upon-a-home. Cinderblocks. We'd seen those Monday, marking a foundation. The storm had snatched away the bright blue tarp, exposing raw yellow wood.

I guided Queen, ragged and worn, to the passenger seat. I squatted beside her and slipped off her pack and mine. Her hands shook. I found the empty water bottle and remnants of the smelly food, the cracker mush. And finally, the plastic-wrapped gun.

At the bottom, in a Ziploc, were bullets. I handed the bag to Queen, who said nothing.

We needed noise. I swung out the cylinder, the way Will had, inserted three bullets, and turned until it clicked. The gun weighed a ton without Will's hands folded around mine. I walked to the center of the clearing, clutching the handle in quivering hands, and lined my pointer finger outside the trigger guard. My gun hand jittered. I pulled back the hammer with my left palm.

Squeezing the gun with both hands, my pointer on the trigger, I lifted both arms overhead, barrel aimed at the sky. I waited for the ear-splitting sound.

I could hardly keep my arms raised. Gun in the air, feet rooted, I sensed my father, who surely had carried a gun, maybe even this type of gun. Something new about Will hit me, and I thought back to that first day when I followed Will around the Court.

Will brought me Dad.

My nose tingled. I prepared for the end-of-the-world blast.

I fired. I lowered both arms, shaky with the weight of the gun, exhaustion, and ten years of worry. My ears rang. Now, bigger sounds. Fireworks from farther away. Wailing, too, the sound of bawling animals missing mothers. No. Those were my screams.

Queen nodded. Her eyes wandered from me to Pearl, to the sky. "Why, we're at *Loblolly*, BooWoo."

BooWoo? Queen's mind. Still on vacation; I hoped it would return home.

Crashing in the brush. I expected boar or deer, instead, two mud-people staggered into the clearing, one was Naomi, wearing a filthy coat that looked like she'd wallowed in mud, eyes unfocused, but she hugged and hugged and hugged, let go, backed away, approached, hugged, let go, repeated. She grabbed my wrist, trying to take my pulse, but could not find, much less read, her watch. She took shallow panting breaths. Did she even recognize me?

Will ditched the garbage bag he wore and tucked Queen in the space blanket from Naomi's first-aid kit. He walked to me and my shaking body, still clutching the gun.

"You done good, girl. I'll take that sidearm." Humming his *Hurricane* song, he emptied the cylinder, pocketed the bullets, and stuffed the gun, barrel first, in his back pocket like he did Monday, a lifetime ago.

"Renaldo, this looks like a piece of trash." Queen fiddled with the silver space blanket.

Will's face, arms, mud-black, made Queen mistake him for Renaldo?

"Naomi, take a load off." Will sounded casual and relaxed. He jogged to the truck and came back with water, regular blankets, and protein bars.

He crouched at Pearl's door and held a water bottle to Queen's mouth, like you'd feed a baby, until she'd taken in water. She pushed away the bar.

Will got up, gobbling a bar. He tore open random bars, urging, "Eat. Eat," one for Naomi and one for me, saying, "Get these down, will you?" He monitored me as I drank twelve ounces, Naomi, too. She got up. He sat her down. I scooted close, and looped an arm around her waist, then waved a blueberry bar past her nose. She nibbled. He draped a real blanket over Naomi. She wouldn't stay still, and the blanket slipped. I replaced it on her shoulders and held it there.

Will looked so fine, like his big heart was shining through the mud, on the outside, but his eyes! Tunnels. I touched his arm. He saw straight inside me like he knew how I felt.

"We'll take care of your mom."

I hugged her hard, pulled back for a quick look, wanting and not wanting, to apologize. She blinked once and darted her eyes.

Will mummied me in a blanket, tied the corners under my chin, and squeezed me in an extra tight hug, pulled away and squeezed again. I wiggled one arm free for chocolate chips between long gulps of water. I made Naomi drink and drink. Their night could've been worse than ours—we had rested in the fairy-fort. They probably walked.

Chainsaws sounded from all directions.

Naomi stared and finally swallowed me in hug-spasms till I nearly choked.

Now Will checked pulses. Frowning, he rolled a log over to Queen and propped up her feet. Hypothermia? High blood pressure, too? Or low? Our hearts, were they working overtime to circulate warm blood? I wished I knew.

"Anytime, Rescue Squad, anytime." He checked pulses again, and knitted his brows.

"My *word*, people, I've forgotten my host duties. Let me welcome y'all to my home—how nice of y'all to drop in. I'd invite you inside, but, as you see, the inside is on the outside."

I wanted to check *his* blood pressure. His face was scraped and scratched, eyes bloodshot, beard, muddy. He was running on adrenaline. Naomi functioned, sort of, or maybe this was pure exhaustion—my wooziness, brain fog, and shaky limbs were about low blood sugar and hypothermia and fatigue, oh, and dehydration. Naomi, a mess in the mud-coat, bloody scrapes and scratches on her face, crazy-big rubber boots, kept her tight hold on me.

I didn't know how or what she had suffered. And Will. Shame surged in my cells: I'd forced people to risk lives.

Now that Will had fed and warmed us, he stood over us and stared like we were ghosts.

Why didn't he yell? I yelled at myself, silently. Me, a kid trying to bury her dad? Or was I wanting to punish Naomi? Oh, God. Jack and Mayzie.

"Will, where are the sibs?" I held my breath.

"With the captain of competence—Belva."

Thank goodness for that woman. Will's eyes wandered around the clearing while we rested on the concrete steps.

"How do we get out?" I asked.

"We wait."

Chainsaws eventually got louder. A chunk of Boneyard Time broke off and floated until finally a rescue truck pitched and swayed into the clearing. "Cleared fifteen daggone trees off that dirt track," said one of two medics, whose nametag read Eddie. They loaded Queen onto a board and belted her.

Will conferred with Eddie, and, though Naomi was wide awake, the medics strapped her, too. "I do not give you permission to treat," she kept saying. "I do not. No."

"Mom, Mom." I jumped up and stroked her hair. "It's quick, they'll give you something to relax, OK?"

"You need medical attention, too, Bud, you OK to drive?" Eddie checked Will's blood pressure and pulse and took his temperature. "They'll give you the works. You OK to drive?"

"*Hell*, yeah, to infinity—and beyond, now that people are safe. Seriously. I'm fine."

How could Will be OK to drive?

"Are you really OK?" I asked him, cutting my eyes at the EMTs.

"Hell yeah. No, hell, no. Oh, forget the outburst. Post-storm euphoria after my journey to the underworld."

Eddie frowned. "Go straight to Rice County Medical, no place else." Eddie said. "You get yourself checked out. I'll tell the ER to expect you."

I hoped he wouldn't wreck! But I knew what he meant, about the euphoria because my blood now dashed around in my veins, too, reminding me Will was right: I was lucky.

27

Uprooted

Will swerved Pearl around roadblocks, power company trucks, and uprooted trees. Why did post-storm days shine so? Strewing brilliance? In Pinesboro, storm surge and high tide had shifted the riverfront's boulder-sized, erosion-prevention stones onto grass. Wind had sliced off a pine-top and deposited branches through the roof of Market Street Bank. Fish jumped in yards because water stood foot-deep.

He drove through the hospital parking puddle, Pearl leaving a respectable wake, and killed the engine. His adrenaline rush had crashed as soon as they'd found their people. He groggily listened to the DJ, who sounded sky high, how else could he keep up his patter? *Storm-night at the station, y'all. That Louis had his eye on us, and we missed the worst, but Rice County's northeast corner took a helluva hit. Dude dumped ten to fifteen inches between midnight Saturday and the wee hours, packing sixty-mile-an-hour winds on the mainland, gusting up to seventy on the islands. Sunday's high tide came ashore with a 5.2-foot storm surge, but y'all, here's the saddest and baddest: Boneyard Island's beach side? History, including the vintage 1940s Palmetto Tourist Court. R.I.P.*

Will slammed his fist into the dash and howled.

In the hospital lobby, a fountain spewed chlorinated water he smelled from the door. The recycled water-geyser climbed up and up, into the atrium's dead space until it fell, exhausted by the ascent, into the pool where he studied winking pennies and nickels and dimes, shapeshifting underwater. Nothing he saw quite clicked, not the thick-leaved philodendron crawling along its decorator brick wall, not the dry, frigid air; nor could he fully grasp the source of the faint keystrokes and whoosh of sliding doors. Only the sound of water reached him, falling, falling.

"Everyone all right?"

The one person's voice Will didn't, but should've, expected to hear. He turned. Belva's wide-open face, her messy braid. Of course she'd be here, she managed the hospital's charity organization; they served anyone who needed help.

Exhaustion tied his tongue. His eyes mechanically shut and he took refuge in the darkness behind his lids. As soon as he heard her question, he understood that *no one was all right.* Not Naomi. Not Lucille. Certainly not Queen, who'd called Will Renaldo. Not even him, though he was the least of his worries.

Belva took his arm and guided him to a couch, rubbed his shoulders and forearms, eyeing him for long, awkward minutes. Her touch unclenched him. The sight of her jeans, T-shirt, and that cockeyed braid quickened his pulse. He stroked her cheeks, arms, head, and finally enveloped her strong shoulders, dropped his arms to her waist, and repeated her name. Under his hands, the miracle of human architecture—skin stretched over muscle bound to bone.

They propped each other up, soaking in survival. She rubbed his neck. "Monk's missing you, he yowled all night."

"Big surprise. I miss him, too. How is everybody?" He straightened, but kept her in his arms while she talked. She told him Jack and Mayzie said, "I want Mom," every half-hour; Mayzie appointed herself Lucille's second-in-command, setting up games, hashing out rummy rules; Renaldo buried his panic with work, repairing leaky faucets or squeaking hinges, and her bathroom ceiling.

"They want to buy Lucille a chocolate milkshake," she finished. "But nothing's open, not even the hospital cafeteria."

Will's eyes followed the droplets hanging in space, refracting light, rainbowing the lobby. Yeah, a chocolate milkshake could improve his mood, too.

Belva asked about Naomi. He started to say fine, but "a mess" came out.

At his feet sat two grocery sacks stuffed with clothes—on top, a neatly-folded red polo. Clothes. God. Why hadn't he stopped at Trip's apartment? Showered? Changed? And he'd *hugged* her. He instinctively drew back. Here he was, scraped and scratched to hell, reeking of the marsh's usual sulfur stink, with the nervous sweat of fear souring the mix.

"I cleaned closets after Nelson moved out, so I brought clothes for needy survivors. You'll need something to wear. The Court is history."

He'd hoped what he'd heard on the radio had exaggerated the outcome. Everything he owned, gone. His mind jumped from Belva to Boneyard to Queen to Lucille.

She edged closer. He wanted his hands all over her, but, God the place was so public. He checked the lobby. A young father in cutoffs and flip flops, a kid clutched to his chest, cuddled a plush unicorn while he conferred with a whitecoat at the mouth of a hall. Soon the automatic doors slid open; father and son exited. Waves of hot air steamed through.

Belva stood. This same whitecoat strode over.

Nelson. He shook Will's hand and said he remembered Will from college. "Let's get you checked out." He doled out a polite smile for Will, and a real smile for his wife. "You've met."

Will stood, his legs, stiffer than two pine logs.

"I'll come back another time." Will randomly remembered that he even had health insurance, the VA's sorry version, but Nelson didn't ask.

"Let me do my job. Come down the hall. Regardless, we need to talk."

"Will, go with him. He's a wonderful doctor, and take these." She pawed through the clothes and presented Will with a pair of khakis and a plaid polo.

Too tired to protest, Will asked himself why he'd come. Nothing was wrong. He only needed news of Lucille and Naomi and Queen and then he'd disappear. But where could he go?

He wasn't a man to barge in, ask favors, and who, besides Trip, could he trouble?

He followed Nelson down connecting corridors, wet boots squishing—the feet inside, numb. He'd never find his way out of this labyrinth. The doc, shorter than Will, cleaner than Will, smarter than Will, also outdid Will stride-wise.

"We'll release Lucille this afternoon," Nelson said. They had patched her up and given her saline. She was napping. They'd keep her mother. "I'm vague on purpose. HIPAA rules. Queen's in ICU, hasn't regained consciousness. Hypothermic, dehydrated."

Will's heart stopped.

They were lucky, Nelson said, the marsh and maritime forest turned out to be the sweet spot on the island. "The Court, the island—everything's gone."

Nelson turned, checked down and up the hall, then told Will a tree had fallen on their Victorian, and trapped Belva in the bathroom. "You two were busy but did she tell you? She concussed. I'm afraid she's a little off her game. That probably explains the way she acted in the lobby with you. She's not herself." They'd scanned her brain. She needed rest.

His eyes stayed on Will. Will got the message.

Will studied his boots' muddy, but sturdy, leather, nothing TLC and saddle soap couldn't fix, they were one, him and these boots. He could make them new.

Had her affection in the lobby been a make-nice goodbye? Will didn't think so, and, as drained as he was, knew he wouldn't let her go easily. He could wait. He had time. This flooded him with peace. He had nothing but time. He yawned as if to prove it.

"You're tired. I'm sorry to keep you." Nelson resumed his breakneck pace but kept talking. "She'll get a thorough workup, but, as usual, wants to care for everyone else first; she's giving her clothes away, mine, too, and making sure you survivors get what you need."

Will flushed and glanced at the bundle in his hand.

In the standing-room-only waiting area, a televangelist spoke staccato phrases, containing words like *believe* and *almighty* and *soul-rescue* and *holy spirit*, while Nelson conferred with the admissions nurse. He introduced Will, and ordered a thorough physical, blood, and heart work. He walked away, then about-faced. "He could have other problems."

Heart work. Check, he'd just gotten that. Will's only other problem was Nelson.

The dark-headed nurse studied Will for a few seconds. He scanned the room for a seat, but she motioned him to a wheelchair. He dropped his butt into it.

"Let's get this party started. You don't look so bad for a guy who rescued storm survivors. It's *our* turn to take care of *you*."

She had it wrong. Will hadn't rescued a soul. Those two ladies walked out on their own.

28

My Mother

Sweaty and scared, I bolted from sleep, lost in the live oak's lap. When I touched Queen she turned to bones, then dust; in another dream, winds screeched and Will marched and marched, trying to save us from rattlesnakes. The closer he came, the smaller he shrank.

A nurse came in and unhooked my IVs, praising me for catching rain in my water bottle. Dark-skinned, with high cheekbones, she was delicate-looking and sweet. "Check the weather, Lucille, before your next adventure, OK? You are one lucky girl."

Scraped-raw knuckles. Bruised spine. A cut, head wound, probably from a broken branch? The nurse thought so. She washed the top of my head.

"No need for a bandage—you should heal fine." She swabbed my bug bites to make them stop itching. I showered and dressed in the pink capris Belva had delivered, along with the short-sleeved shirt printed with green palmetto trees, an outfit, way too girly-girly, but inside Belva's clothes I felt weirdly snug-safe and protected and *able*.

On a chair across the room sat my bagged dirty track clothes, spreading their mud smells spiced with rabbit tobacco. One shorts leg had ripped clear to the waistband after a broken limb grabbed me. I'd keep these clothes forever.

I removed the Flexcut I'd stupidly used to mark my path. Palming its smooth, curved wood handle, no bigger than a tiny bird, observing its beaklike blade, protected in plastic. When I'm old, like Naomi and Belva and Will and Queen, if the planet lasts, I'll shake off the mildew and flatten the shirts and shorts, and dream myself for real across the muck to the tangled, wild side of somewhere, only this time I'll prepare for a storm with water and food and waterproof gear. Sleep in the fairy fort. I will have no children to tell — who would bring a child into this effed-up world?

Naomi's room was all plastic tubes and inverted bags of fluid. She slept. I didn't care what drugs they'd pumped into her, she'd needed this rest for nine years, maybe her whole life. To stop staring at her face, the face more familiar than my own because, duh, I was always looking at her and not in a mirror, I inspected the floor, which pretended to be stone but was fake. Seeing my mother hooked up scared me and shook my insides.

I will start to think Naomi as *my mother*, not because she had changed, but if I called her my mother, would she *act* like my mother?

"Psst. Lucky." Will took up the whole doorframe, in clean khaki pants and a preppie polo. So he also got clothes from Belva. Under-eye bags ghosted his face, but he smiled that lips-closed-corners-upturned smile, mouth pulled to one side. His mischief smile.

My heart lifted. I floated to him. Nobody ever got me, but Will *really got* me.

"Let's us go —see if Boneyard is really gone," he whispered.

I froze. What? Was I responsible? Was I, like, a prophet? I'd predicted its death.

Just then my mother's voice said, "Do I have that ridiculous tube up my nose? I'm taking it out." She moved her hand and I rushed to her bedside.

"Don't. You'll get the nurse in trouble. You know that."

I took her hands, squeezed them, and told her I was sorry, but as the words fell heavily from my mouth, I wondered, was I sorry? Why couldn't *she* say *she* was sorry? Tons of bone-deep anger and sorrow burned; inside, I was raw and exposed.

"How does my hair look?" She sounded half asleep. Her lids shut.

Oh. She wasn't all here yet.

Will and I found a closet-sized waiting room.

"Tell me everything." I handed him the Flexcut.

Will raised his eyebrows. He cut his eyes to the ceiling. "Thank you for keeping it safe for me—the sea would've swept it away." He tipped his chair back and related the story of how they found us missing. Of course, Mayzie couldn't keep her mouth shut.

"Queen," I interrupted, "was full of energy, excited, and so happy. Her memory stayed sharp until the dehydration and hypothermia. She called me BooWoo. Who is that?"

"Some long-lost relative." His words filled the claustrophobic space, and I leaned against a wall, fading in and out, catnapping. The little space stank of sickness and desperation and it choked off my airways. Will's words wove the story's threads, and formed pictures that collided and blended with scenes of my own, but soon, he nodded off.

I woke. The clock said four in the afternoon. I crept back into Naomi's room, where a nurse was taking her temperature. "Visiting hours are over," the nurse said, but I puffed up and told her this was my mother. The nurse removed the thermometer and left.

"Do you remember talking about the ozone layer?" Naomi asked. "You were maybe nine, and you walked around saying, 'We've got to detox the planet.' Where'd you hear that?"

Marco always planned science lessons about toxins like fossil fuels. I needed to call him—tonight. He surely knew about the storm.

Will knocked lightly on the door as he walked in. "Sorry. Conked out in the middle of my own story, Lucky."

"Who's Lucky?" my mother demanded.

"Your superhero daughter."

"Bring Jack and Mayzie with you tomorrow," she said. "And, Lucille, thanks, for coming. For everything."

"Course. You're my mother."

She loosely wrapped her non-IV arm around me. I pulled back. My vision blurred, my adrenaline kicked in and I started a round of squats; maybe they'd help me return to my old self.

29

The Book of Will

We got permission through Trip for a Coast Guard seaman to pilot us over the water, past floating islands of grass in the creek. Storm waves had battered the old bridge so badly, Will said, it couldn't hold the weight of even one car. Fishermen haunted the bridge beyond the barricade, their lined and weathered faces shocked by the island's gone-ness, casting lines and nets like robots; one guy hooked a sneaker, the woman with him hauled in half a cooler.

High tide now covered all but a wide swath of firm sand. The ocean swished and swirled, restless; the tides and currents had forgotten how to act. Sunset purpled and reddened the creeks, just now remembering their beds and boundaries. The Boneyard Beach I first saw more than a week ago had cracked all over. Water rivered every which way. The surf had shoved the big beach dune across the road and dumped sand that had half-buried the Court's famous neon wave and palmetto sign, now rising cockeyed. No crashing blue waves, no jittering green fronds.

I raced past Will, up, up its soggy slope, but slipped and slid; my feet and calves mired in sand and water. Cottage foundations sat, giant square shells, half-flooded. The ocean had left shaggy piles of debris and jagged pieces of what were once doors or window frames, chairs or tables or shingles. Tangled black electrical wires. For a good long while after that, weeks, months, and maybe years, the tide would wash in junk-microwaves and toaster ovens along with the usual ribbons of seaweed and dead tree-bones, until another storm and another and another would wipe the whole island out of existence.

We picked our way, half-wading around the Court's carcass. The historic old-school cottage, its peaked roof, columned porch, belonging to Queen and Renaldo—another home lost.

"What does the back side of the island look like?" Only hours ago, I was there.

"The forest survived. *Mudhole* made it. As you saw. Marshland is miraculous." Will trailed me close, hands deep in his pockets, afraid, maybe, I'd be swept away. He seemed content, a weird look for Will, like the only thing worrying him was trudging the wet sand. His cottage at the Court was his home, his studio. Sure, he had *Mudhole* but he *lived* at the Court.

"You can concentrate on your art and rebuilding your house, without us distracting you." Maybe it was the clothes, Belva's husband's—khaki pants and a plaid polo—plaid!—making Will look different, calmer. I wasn't sure about this new Will.

I hated that Will's beach was dead, killed by a barbaric civilization.

"What'll I do with no art advisor?" His voice sounded serious, not teasing. "Tell you what, Miss Queen of Art, I'll miss the commotion. I'm not as interested in *Mudhole*—still no money for the rebuild, nothing's changed—but me."

What an idiot Will was. "Home isn't—," what word did I want? Did that word even exist? I settled for "replaceable."

"Of course you'll fix *Mudhole*. You belong there. You can do the work yourself, you and Trip. You've already started. *Mudhole's* no worse than before the storm, is it?"

"I haven't inventoried the damage."

"At least *you* have a place to come to." Like Tabby Town's crumbled walls that Queen still loved. But maybe Will was right to question home. I saw with my own eyes how structures don't last, man-made or natural. People don't last either.

The sand washed out from underfoot, forcing us farther from water. There was no escaping the tide.

"Landscapes change and people change."

Wait. Was that pity in his eyes? For himself or me?

"What about *home*?"

His expression turned sorrowful, on what little of his face showed. His beard must've thickened overnight. I shot him a solid stink-eye.

He smiled. "I needed that. Home gives you, for sure, a good start, like turtles, after you hatch, you're on your own. Maybe I just need to swim away."

But he'd already gone away. To fight! I'd thought of turtles, too, we even nosed around spots where the nests might have been. Useless—the storm had yanked stakes from the ground. My feet dragged, heavier with each step, and I worked to stabilize my feet in the shiftiest substance on earth besides water. Sand.

Even wanting roots seemed stupid now.

"Naomi's old flame Tom called, to make sure y'all survived. Bet you're glad nothing came of that. Or did it?"

I shook my head. "He wasn't that nice, and even she realized she was only interested in the novelty—get this, he ditched her for another woman.

"I was glad —I'd hoped Naomi was over that idea that a man could distract her from herself. Maybe she learned her lesson, after this Tom. What's happening between you and Belva?" Was that OK to ask?

"I'm not sure. She's married."

"Oh. So, it's over?"

"He left her, that's what she told me, then said she was glad because she'd been 'unfulfilled.' What does that mean, Lucille? You're smarter than I am about people."

"Fulfilled is one of those words that defines itself. Flip it, and you've got *filled full.* Like eating food you love, and having enough. Like working your wood—you fill yourself full of skill and ideas to make art. I've never been married, but maybe it's the same idea. You fill yourselves and share and make more love. Like that sunflower reseeding itself."

"Can one person fill another person?" Will asked.

"I doubt it works that way, from watching Naomi. She's a black hole of grief. Belva's not a black hole. She might just need time to figure out what's missing in her fulfillment package. Hey, ask her!"

"Why didn't I think of that?"

We shut up about love. But every time I thought of Renaldo, my feet lifted from the ground. I wanted to ask Will something. We'd discussed love, sort of, and I wondered if he'd be my lover, not because I loved him *that way*, but he could prepare me for when I did finally someday have sex. I was a planner, and hated surprises; all around me grownups did stupid things related to sex, especially the way Naomi couldn't stay true to one man. People thought I was too levelheaded and practical to have hormone urges, but I had those already.

If I confided these thoughts to Will, he might fold up inside and disappear. I kept quiet. It would be a compliment. He might not see it that way.

The boat bobbed a few yards away, our private time, like tide, ebbing.

"You know, Belva's a big shot in town. She could fix you up with a summer job at the turtle research center."

"I wouldn't want the job if I didn't earn it."

"You've earned it, girl, you're a Boneyard legend."

"Because I was too stupid to head back here while I still could?"

"You stuck with Queen and used your head."

Will was wrong. I used Queen's head. She knew how to survive. I'd never have had the guts to stick it out in that old oak tree.

"Seen enough?" The boat guy smiled.

"No." I wanted more Boneyard time. Beyond tears, I studied the island. Wild weirdness. The calamity of the Court.

"I can get us over here anytime," Will bragged. "Then you can run, run, run."

"On what? Water?"

"We'll explore the back side when you visit me at *Mudhole*. Girl, you're going places."

I tried to imagine a future, mine and Boneyard's.

Will stood a foot away, his back to the ocean. I memorized

his brown hair flopping on his brown forehead, his caterpillar eyebrows, that beard-face, even the silver gulls behind him, swooping and diving. "Nobody can stop you—you'll run a long way in life."

That sounded too much like the ending of a book, and I didn't want the *Book of Will* to ever end. I shut up.

30

Nontoxic Male

Labor Day morning, Will left Pearl at Trip's apartment, where he'd slept the night before, and hoofed it the few blocks to Belva's, navigating by instinct around downed trees and power lines, bucket trucks and hard-hat workers. At the old Victorian, foregrounding the cobalt sky, yep, there it was: the massive oak that had punched in the roof. Leafy limbs, contorted branches, smashed bird feeders, and mangled lawn chairs trashed the yard.

On the porch, the racket coming from inside told Will Jack was winning. Will pushed open the wide, solid-wood door. Monk greeted him in the hallway, talking man talk, and climbing his pant leg. Will swung him up to his cheek and asked how he was doing. The kids lay sprawled in the giant, dark living room, dimmed by heavy drapes.

"Lights! How can you two—"

They ran at him, twin twisters with wide-open mouths, screaming, each claiming a leg. He hoisted first his left, Jack attached, then his right, with Mayzie, up and down. Leg hugs worked for Will. He squatted for real hugs, still cradling Monk. Mayzie grabbed Will's beard and Jack tugged his hair. *Will, Will, Will, Will,* they chirped.

"Thanks for the welcome. Where's Big Sis?"

"Visiting Mom. Can we go?" Jack hopped foot-to-foot, with so much to say.

“Soon,” Will promised. “Count to four million, four thousand, four hundred, and forty four first.”

“No! *You* count to that much million.” He pulled at Will’s hair and wouldn’t leave. Renaldo hurried down the steps, asking about Will’s health.

“Good God. Do I look worse? Resting heart rate of, oh, about sixty, could be better, but I’ll live.” Even Renaldo found a spare inch of flesh—an elbow—and squeezed.

Renaldo’s eyes searched Will’s. “Queen’s still in intensive care, and the Doc says she’ll be there awhile. Lucille took off early this morning—running—for the hospital, with her book, in those beat-up shoes.”

Renaldo had gotten the lowdown about the trip to Boneyard. “Lucille painted the whole picture as a wasteland that night. Wild.”

“The place is my heart and soul, skin and bones, but barely hanging on. On a happier note, Lucille’s birthday is today, Labor Day, the workingman’s holiday. She mentioned it so many times last week, the date stuck even in my weak cerebral matter. We need a cake, a gift, and what else?”

“Key West? That’s her big wish, guess that’s not happening.”

“But Key West,” Will pulled on his beard, “should be around at least another year.”

“Your place survive OK? Bet it’s sitting pretty above the marsh. Isn’t that something?”

Will nodded. “It is. Louis tricked us, big time.”

“People died.” Renaldo stared at the floor. “An eighty-five-year old man fell off a ladder, preparing for the storm.”

People died stupidly even without life-threatening storms, but Renaldo already knew that. His father—unknown, and his mother had all but abandoned him to Queen. Renaldo’s thin face and gangly frame reminded Will how young Renaldo was. He touched the arm of this damned decent young man.

From the window of the spacious hallway, they took in the debris-filled yard and the tree lying atop the iron fence. Even iron couldn’t withstand that oak’s force, two hundred years old, so strong, with roots weakened by tools of civilization—concrete, careless pruning, lack of breathing space.

"That tree was here before this house," Will said.

"Maybe the tree and the house grew up together." Renaldo's face looked like it had Saturday—innocent, scared—when Will had schooled him on the generator and evacuation procedures.

"You got plans? You graduate next spring, right?"

A long, restful silence—a welcome break in the action—folded the men together.

Renaldo studied the pattern, or something, in the carpet, a woven Oriental masterpiece.

"Queen's in bad shape. I saw it coming but she's such a tough bird."

"She may pull through." Piss-poor phrase—pull through. What did the boy see in that carpet's intricate design? Something soothed or moved him. Will silently thanked him for being alive and vaguely related.

"She saved for my college." His Adam's apple wobbled as he spoke and swallowed. "I'll start those applications; there's help at school."

Will reined in nagging worries about not only his future, but the futures of those he now loved and felt responsible for. "We'll figure that out."

His eyes held fear. Will recognized the look.

"Where do we even live?" His words rushed out, breathlessly. "She has life insurance."

Will's pulse raced but his mind, slow and dense, stuck on those words: *life* and *insurance.*

No way money compensates for life.

"Wherever I am, there's a spot for you, Renaldo. I'll need to rent something or hustle to get the *Mudhole* up and habitable—if I even stick around. Might try and find my father, though God only knows where he is."

"My mother finally got through, worried."

Will had lost touch with Vanessa, Queen's daughter; though once they'd known each other well, a cousin, like everybody else, who now only visited once a year.

"She wants me to move to Atlanta, and Queen, too, if . . ."

"What do you want?"

He shook his head. "My teachers told me to apply to Tech. They said, maybe, probably, even, I could get a scholarship." He favored Will with a tiny smile.

Good God. Georgia Tech. Who'd've guessed?

"Do it. That's some high cotton, as your grandma would say."

"I'd rather stay here."

"Don't write her off. She could surprise us all."

"Will, I've been thinking how hard life is, you know? Think about Queen's life in Tabby Town, how hard up they were, how racist people are now, so imagine what they were like then? Klan rallies, raping black women, and lynchings? She got herself educated back when black women, mixed race women like her, just didn't. I envy Lucille—going back of the beyond with Queen. Should've been me."

"Tell Lucille that, will you? She blames herself for Queen's condition."

"We could write grants—with money, we could make Tabby Town a park. Tours. Environmental education."

"Nice thought, but Lucille's right. It'll be underwater sooner than we want to believe."

Mayzie skipped into the hall, and yanked on Will's shirttail. "Will, come ON!"

"One minute, you big card shark. Can I see Belva first?"

Mayzie dropped his hand. "She's resting in her office. She's supposed to not get excited, so, nope, you can't see her."

"Me? Exciting? I'm a dull knife. I'm a boring movie. I'm unsweetened yogurt. Where's her office? And y'all deal me in, next hand. Whatever you're playing, I'm beating you. And thanks for helping Renaldo with Monk."

Mayzie frowned. "Wish I had a kitty cat."

Renaldo, Jack, and Mayzie escorted Monk and Will to a tiny study off the living room—loveseat, ladder-back chair, antique roll-top desk. Belva sat at the desk, her back to Will, hair in a sloppy braid, in that same thick robe from their night, dingy, not fresh-bleached and white, but the sight of her neck—a pale stem with wisps of hair—unglued him. She clicked away on a keyboard.

Renaldo shut the door.

"She never stops working, how about that, Monk? Doing business after a hurricane, and her doctor says she's even had a concussion." The cat rolled over and pawed the air. Will kneeled and massaged the cat's belly.

"What'd you expect? You're OK? Everyone said you were wonderful out there." She spoke but did not turn. "Guess what? Downtown's not so damaged we can't hold the market this weekend—today's only Monday. Everything will be OK by Friday and Saturday. We're adding September this year? The weather's always balmy in September, despite the occasional 'cane, so why not? Are you interested, Will? I've got your work in the Prius, your carving tools, too. Sorry I didn't have space for the table saw and that grinding wheel, attached to your workbench."

Like who else was "out there" but Naomi, who would not describe Will as wonderful, but the excitement in Belva's voice—and after all the ruckus—pleased him.

She swiveled her chair, antique oak, expertly carved, forearms resting on its sculpted arms, and stared at Will, trying not to laugh. "Nice outfit. I've never seen you look quite so presentable."

"Preppie's how Lucille described it." His face flamed. "Oh, come on. I wore khakis that night we went to dinner. Thank Nelson. What would we have done without him, and, of course, you? As always, your presence was essential."

"What? You lost everything."

His stiffness melted. "Except my work. Those pieces you rescued are all I've got. Lucille and I boated to Boneyard yesterday—nothing but foundations left—."

She sighed. "People are so willfully ignorant." She about-faced to her laptop. "Let's see. How about you exhibit Friday and Saturday? Primo spot. No sidewalk sales, though. I have a card table you can use."

"What's going on? No one else registered?"

"You guessed it. It'll be you and me."

Whimsy in her voice. She turned and cut her eyes at him. Hope, or something like it, flickered through Will, that and a charge of electricity.

"I might as well stand at an intersection and peddle the things, or give them away. Do you. . . have I told you about my art dealer?"

Will couldn't stomach this distance. He had no idea how things would play out. What if this was his only chance? He placed Monk on the floor, stood behind her chair, and reached down, hands meeting chest level.

"You OK?" He spoke into the robe's collar. Life is a scruff of cloth, a touch of skin. He mentally stepped back, but could not physically budge, though Nelson had made things clear: She'd been out of her head when they cozied up in the lobby.

She stayed seated, tapping, tapping, as if his two hands weren't locked at her heart.

"What's wrong?"

"Nothing," she said. "All good. Sit down."

All good, his ass. He stepped back and shrank into the corner ladder-back.

"Nelson's killing himself at that hospital, presumably he's catnapping there. They were short-handed, what with the holiday, and doctors away. Nurses, too. I only wish I could help. I'd love to be of service."

Service. Her calling. Will was sure she'd wanted to do more with her life than run the market, but she'd made hay with the enterprise. He'd seen the ambition in her face. His own ambitions had imploded after smoke cleared, crumpled like the uniforms of wasted troops.

"This storm—it's changed my thinking, too," Will said. "Maybe it's the urgency—marine life in jeopardy, consumerism gone wild, shootings. Lucille opened my eyes. So much needs doing. Carving wood seems, well, useless."

"But your work—it's raw and fresh. Art makes people think in ways that lectures or news articles can't. Weren't you about to tell me something good? I need upbeat news. Please?"

She stopped typing and swung her chair around.

Heat had permeated the walls clean to the plaster, which sweated as profusely as Will did, and he hadn't showered this morning—there'd been no electricity, but he could've taken a cold shower. He saw himself in her husband's ill-fitting clothes, uncombed, undone, though he'd spit-washed, he probably still stank.

"Trip's aunt introduced me to a dealer who says my work will make him money."

"Will! A dealer. What's her name?"

"A guy. Dick. I don't remember his last name. They fled before the storm—back to New York, and I wonder if I'll ever see the guy again." Will had figured if Dick sold his work, he could document that income, get a loan, rebuild *Mudhole*, construct a decent studio, and sell art, but the storm complicated those plans. Now, he could hardly make himself *care*.

"They'll be back. Do they live on Boneyard?"

He nodded. "On the back side near my place. Her house—Sunbow—probably survived in the storm—mine did—but with the beach gone? The inland marsh side is surely next."

Her face darkened. Why? They'd spent barely four or five hours one-on-one—mostly in bed—strange how you convince yourself you know people, fall for them, especially when you'd explored each other's intimate spaces. He wanted to bury his face in her neck right this minute.

Let her go. Leave this effing town. Go find yourself. Will didn't want finding, he argued. He wanted losing. Maybe in her.

"Heard you and Nelson patched things up. Nelson told me yesterday, walking me to Emergency." The sun lit the bare heart pine, a small rectangle between them. His eyes tracked the wood grain leading to her feet, pale, bare, and—what? God. Bruised, soles flat and motionless on the floor. "What the hell happened to your feet?"

"I can't walk too well—mauled these last night when I tripped."

"Did somebody beat your feet with a club? *After* or *before* your concussion?"

"The concussion's why my gait was so unsteady. One foot

lodged between slats coming down the staircase—you remember the stairs?"

"I remember." His voice was tight. "The other foot looks better, but . . . that ankle."

"I stumbled. My foot stuck, my ankle twisted, and the rest of me flopped down the stairs, or tried. I pulled myself up, using my hands, step by step, and managed to free the foot, then tumbled the rest of the way down. Mayzie heard thumps and came running. She helped me try to stand, but I slept down here, on that loveseat. I love that little girl."

"Where was Renaldo?"

"Asleep, poor bunny, first sleep he'd had since the storm. I didn't want to wake him."

"Can I help?"

She closed her eyes. "Actually, yes." A moment. "I hate to ask, but I need the, um, toilet; I don't like interrupting the kids—they've got so much to worry about—and Renaldo's trying to seal the upstairs bathroom ceiling with plastic until the tree is removed, which could take weeks, maybe months. Besides, he . . ."

"Say no more. One of my unrecognized talents is helping women to toilets. I cared for my mother during her . . . cancer." Never mind the dead bodies he'd hefted, the wounded he'd tried, mostly without success, to move without further damage.

"You?"

Will heard, from somewhere, her words, and waded through time, which wasn't so much puddling as spasming.

"Am I shocking you? Thanks for your confidence."

"I'm talking about you caring for your mother. How counter-cultural is that!"

"Yeah, I'm the poster-boy for non-toxic masculinity, but this is no time for anthropology research. Let's go potty."

Avoiding her feet, he leaned and placed his hands under her armpits, amply cushioned by the robe.

"I can sort of shuffle, it's just so hard to keep the weight—"

"How have you managed so far?" He test-lifted her.

"Renaldo. He's thin but wonderfully strong and gentle. A gem."

That kid never failed to step up.

One second and he'd swept her into his arms. "You OK with me carrying you like this? Yeah, yeah, it's romance-level bullshit and sexist, but gets the job done less painfully, I hope."

"Might work." Her face screwed up; the woman hurt.

His arms under her knees, her shoulders, hers ringing his neck. He risked a look at her face, checking for pain, found her biting her lip, and glanced away. A chaos of scents and sounds and feelings overpowered him—the hum of an insect on the wing, somewhere in the room, her warmth, her Belva-scent seeping from the robe. Risky territory.

"You're not well," he told her. "You need to take care of yourself." At the moment, he was the one who wasn't well.

She touched his face. "Let's talk later. '*Things*' are not '*patched*.' But I need to pee."

"Oh, God. I'm sorry." He hurried, slowly. In the living room. Mayzie and Jack leaped up and ran over. "Stay back, you varmints. Comin' through with wounded."

"Belva, Belva, are you OK?"

"I'm fine, kids, just a little trouble walking."

"Where are you going?" They chorused. Mayzie sucked the end of her braid.

"Nowhere, troops, she hurt her feet, remember? Go on back to your game—Miss Belva's going to the ladies' room while I'm planning how I'ma beat both y'all at rummy."

They giggled. "You cheated," Jack told Mayzie.

Belva directed Will to a half-bath off the kitchen. He set her down in front of the toilet.

"You OK in here alone? You shouldn't need to move your feet. Need help with your underwear? Anything?"

She shook her head.

"Holler for help."

"This is perfect. Shoo."

He shut the bathroom door and waited in the kitchen where a jumble of dirty dishes buried the counter, sink, and the fine maple tabletop. Kids must've eaten spaghetti three times a day since Saturday. Will liberated the sink, filled it with hot soapy water, and scrubbed a dozen plates and put them away, wet, in the cabinet till he could clear space.

The back door opened. Nelson. The guy wore exhaustion—raccoon eyes, gray skin. He loaded the coffeemaker and pushed a dirty cup under the cone, drummed his fingertips on the counter, and waited for the drip.

"Hi, Will. Queen's in bad shape, FYI. Pneumonia. Does she have a living will?"

Will shook his head. Renaldo would know. "I only stopped—"

"To wash dishes. You're all right, Will. I've always liked you. Glad you're alive."

"You?"

Nelson nodded. "Surviving. Can I tell you something?"

Will opened his mouth to demur; whatever it was, Will didn't want to hear it, but Nelson kept talking.

"I've screwed things up. Not at work. No, work's what I do. I thrive there, crave the adrenaline kick. Here, in my real life? Problems. I've got only myself to blame, but I hope it's not too late to make things right." He alternately eyed his cup, filling with the acid brew, and Will. "Where's Belva?"

Will pointed to the bathroom. He scrubbed hardened tomato sauce from a dinner plate, soaped, rinsed, and dried that, and tackled a metal pan with steel wool, the two metals scraped the air. This pan, these ancient stains, accumulated over years, maybe decades. Everything in the house smelled off—kitchen leftovers, mildewed and half-burned, discarded but not bagged. Who'd eaten what, when? How long ago? Lives, so many intersecting under one damaged roof. Nelson hadn't seen his wife's bruised feet. He knocked on the bathroom door and cracked it open. He was seeing them this instant.

Will strode quickly to the living room, wiping his hands on the butt of Nelson's khakis, sealing away thoughts of Belva. "Jack, Mayzie, let's boogie. We'll go see your mom and Lucille. Bring the deck."

"Boogie, let's boogie." Mayzie danced over. At least the storm brought a moment's joy to somebody. "Look at me, Will, Miss Belva said I could keep this! It sparkles." She opened the drapes and twirled. The girl glittered, and now she ran toward him, a sweet, shiny swirl.

"You're a sight, Mayzie—our holiday sparkler."

Labor Day in Will's old world was customarily a day for brawls, hollering drunks, and fireworks at the Court. Today's chores, looming larger and more delicate, nagged him. He would talk straight with Renaldo about Queen and to Naomi about her plans. Topping the list, toughest of all, was a good-enough remembrance for Lucille's fourteenth.

31

Labor Birthday

I FaceTimed Marco from the hospital first thing this morning. Face and Time, a "connection" with someone you see but can't touch. Like Mom.

"Happy birthday to me," I sang when Marco picked up.

"Lucille! Where in the world and how in the heck? Everybody safe? Jack? Mayzie? Naomi? What is the deal down there?" His voice sounded breathy.

"Boonies. Town called Pinesboro." I gave him the lowdown on the hurricane.

"Am I close? Wait. Here it is, on the map. Yeah. I can be there in an hour? Maybe not. The motel manager's saying there's traffic."

"Do I look as funny as you?" Marco asked. "Never noticed how every single freckle on your nose, I swear, is different. Love that."

"Listen, Marco, you need to talk to Naomi."

"What's up?"

"You'll see. She's in Rice County Medical. Come straight here." I wasn't going to be the one to tell him about Tom or rehab.

Next, I broke into the ICU. Head high, in my Belva-clothes, which made me look forty not fourteen, I slipped silently and unnoticed to the third floor; it paid to stand tall and wear clothes meant for matrons. Inside the dim room, Queen lay completely still, between bed rails, taking up, like, no space, covers to her chin, hair like froth on the pillow. I stood beside the bed and smoothed her hair, made it neat, like how she wore it. I stroked her face, longing to lie with her the way we'd cuddled in the tree, but she was hooked up. I might hurt her. Tubes and wires connected her to—life? What did they do? One machine breathed in and out, like a person, and another made the high-pitched beep then the beep then beep-beep like it was keeping time.

No one could keep time.

Wait. Did Queen make a sound? I angled my ear to her mouth. A breath but no voice. Jaw slack, mouth slightly open. "Hey, it's me," I whispered. "We made it. It's my birthday."

Fluid bags hung in the bluish light, tubes wound into nostrils, and all this equipment tangled me in despair. I had to get her out of here because this place was way worse than the oak, the storm, and the mud. She was so happy that night, even in pain. My feet found a chair, my bottom found the molded plastic seat, and my eyes stared at the only part of Queen visible, the rumpled skin on her dark, ancient face.

I pulled from my pocket my mangled sprig of Life Everlasting, and found voices for the "Wayfaring Stranger" and Still Waters, the words in my brain activating my own song about women wading and tossing ashes and clipping rabbit tobacco; others crowded the room, and they were spirits. That's what Queen would say. "Shhhhh," she'd say, and this body sitting on hard hospital plastic—me—believed that spirits were near. Naomi talked enlightenment but Queen spoke spirits. They lived where she lived.

Using words spirits might understand, language Queen used, I spoke to them. "Leave her a spell, she's got work here, the world's in danger, so are the turtles and the islands. We need to stop our own fool selves from killing the planet." I dream-dozed, but, like dripping rain, the prosecutor in my head kept saying *she was old, she wasn't all there, you should've said no, you could've forced her back. She might die*. Another voice said *let her go*: "She's happy." I'd recognize Dad's voice anywhere, and turned, but, of course, he was inside me, denying the prosecutor until accusations stopped flooding my brain.

Inside the silence, space and time splintered around us, me curled in the chair, wanting to climb in bed with her; but that might interfere with her recovery. I dragged the chair nearer her face, my knees to my chest, and studied her skin, nearly transparent.

Hours later, I wandered down the staircase to my mother's floor, where a nurse said, "Come back tomorrow, Hon, during visiting hours."

"I'm her sister." I popped in my mother's room before the nurse could stop me.

"Snuck in."

My mother laughed. She was no fonder of authority than I was. Pale and pretty, her ears trailing buds, she listened, and, hopefully, enlightened herself, while I read my book, thinking of Queen, who reminded me of Zora Neale. When I came to the part about how Tea Cake rescued Janie, my breath went fast and shallow, reliving our storm. *Havoc was there with her mouth wide open. . . In the city it had raged . . . Tea Cake and Janie . . . looked over the desolation.*

I prayed the cost wasn't Queen.

"Mrs. Lamb?" A woman poked her head in. "I'm Tracey Young? I'm the hospital case worker? OK if I come in?" She didn't wait for permission. Tracey reminded me of student teachers at my school, cute and smiley and small, with short, dirty-blonde hair and glasses, making statements into questions.

"Why not come back, Ms. Young, once I've checked out?" my mother deadpanned.

I ate my lips to keep from laughing.

But Tracey hooted and wagged her finger. "Mrs. Lamb! A sense of humor, that's healthy. Call me Tracey. Is this your daughter, Lucille?" She turned and beamed. I lifted a hand.

Her eyes glowed like she loved her work.

"Why are you here?" Naomi asked.

"I make sure patients not only get great care while they're here, but find them help, should the need arise. We could, for instance, get vouchers for food and other necessities, shelter, too, you've lost everything, correct? You were vacationing at the Court, destroyed in the storm?"

My mother nodded.

Tracey turned. "OK if I call you Lucille? And may I say I admire—"

"Ms. Young, all I did was get lost and cause a ton of trouble for people I love."

"You kept your cool, that counts. Can you give your mom and me maybe fifteen?"

My mom's attitude already had seeped out of her and into the room. I shot her a look.

"OK, I'll be outside the door," which Ms. Young closed, but I caught bits and pieces—*family structure, single mother, short stay*—and filled in blanks myself. A curious social worker was a dark turn. Did Trip rat us out? Did hospitals question all patients? The last thing I needed was for Marco—I hoped he'd never do this but who knew—to insist Jack and Mayzie live with him because of negligence. Where did that leave me? *Foster care*? I was fourteen today. Technically, I could stay overnight with the sibs, in Georgia. I never cried, but stupid tears gathered behind my eyeballs, waiting to pop, making my head, especially my nose, stuffy. At the end of ten minutes, Ms. Young would know my mother had no for-sure job, three children, only two of whom had a father, and no husband. Social workers fish—for neglect.

Ms. Young nearly banged my head when she opened the door and motioned me to the stale closet of a room where Will and I sat yesterday. Nobody'd cleaned. I sat in the straightest-backed chair and gave Ms. Young the easy chair.

"First, how *are* you?" she asked.

"All rested."

"And you're staying where?"

"Do you know Belva? Her husband's a doctor."

"Ah. Everyone knows her. She brought used clothes to my office yesterday."

"I'm wearing her clothes."

Shut up, Lucille. Wait for questions. Don't volunteer answers.

"I'll get to the point. You held down the fort, so to speak, while your mother stayed at Cumberland Island, Monday till Friday. Correct?"

I nodded.

"You do this in Detroit when your mother works the seven-to-seven shift."

I nodded.

"And you're young, to be responsible for a five-year-old and, how old is Mayzie, eight?"

"I'm fourteen. Today's my birthday. We weren't alone. The manager of the motel was there, and Linda, who works at the bait and food store, watched the kids one day, and Queen, Renaldo . . . , oh, and Mrs. Pitts, who smokes, and Will's always having to confiscate her . . . well, anyhow, I kept telling him we didn't need him."

"I see. Oh. Did he force you to . . . obey him?" She flipped open her pad.

"He thought he should keep his eye on us. Probably because he's ex-army. No one left behind." His name would've been on the news because he managed the wiped-out motel. "He worked and showed us wood-carving techniques, to keep us from fighting and getting on his nerves. Ms. Young, I've got my life planned through college."

"Did you plan *this*? Did you and your mother work out a schedule, a communication plan, an in-case-of-emergency plan?"

"We have an understanding. As I pointed out, we were staying at a motel where there was a grownup in charge."

"Yes, I'd like to speak with the manager. Were there problems getting in touch with him? What was the nature of your relationship?"

"He lived there. His cottage was across the parking lot. He was busy but we managed. We played on the beach, we just . . ."

Her pen scratched noisily then stopped. "And?"

"Goofed around. It's not hard, we're kids. We play. And Queen, the lady—"

"Yes, she's famous."

"She came and got us so we could watch the hatchlings. She's a turtle guard."

A pause. She flipped pages and looked up. "Do you ever worry about your mother?"

"Nah. She's a survivor. Like me." Lying out of necessity felt OK.

"You inherited your strength, from her, but do you worry about her?"

I shook my head.

"How about you? Ever worry about you?"

"Pimples, finding a college, saving the planet, which is about to burn up."

"Catastrophe."

I nodded. "Everybody should worry. You, too. Do you drive an electric car?"

She smiled. "Do you worry because things are out of your control?"

"They're not. We could stop global warming but we won't. People won't listen. Probably even you. Do you pollute? Did you drive here?" Probably shouldn't have said that last, but Ms. Young was trying not to smile.

"Would you describe yourself as anxious?"

"Yeah, but I don't take meds like my mother does."

Shouldn't've said that either. Wouldn't she have studied Naomi's medications?

"How do you cope with your mother's anxiety?"

How much did she know? Who else was she talking to?

"Think about it—call me anytime."

"I hope we're leaving tomorrow for Key West."

"Oh, a family trip."

"Not sure who's going besides me, but I'll go alone if I need to. I've saved." I stood, breathing hard. "The Florida Reef. I've got to see the coral before the reef—some corals are already dead—" I filled my lungs again and blew out—"before it becomes Atlantis."

She raised her head. "The sunken civilization. Oceanographers say that's a myth."

I leaned in close enough to see her roots needed touching up.

"Thank you! Ms. Young, you are the only person who understands Atlantis. See, the lost civilization of Atlantis captured people's imaginations, even though it *never* existed, and our silly civilization, with fossil fuels and stupid greed, will *be* sunk—a for-real Atlantis."

Ms. Young shook her head and pinched her nose. "It's frustrating, isn't it? I agree and, for what it's worth, deeply care." She thanked me and gave me her hand. "Stay in touch, Lucille. I'll arrange for clothing and toiletries. Shampoo, deodorant?" She held out her card.

Toiletries would not help our family. "We're leaving. Soon. Ms. Young, you're pretty cool." I took the card from between her fingers, with nails the color of a peach.

"Lucille, you're smart. What do you think your family needs?"

I gulped, my mouth cottony. Since Saturday, no matter how much water I drank, my tissues wouldn't hydrate and fluff up. Had I withered inside?

My eyelids closed all by themselves.

"Ms. Young, my mother needs drug rehab, but she's going to refuse." I opened my eyes.

She nodded. "Lucille, call my cell anytime. Can you call me Tracey? I will do everything I can for your mother. Do you believe me?"

"I'll try."

"OK, you try, I'll try, and we'll call each other if we have problems." She squeezed my hand and left the room.

I waited, listening to the squeak of her soft-soled shoes fade, hoping it wasn't a mistake to trust a grownup, especially a social worker.

The nurse's aide served lunch—watery applesauce, dry chicken, undercooked rice, with a garish yellow square of cake topped with cherries, sopped with syrup the color of blood. The morning had disappeared. Hospitals warped time, too.

Jack and Mayzie pushed the door open. "Hello, hello." Their eyes landed on the cherries.

"No way you eat those, you hear?" I said. "They're filled with *dye*. Who brought you?"

"Me." Will entered. "Sorry, but couldn't keep the varmints away."

Naomi shoved the wheeled table aside and patted the bed. Jack and Mayzie climbed up and bounced.

"Mom, why not go to rehab?" I threw the word, with all present and accounted for, on purpose. OK, so I shouldn't talk about rehab in front of the kids, but she needed six weeks.

"That is none of your business." Naomi glared at Will, probably because she figured I'd gotten the idea from him, but we hadn't even discussed how she behaved during the search.

Jack and Mayzie fought over the cherry.

"Stop. It's off limits!" I scraped it into the trash.

"What is the big deal?" Naomi asked.

"That red dye—it's poison."

"I mean the drugs. These aren't opiods, for heaven's sake, these are legally prescribed."

"We can't force rehab on you." I nearly choked. "But it would put you on the right track." I took her hand and held it between both of mine, and massaged the spaces between her fingers, tugged the ends, and rubbed her palms, an acupressure move she'd shown me. "Want me to brush your hair?"

She nodded. Will played rummy with Jack and Mayzie, on the floor, and his knees creaked and cracked when he tried to move his long legs into different positions. I pulled the brush carefully, smoothed the butter-colored mass, twisted it atop her head and knotted it. It couldn't last, but the point was pulling the bristles gently through the fine strands. Every so often, Mayzie walked over, nibbled chicken, watching Naomi like she might vanish. When it was Mayzie's go, Jack called her to the game.

I lowered my voice. "OK, you're not addicted—maybe—but

why'd you take a leave from work? Why are you so moody and unpredictable?" My inner voice urged, *Tell it, sister, all the time it affects you.* "And you can't remember important events." *Like your birthday, today.*

"And you're short of breath, I've read the symptoms."

"Let's talk later."

She always said that, or this: "Occasional side effects, not symptoms of addiction." Yeah, like broken bones, traffic accidents, and risk of falls. Now, she said, "You worry about my prescription medications. OK. I'll stop. Happy?"

I snatched my hand back and left. I bugged the nurse about a box of tissues, in case someone, like me, started crying, and re-entered. By then, Jack and Mayzie had licked the red goo from the plate.

Will had moved to a chair, and sat, dumber than dumb, not even smiling. He hadn't seen her since dawn Sunday, more than twenty-four hours ago. Mayzie twirled in that too-long dress of Belva's, revolved this way and that. She fell on the floor, curled into a ball, and sobbed. And Jack held onto the end of the bed and shot himself into space, barely missing Mayzie when he landed. Were they getting sick? No. They were infected by grownup *worriment.*

"Come on, you two, let's let Mom and *Will* visit. And guess what? Marco's on his way!" I threw Will an apologetic glance that said, "You'll be fine." He blinked.

32

Jeopardy

Will shifted and twisted, crossed and uncrossed his ankles.

"These are perfectly good meds to calm jitters or induce sleep. Have you ever gone a week without sleep?"

"Hell, in the sandpit, we got so damn tired, even if we just sat around cleaning our M-1s, I slept like the dead. I was dead. I'm sure you understand that from your husband's experience."

"Did I know you'd served? Can't remember."

Her tone, vague, her voice, scratchy. Will wondered what she was on. They'd discharge her today or tomorrow, full of saline, checked out, on the physical mend, healthy, but her mental state? Her disoriented stumbles during their night from hell? He felt for the woman, but at the same time didn't, weird, but there it was—she was another job to get done. They'd managed to walk out together. Worn out, she lost her fight. Once she saw Lucille, she came half-alive.

"Here's your chance to make things right." He wanted to say more. Was it normal to leave your children on a family vacation? Deputize your daughter as your *in loco parentis*? But what, he argued her side for a moment, did he understand about widowhood? Women did life's dirty work: They grieved and cared for people. His mother had kept his father at least half alive after the jungle.

"Say something. You quiet men make me mad, like you'll suddenly explode."

What did she expect? Apology? Sympathy? Empathy?

"When my husband was killed, I was happy for him because his brain was so fried from previous tours." Her voice dared him to express shock.

Will knew the officer died there, but saying she *wanted* him dead?

"Tough on you—needing to grieve and having to fake it."

She exhaled. "It's true. Where did you—um—serve?"

"Does that matter?" He was driftwood inside and out—light, hollow, empty.

"Never mind." She turned the TV on mute and stared at a Jeopardy contestant. "Besides, who could grieve for *ten years*? He suffered traumatic brain injury. Do you know why Lucille ran away?"

He positioned his chair so he could watch TV. *Final Jeopardy*. The winner, up by thousands, bet nothing. "She didn't run away, though, did she? She needed to bury her father. She was doing her job."

"I would've scattered the ashes or whatever, I simply hadn't gotten to it."

He nodded. "Understood. Tell me the 'or whatever.' That's familiar territory."

"Waiting for the right time?" She observed the ceiling. "Arlington's nice. You could be buried there." Her voice sounded odd. Perky, devil-may-care.

He gripped the chair arms. The sun blasted the blinds; sun stripes quivered on his arms and legs. "Good one. Keep going."

Trip, and Will's ex, had lectured Will about AA and rehab, but their efforts failed. He wasn't about to tell Naomi what to do—that could mean time and money down the drain, and give Lucille false hope when she needed extra vigilance until she turned eighteen.

"We needed his presence? I didn't want her to forget."

He concentrated on the TV. The weakest contestant wagered everything—and won.

"That what you told Lucille? That bullshit satisfied her?"

Naomi slumped, her ghoul-white face blended with the bed

linens. "Till lately. Finally, he's buried." She stuck out her chin. "We're fine."

"We're all fine until we're not, and that's when we need each other." He'd forsworn platitudes, but they eased people over hard times, when speech was necessary but too difficult.

She glued her eyes to *Jeopardy*. "Here's where you'll deliver your rehab pep talk. OK. I admit my mistake, going off with Tom. We'd been friends for more than twenty years, but I didn't know him. He took off with another woman."

"I don't care about any of that. I got the opportunity to—hang out with your children."

She closed her eyes, pinched the bridge of her nose, and re-opened her eyes. "I owe you. For your time. It's the least I can do. My purse—the drawer. I can't quite reach it. I've got cash. I spent nothing on Cumberland, and Key West is off the table because school starts tomorrow, and we'll need to rush back to Detroit. Even so, the kids will miss a couple of days."

"Money crossed my mind—at first." He stopped there, no need for *they gave me more than I gave them*. Enlightened him. Worried him. Evoked human instincts he didn't know he possessed.

"Tell you one thing that happened—did I see you Friday night? Honestly, I can't recall. Why?" He walked to her bedside, looked down at her, and dug deep in Nelson's pockets. "Sober for the better part of three years, I got wasted Friday night, even the thought of my kid responsibilities didn't deter me from one Scotch after another. If you saw me that night, you smelled booze. I got a piece of good news, see, I got a dealer to represent my art. Imagine . . ."

"I'm glad, for you and your art, but fail to see how this news helps me—you made a mistake—you'll survive. Whenever I double my dose—some days are just double-dose days—I get up the next morning . . ."

"I understand how you feel."

The sun stopped striping the room, now dim with only the *Jeopardy* glow.

"I understand how you feel because that's how I felt Saturday morning. I would've heard Lucille leave because I rise early, but didn't because I'd slept like a drunk. You might have heard her, too, but, correct me if I'm wrong, Friday was a double-dose day? After the Tom episode, everything seemed too hard? Am I lying?"

She shook her head.

"I sleep-walked, doing hurricane chores, and took too long to grasp the urgency—Lucille fooled me the way she fools you—she convinces grownups she's more competent than we are. She's a kid. A *good* kid. Not a grownup."

He stayed at her bedside. Vigil or guard duty. Over there, he'd worked to stay awake and alive. Naomi needed to wake up to her own life, her children. She might not fully grasp or appreciate his words, but he needed to try, for the kids and his peace of mind.

Time passed. He broke the silence.

"I hate AA, hate the up-talk, hate the confessional atmosphere, fluorescent lights, church basement vibe. But I'm going back.

"You play this any way you want, but you're fucking with your children's lives."

His legs had numbed, but somehow they transported him to the door.

"With your permission, and Marco's, I'd like to drive the children to Key West for Lucille's birthday. We'll leave tomorrow. Talk to Marco. Vouch for me—if you can—I'd hate to send my kids off with a stranger."

She acknowledged the words with a head-tilt, and, though her face stayed expressionless, her eyes lasered his. "Are you sure?"

Doubt charged through him. How could he fit all four in Pearl? He had no clue except the usual double buckling. How would he fund the trip? Ideas, but nothing certain. "I'm sure." He tried to sound confident. "I've never been surer." They, himself included, deserved Key West.

Outside, muggy air smacked him. He heard and tracked the three kid voices.

"I'm it!" They dashed around the small green space, shrub-separated from the entrance, and ganged up on Will; even Lucille pelted him with tufts of grass while the little kids climbed and pulled and pushed until they collapsed in a heap, rolling in the soggy, sorry grass, staining Mayzie's Belva-dress, Jack's thrift-shop duds, Lucille's Belva-pants, and Will's Nelson-khakis, trying to laugh, exhausted.

"Let's go see Queen?" Mayzie asked. "Please? May we?"

He shook his head. "They're keeping her quiet. Sometimes when old people get too cold and too thirsty," he started, stopped, and prayed silently to the blue sky.

"You can die of thirst," Mayzie said.

"You can, but they didn't. Lucille did Queen this big honor, escorted her to the place where she grew up, a long time ago. She may have gotten pneumonia, that means her lungs could fill with water."

"But you said she didn't get *enough* water, she was thirsty," Mayzie argued.

"That water goes into your bloodstream; water in your lungs slips in because your lungs aren't working."

Sorrow closed around them. Queen. The realest of the real—that and the possibility of her permanent absence had never once crossed Will's mind. His mother's cousin knew everything, spoke plain truth, and had lived large inside Will for as long as he'd existed.

He crammed them in Pearl, double-buckled Mayzie and Jack, and drove to Belva's.

Renaldo had found a half-frozen cake—no one had electricity—and cleared a spot on the table. They lit a two-burner white-gas stove he'd dragged from the basement. They heated water for noodles and warmed half-frozen broccoli. They ate out-of-date pickles.

After dinner, dirty dishes piled, Renaldo carried Belva while Will hauled a folding chair from the basement. Without electricity, the sky turned velvet. Stars, even recognizable constellations, shone like detailed deep-space maps. They formed a half-circle around Belva's chair, in front of Will, who turned his back, fished a lighter from his pocket, and lit the sparklers he stashed Saturday under Pearl's seat.

He snapped and snapped the little lighter, and flame flared, but the sparklers only smoked. "Oh, hell." He threw up his hands and laughed. Once he started, his laughter built until he truly could not stop his bellyaching, tear-inducing laugh—the kids' mouths gaped open, Belva's, too, and, soon, they laughed at Will laughing and kept on, until the laughter spread and Will imagined it drifting out over the neighborhood, unstoppable. They watched each other laugh, whoop, and holler, and made it last, who knew for how long, but today, there they were, a makeshift, momentary family, convulsing. With laughter.

Their howls subsided. A shape ambled through the dark, head down, shoulders drooped. Will could not make out the face in the gloaming, not from twelve, ten, now six yards away, even Mayzie and Jack quieted. It took forever for the stranger to cross.

Will jogged over. "Hey, man, need help?"

"All set, thanks." He strode past Will in the sodden grass.

Mayzie screamed first.

"I've missed that scream," Huffing, he kneeled in mucky grass, a kid inside each arm, pushing him over, and rolling in the wet.

Will's tears gushed, too, tears he'd saved all week, maybe all his life. He and Lucille stood aside. Belva stood, holding onto her chair.

Marco poked his head from the flesh mountain. "Would've been here sooner but needed a birthday gift for *somebody* who should've stayed in touch. Somebody who is fourteen today and wants badly to see the Florida Reef."

Lucille tried to silence her blubbering but hiccuped, loud.

Will slapped her on the back.

"God. Stop! What are you doing?"

"Scared ya, though, huh? Gone?"

"Yeah."

Belva urged, "Go on, Lucille, pile on."

"Yeah, I can take it—I'm starved for kids. How boring my life has been!"

Lucille hung back.

"Get in there, Big Sis," Will said.

"Come on, Luce. I'll fuss later."

She grabbed Marco around his fleshy middle.

"A right good end to a sorry weekend. You must be starved, man," Will called. "Here's cake, how about soggy broccoli? Nothing too good for our friends. We're taking off tomorrow for Key West. You're welcome to join us."

"Thanks, but I'm sticking around with Naomi—I stopped at the hospital and she told me *everything*. But why didn't you stay in touch, Luce?"

"I'll back up any dead-zone claims. Weird Wi-Fi and no cell."

"I thought you'd be too happy to be mad, Marco," Lucille said.

Marco wrestled in the grass with the little kids. Will and Lucille crouched at Belva's chair, and Belva stroked Lucille's hair. "You accomplished so much this week. Put your dad to rest. Your mom may be getting the help she needed. Lucille, I volunteer at this hospital, and nurses work well beyond a safe number of hours. When hospitals operate short staffed, nurses fill in the gaps, too tired to function. They lift heavy weights, patients even, when no one's available. They suffer needle-sticks, and, all day, stay on their feet. Depression like your mother's is a serious, common occupational hazard. She is burned out."

"Naomi talks about staying late to update electronic records. See, I think she made a mistake." The poor girl said this like someone dying to spill a terrible secret. "She doesn't know if she can work again. She won't say what it was. She keeps it inside."

Belva stayed quiet. "A terrible burden."

"She'd been super-odd since my dad died, but this sent her over the edge, last spring. She doesn't trust herself. And now, *she's* on drugs. She always took a little of this and that, over the years, but she's taking everything all the time. I'm exaggerating, but, you understand what I'm saying? Don't you?"

"Getting the idea. Who's around to help you, Lucille?"

"Marco, but she left him. I don't want to go back to Detroit unless rehab cures her. The social worker Tracey said she'd see about rehab for Naomi."

Will kept quiet. One tragedy, two, maybe more, setting others in motion.

"Lucille, love, think about coming here next summer and working in the sea turtle center. You're welcome to stay here. From the spare upstairs bedroom, you can see the water."

"I can't imagine anything better than a turtle summer. How are you feeling, Belva?"

"My brain's recovering."

"Uh oh." Will broke his silence. "I figured if her brain stayed winky, I'd have a better chance with her. Right, Lucille?" He walked around and touched Lucille's shoulder.

"Will is truly terrible. Stay away from him." Lucille rose from the grass, threw her arms around his waist, and buried her head in his shirt.

33

Float

My chartreuse jacket bulked under my chin, and the mask—printed with octopuses? It dwarfed my face, and slid down my nose until the strap magically tightened. Oh. Will, grinning. Knee to his chest, he waved, then jumped, butt-first, splashing and soaking me. Idiot. Seconds later, he popped up; his arm motioned me in. I was terrified.

She tap-tapped each rung to test her footing. That damned mask was too damned big, which was Will's damned fault. Okaay, bottom step, good, good. He scouted left, for Jack and Mayzie. Shallow-snorkeling. Their guide air-high-fived Will. Everybody was good. So go, go, Lucky.

Why was Will staring at me? I was *almost* ready. Almost. My mouth closed around the tube, lungs puffing, like I was rehearsing. I stuck my mask-shielded face on top of the water. Jazz-bright down there, a kaleidoscope. My body dropped in, slapping the water.

Ow. At least the life jacket cushioned the belly flop. Will stifled his laugh, and, when he did, inhaled water through his own snorkel.

Lucky's head stayed in the water. He'd love to hear her thoughts; this was his first snorkel, too. Afloat, above the sea world, was she pondering the reef's lifespan? Coral bleaching and dying? She'd spouted facts yesterday for nine, or was it ten, highway hours? *Living tissue binds coral colonies with thousands of polyps.* Fact and Fact and Fact.

What really got me? The bright sunlight drilling deep, refracting light and making patterns. Corals iridesced and phosphoresced and incandesced—jewel-words I memorized yesterday. Jewels, these neon creature-fish— precious jewels. Angels and parrots and clowns and aqua-blues—flitting like birds, under the sea, flying among orange and yellow, pink and red. A see-through something ghosted past. Will kicked a circle around me in giant swim-fins. When I smiled, I choked and re-surfaced, gasping for breath. Will shot up and yanked off his mask and snorkel.

I beat my chest, treaded water, and checked, re-checked my mask.

With my lips around the snorkel and my head lowered, I flapped my floppy fins. Lucky me, weightless.

Will swam ahead like a dolphin, his skin the color of raw brown earth. Could he dissolve? No way. He bulldozed through the water.

I glued my gaze to the seafloor, and got my reward—a loggerhead skimming the bottom while a nurse shark passed between the loggerhead and me.

Lucky me. Suspended between now and what comes next in this floating world.

34

Shellsea

That afternoon at the Shellsea—the cheapest motel in Key West—I flipped through a women's magazine, and caught a headline about drugs and loved ones. It snatched my attention and brought back the seining memory I'd kept alive: our first evening on Boneyard when Naomi and I had plodded through mud and water, just us two.

How could she vanish with Tom after that? Why'd she go haywire on me? And today, bathing in a muggy sunglow, it hit me that Naomi would never check herself into rehab unless somebody tied her up and gagged her. She loved babies, and would've needed drugs to survive an "incident."

Swimming and snorkeling had cleared clouds from my head, and now I knew that her high school friend, Tom, maybe ditched her for someone else on that fancy island, maybe he didn't. I couldn't trust her. Had I ever? Could Naomi straight-up refuse rehab? Could Tracey help? Who would pay? Even if they couldn't force Naomi to rehab, Marco could get custody of his kids. He had space in his two-bedroom apartment for Jack and Mayzie. None for me. My heart stopped. I forced a breath, then two.

Right this second, in fact, Tracey and Marco could be discussing custody.

My brother. My sister. Halves. But to me they felt whole.

I jumped up. God. We had no time. "Will!" I tapped Tracey's

number. After a million rings, she answered. I went on and on and on. "We're making progress, Lucille," she said. "That's all I'm allowed to say because of privacy rules. Your mother will explain. Are you allowing yourself to have fun?"

"Sooo much, I haven't had phoned Mom. We snorkeled today. I belly-flopped." The motel wireless worked, so did the service at the hospital, but I hadn't stayed in touch. I loved my vacation from Naomi, who stirred me up over things I couldn't control.

I found Will in the Shellsea's outdoor kitchen making his third Cuban coffee.

"More? You won't sleep a wink."

He stirred and stirred. "Lucille." He laid down the Styrofoam cup and stick. He parked his palms on my shoulders and stared into my eyes, into me. "Queen passed away."

I'll never forget that moment if I live to be as old as Queen. Straight delivery. I didn't know what to make of death—one minute she was alive, the next, dead. I'd gotten used to my father's absence, but Queen fired me up, and showed me what I could do. In less than twenty-four hours, she'd beaten a life-path for me. I'd faced fear because of her.

The thought that I killed her nagged me. "How could her death not be my fault?" I asked Will, pouring hot water over a Lipton's bag. He shook his head. "She was ready. You took her home."

I pushed my bare feet through tufts of the green plastic, a rug pretending to be grass, until I reached a big wooden chair. I adored this Shellsea Motel. The Wi-Fi *worked*. Friendly guests: big-bellied bikers with scritchy gray hair on their chests, bald spots, and tattoos of big bosoms on biceps. The manager, Sarita, with her waist-length black hair and smiley eyes.

Queen would love it here.

I whispered *Shellsea, Shellsea,* to Queen. So much to love in Key West, besides the snorkeling, Cuban coffee, with sugar and milk. Mayzie and Jack slurped it up, too; maybe that's why nobody slept last night. We were wired, especially Will. He drank three yesterday.

Even the stupid Styrofoam—which, like, never, *ever* breaks

down—didn't rattle me—not with Queen memories dripping on every thought. I'd managed Naomi! I could've managed Queen. We could've scattered Dad anywhere, even Key West. He wouldn't have cared. Why did I let Queen come along and get hypothermia?

But without the trip, would I have shed my cocoon?

I raised the squeaky Styro to my lips. A bizarre screech-scream ripped the air. Mayzie. I dropped the cup in my lap, hot tea reddened my thighs—first-degree *at least*. In our room, Jack lay on the tile floor, cradling his arm, oddly askew. "Owww!"

Mayzie turned to me, crying. "It's your fault. Everything's ruined! First you disappeared and then there was a hurricane and then we finally came to Key West, and now Jack might die."

I put my arm around her. "He's OK, Maze, don't worry. Think of some *Wire* lines."

Will kneeled. "Hold on y'all, nobody's dying. I'll get him to urgent care—about time for a crisis, I was getting complacent. Y'all get yourselves something to eat." He tossed me a twenty. He and Jack climbed in a taxi.

I couldn't imagine food in my belly. To distract Mayzie, we wandered around Duval Street for two hours, buying cheap T-shirts for Renaldo and Marco and Belva—and a butterfly hair clip for Naomi, to go with the fishing-lure earrings from the drowned Boneyard Bait and Grocery. We never spent time together, just Mayzie and me. Why?

I gave a teenager my phone and she snapped our photo in front of the concrete buoy marking the southernmost point in the United States.

Mayzie would only be eleven when I left home. We wouldn't live together as sisters when she was fourteen, like me. But if Marco got custody, we would separate sooner. Duval Street's glow dimmed.

We hiked to a food truck Sarita suggested on Simonton Street. The line snaked down the block. An hour later, Will and Jack rolled up in an Uber before we finished, Jack swaggering, his arm in a lightweight sling—"Broked it!"

"Cracked," Will adjusted the sling. "Tiny, clean fracture." We sat under an umbrella.

"Best food I ever ate," I told Will around a mouthful, suddenly famished. When I thought of Queen, food stuck in my throat like wads of newspaper. Big grilled shrimp. Black beans. I'd never tasted black beans; these came in a Styrofoam cup, which at first I sent back, thinking it was coffee. And, yellow rice.

"How do they turn rice yellow?" I asked Will.

"Saffron. Super pricey, grows somewhere in Asia or Africa? Isn't it great? My mom loved yellow rice and so did I. I haven't eaten it—" his face froze for a sec, and then said, "in forever." Will's mother died, not so long ago. Gosh. Will and I kinda-sorta had that in common. Both our mothers, only mine wasn't dead, only absent, like Will's father. Will was almost thirty. I was fourteen. Did people need parents at thirty?

Now that Jack was OK, I worried about money. How did people pay for medicine and doctors without money or insurance? I swore I would sit Naomi down and talk finances and marriage and mental health. If we again became our own family.

Will weirdly ate almost nada. "You're too skinny," I told him. "Did the ER cost much?"

"Can I have your shrimp?" Mayzie asked Will.

He slid his plate over. "I'm a lightweight. And, as for your question, Lucky, I have no idea, because—ha ha ha HA!—Marco gave me his insurance information. Grownups aren't as stupid as you think. Jack scared us, but he's tough."

"Yeah." Jack lifted his arm. "Hurt like *hell*. No big deal."

I slipped out my wallet and secretly paid the bill, which was only thirty-five dollars, plus tip. "Don't tell the big guy." The waitress smiled and a giant piece of tres leches cake appeared on our table. She explained in Spanish how the cake recipe contained three kinds of milk, but I already knew tres and leches from eighth-grade Spanish.

Back at the Shellsea, we packed. Jack tore the place apart until he found Pterodactyl, only because Will had pocketed it.

35

Fulfillment

Belva's door was unlocked, though it was midnight. Lucille remembered the layout and shepherded Jack and Mayzie upstairs. Maybe four people were sleeping here, seven now with the children, a dadgum boarding house. Will stood in the hallway fighting sleep, and followed the kids' progress upstairs with his eyes. They'd be fine, but watching them go felt like the first goodbye. Lucille lifted her hand and gave him a peace sign.

"Tomorrow?" she whispered.

"Tomorrow." Who slept where? Marco? Naomi? Had she been discharged? Had she agreed to rehab? Will hadn't even called Belva. Renaldo had called about Queen's passing.

Marco appeared in the hall, he'd been asleep on the couch in the adjacent living room. "Thanks, man. I'm sure they had a blast. I'll go say goodnight. Got a place to sleep?"

"Yeah. The sheriff's. Jack busted his arm. Lucille said she left a message."

He nodded. "Kid's accident prone, thanks for coping. Probably post-hurricane stress. You've done so much, for Lucille especially. She found the father she's missed."

This thought had briefly crossed Will's mind during the search. Could he adopt them? No. Fatherhood seemed remote and unfathomable, but weirdly worthy.

"Night." Marco went upstairs, passing Belva, stepping her way down, clutching the handrail.

"Where are you sleeping?"

"Trip's." Fatigue slammed him full force, but his feet moved his body forward. He met her at the bottom step. "Last time we met, I delivered you to the potty. You OK?"

She laughed. "Better. I haven't left the house. Thank goodness for Renaldo."

Neither mentioned Queen's death. "Your feet function, at least. Hear about Jack's arm? I'm the last person anybody should trust with kids."

She clasped her hands. "Kids break bones. The worst injuries are those you can't see."

"Hope I didn't cause those. We had a blast, even at urgent care. Kid's a scrapper, too. They all are. How's your brain?"

"My brain's lighting up. You could even sleep here."

He jolted awake from hours of road stupor. "You've got a house full."

"With me."

Tired and clueless, Will nevertheless registered the invitation. "I'd like that."

"So would I."

No need to rush. And he wasn't even sure he'd stick around the marsh. That notion of fulfillment, once she'd uttered the word, had stuck with him. He had registered a rich, full feeling in Key West, even at urgent care. Was that fulfillment? Like putting his feet under his mother's dinner table at Loblolly, surrounded by layers of love and warmth and smells and tastes?

"Can I take a rain check?" Stupid phrase but he specialized in stupid. "We have plenty of time. Right?"

"Yes." She started back up the stairs.

"How much time?"

Over her shoulder, she said, "Who can say? Time is slippery."

"Winter's coming. That's when I usually hibernate, but my cave crumbled."

Belva, halfway up, grabbed the railing, and turned. "You're a wild one, Will, where in the world could you hibernate? See you Saturday. Your work's in my car."

"I don't know where I'll live or what I'm going to do, but I'll join you tomorrow."

She reached the top. She disappeared from view. Carefully, quietly, he let himself out of her house.

36

Secrets

The next morning in Belva's kitchen, somebody must've been up awhile because they'd brewed coffee. I poured mine, added milk and two teaspoons of sugar. My bare feet stuck to the floor and clammy air coated my skin. The electricity worked now, but the A/C had died. I could've eaten the air, it was so thick.

Naomi wandered in, looking like somebody'd run her through the dryer and left her there all night. Where had she slept? I hadn't seen her when we came in. Marco had stopped in our room to say goodnight.

I didn't ask her about rehab. She wouldn't outright refuse, that wasn't her way. She'd go about her business like she was at this moment, eating scrambled eggs, making toast, pouring coffee and offering me orange juice, and somebody would eventually ask her point blank, and she might or might not tell the truth. It seemed, well, so freaking normal. I should've told Tracey more about Naomi's M.O. But Tracey was a professional, I reminded myself, as I sat at the sturdy wooden table.

I'd hoped for *alone* with Naomi, but here came Marco, as I sipped. Marco quick-hugged her. I'd always had trouble reading her reactions to men—what was real, what was fake. She crossed the room to my observation post. I'd gotten halfway through my Cuban-style coffee drug when she kneeled and laid her head in my lap, arms around my waist. I wanted to cry, but hated crying, hated that women got dissed for crying, which was normal, and, personally, I thought if men cried more, the world would improve.

The weird thing was how resigned I felt; her gesture told me everything I didn't want to know. I stroked her head. "Your hair needs brushing." A bouffant nest. My thighs, still sore from the hot tea spill, chafed with the weight of her head. I slurped the sugar at the bottom of my cup.

Marco sat in the only other chair. Naomi got to her feet. "I need to talk."

My muscles tried to jump me out of my chair but I commanded them to stay still. Her eyes looked weird and jumpy, fireflies trying to escape a jar. A dark fog's rolling in, I told myself, prepare.

"I have news. Do you remember when the officers came?"

"Don't use that dead image." It was Queen I mourned now; Dad was home. "What could you possibly have thought of in the past 48 hours or during the night you spent with Will that could make you want to bring up the past?"

"It's not over. The past goes on and on."

She'd never before referred to grief. "Why? What's different?"

"Me." Her face sagged. "You are my daughter. I found that out Saturday night."

"And my father's."

She smiled, not at or for anyone, but to herself, a secret smile. "You are him in so many ways."

I hoped she'd say how, and not just that he'd be proud of me. I knew that.

"The spit. The fire. I never talked about him, not because I didn't want to, but because I needed to forget. I could no more do that than deny my own presence. Plenty of times I've wanted to check out."

"And did."

"But you were always doing your sweet, stubborn little-girl Robert thing. Part of the reason I came on this trip."

I interrupted. "Are you quitting drugs? Or not? If you're not, I'm not going back to Detroit with you. I may not even go if you do quit. I like it here. I have friends. I'm only sorry Queen died and that I helped—kill her."

For a moment, the only sound was Belva's coffee dribbling into her cup. I hadn't even seen her enter the room, but there she was, in the dirty bathrobe. Solid.

"Lucille," Belva said. "Queen would be horrified if she heard you. We worked together on sea turtle protection. I knew her well. You honored her. She had often talked of Tabby Town. I wish I'd taken her there myself. But you did."

Right. Maybe I'd see it that way when I grew up. "Thank you."

"I've been seeing Tracey?" Naomi said. "You know? The social worker? She's a counselor?"

We smiled at Naomi's Tracey-imitation.

"I made a mistake. It scared me, so I asked for a leave of absence."

I straightened to give the butterflies in my stomach more flutter space. "Why? Were you suspended? Drugs? Did you steal drugs?"

Naomi's eyes closed. I'd given her too many chances. She hadn't been my mother in nine years. Four more years till I'm eighteen. I shut my eyes so tight I saw stars. I liked this view inside my eyelids.

Even when her voice started again, I studied my light-spangled lids. "How bad was this 'mistake'?" My voice went catty.

"I administered oxytocin instead of magnesium." During labor, the bags weren't labeled clearly, and during the labor, things got hectic. Preparing and administering solutions. "Twins."

My eyes flew open. "What's magnesium? Couldn't you correct the dose? With an antidote? Was it poison?"

She inspected the floor. "They survived. After five months in NICU."

I sucked in my breath. Naomi and I, blaming ourselves.

37

Perdita

Will loaded Mayzie, Lucille, and his sculptures in Pearl's bed, and, with Belva riding shotgun, drove the two blocks to the market. Jack and Marco stayed behind to pack. They'd leave today for Detroit, where Naomi would enter rehab. Marco would keep the little kids and Lucille. Will couldn't stop their leaving; they were a family.

"Let's keep the exhibitors in this one spot, not spread them out." Belva got around on feet that were mostly healed, while Will unloaded two folding chairs and made her sit, to direct her minions, like Will. She'd even arranged for food trucks and a classic rock band.

Lucille filled a giant coffee urn with two gallons of bottled water because she insisted the water from the public spigot was probably contaminated.

Will walked the market end to end—the east end, nearest the spigot, had suffered not only hurricane but tornado damage—its roof angled and slumped, but the main sections had stayed solid, and the city inspector OK'd them. Exhibitors arrived one by one. They cleared the concrete of sticks, dried mud, branches, pine needles.

The city had delivered twenty folding tables because twenty exhibitors had committed. Will couldn't imagine customers coming much less buying. Tourists or casual shoppers or gallery owners? Unlikely. He hoped he was wrong.

"If that fried pie lady would only show up." Mayzie had come strictly for those pies.

"Hope she's got sweet potato. Yum." She rubbed her belly. Sadly, the storm had gobbled Mayzie's wild outfits, and now she wore regulation girl-shorts Belva had culled from somewhere, with a T-shirt. Mayzie didn't seem to care, but Will missed her offbeat duds.

By eight, the coffee smell had permeated the place and the displays, artfully arranged, had created a cozy, small-town vibe. Perdita, the Guatemalan crafts dealer, and Sid Turner, the artist who transformed books into boxes of social commentary, and a dozen others, had unloaded wares and knock-down display units, a cabinet or two, shelving systems, and pedestals.

Everybody flew high not only on Belva's rich, strong, organic Guatemalan coffee, but each other, glad to be alive and making art; they priced and placed each other's work, until the cordoned-off section resembled a halfway respectable gallery. Even Will's *Out There* sculpture commanded attention, prominently propped against a six-by-six post.

"*Lucky Us.*" Sid pointed out the title of his newest "book," between whose covers he'd placed tiny, hand-sculpted figures that shook hands or hugged or slapped palms or high fived.

"That's the sunniest piece of yours I've ever seen, man. I love that darkness in your work, though. No pretense."

He nodded. "Right. I don't do sunny, but today's a different day, friend."

One week ago, the storm. An end. A beginning. The day fully cooperated: Early clouds parted for a cerulean sky. The space crowded quickly. Maybe people needed to get out of the house, hungry for company or a reprieve from debris clearing, roof-fixing, chainsawing.

A break from disaster.

This whole shindig and setup, he marveled, was a win. Belva had done it again.

He loped back under the roof. Perdita caught his arm and led him behind one of the posts. She whispered, "Will, I need your help."

"Sure. Need me to carry boxes?" He wished now he'd made more of an effort to befriend Perdita and the other artists. "I'm happy to help."

"Not me, my friends. I saw on the TV, someone had filmed the place where you found the missing girl and the old woman, is that your home?"

He shook his head. "Yes and no. I haven't lived there in several years. You surely saw the condition of the place." Weird. He hadn't seen any TV, much less *Mudhole* footage.

"No matter." She looked around. "We need to keep this quiet. Can I trust you?"

"Depends." What could she want? They'd seldom spoken over these past summer weekends; he knew nothing about her.

Her eyes roamed the surroundings. Her voice went whispery. Her caution was contagious; he steered the small, brightly-dressed woman farther from clots of people. "We would need for no one to know. We could fix your place in exchange."

"Whoa. Whoa. Who? What? Who's we?" He scrunched his face, shaking his head.

"Only for winter." She leaned in and whispered, "Immigrants. Illegal."

Oh. Trip talked about illegals all the time, but their plights, to Will, seemed distant, vague. "Why? What would change after winter?"

"We're working with lawyers to file for legal status—green cards or citizenship."

Will considered the enormity of the request and registered her desperate tone, doubt lacing the word *citizenship*, as she drew out the four syllables. The process could take years. Money. Maybe she didn't understand. He didn't.

"How many people are we talking about?" Will asked.

"A family. Five. My brother has work with a roofer." Perdita raised her arm.

Will's legs went weak. He leaned on the post.

A man materialized from somewhere. "We need a place."

"This is Miguel—Mike," Perdita said. "He can explain."

Mike shook Will's hand. "Thank you for helping. Tom Barnes suggested I talk to you."

That raised a red flag. "Doubt I can. I'm Will, by the way. This is tough territory. Tell me what you need." Perdita had already explained; Will needed to hear it again, even though he'd rather join Mayzie, across the space, chewing a fried pie.

"We are without papers, or green cards, or a place to live. We could work on the house, in exchange for shelter. I have a job with Tom's company, but my employer does not file paperwork. My wife and baby recently arrived, and we are staying at a local church, but it's not—," he shook his head. "I fear that authorities may raid church sanctuaries."

Which authorities? County? City? State? Federal? Will shook his head. "Doesn't Barnes have rentals? Have you asked him? No can do. I'm rebuilding the house. It's uninhabitable."

Illegals worked all over the place, boats, farms, construction sites, everywhere. An open secret. This was not Will's problem to solve.

"And you can't—there's boar hunting in the fall. Besides, the sheriff's helping with construction, so, what could I tell him? To stay away?"

"Even a few weeks?" He pleaded. "Tom says he'll help but has nothing now. We can make ourselves invisible when it's hunting season. We know how to become invisible."

Will supposed he could post his land. No Trespassing, No Hunting. But how can a family become invisible? Impossible.

From across the space, Lucille motioned to Will. She seemed miles and miles and miles away, though it was only a few yards. She lifted her shoulders in a questioning gesture. She skipped over.

"Hi," she said to Mike. "Remember me?"

This man grinned in recognition. "The girl who destroys beach towels because she hates the racist Confederate flag."

Will cut his eyes at Lucille. "When this one calls you out, man, she's usually right," he said. "I'd love to hear the rest of *that* story, once we, if we ever, get sorted."

WTF! The last thing Will needed was the worry and

responsibility of another family. He shook his head, considering not the proposal, but his own future, fuzzy now that he'd lost his craving for solitude—it led nowhere and to no one. He was no longer the zookeeper, observing the human race. Now, he lived in the zoo. He studied the crowd and liked what he saw: shapes, colors, moods, even that kid giving another kid the finger felt normal.

If he lived to be a hundred, life's messiness would never get all-the-way sorted. He saw that now. But why not stick his neck out? He thought of Belva exposing hers, two weeks ago when she caught him sneaking from her house. He thought of Queen. Her wise woman words could have cracked his way through this conundrum, but somehow he already knew them.

He signaled Belva. She didn't notice.

"Give me a little time." Will shook hands with the man and walked toward Belva, whistling the only tune that came to his lips, "Rock You Like a Hurricane."

Lucille fell in step. "You need to learn a different whistling song."

"Such as, Lucky? 'Somewhere Over the Rainbow'?"

"So. What? Are you going to hide them out at *Mudhole*?"

He raised his eyebrows. "I need you to think of a title. Got a minute?"

"A new piece? Or an old one?"

"New. It's not a sculpture, though, it's a feeling. Can you title feelings?"

"I'll try." She shook her cascading flame of hair.

"You might could call on Queen's spirit for help."

Her eyes shone and her voice wobbled. "Why'd she die, Will?"

Lucky would ask this question many times. Today, Will could answer. He was here. "She wanted to go home. You saw her through, not a departure, but an arrival."

She picked up her hair and wound it around her fingers.

"The county's planning a memorial celebration for Queen once the storm debris gets cleared and things quiet down. She was a trailblazer in this community. We could fly you down? I can make that happen."

"Right. What would you use for money?"

"That's not your problem. If Dick, my dealer guy, has lost interest, I'll go back to reproduction carving in Savannah till I get on my feet and decide whether I even want to keep *Mudhole*. These folks," he said, in a low voice, looking around, "won't be here forever. They'll need to move on."

"Move where?"

"Out from under Trip's nose."

"What'll you tell Trip about *Mudhole*?" she asked.

"I'll suggest we wait to rebuild, until I get on my feet and decide my next step. I'll rent a place in Savannah, earn my grubstake, and come back. Or not."

"He'll believe you? I'm not sure I do."

"If not, we'll find them another place."

"We?"

"Me, myself, and I, and a few others I trust. Belva. Renaldo."

They reached the check-in table. Battered guitar cases and a few men, sixty-ish, wearing worn jeans, tie-dyed shirts and big, scuffed leather boots stood around Belva, sharing a playlist for her approval. She nodded. "Anything as long as it's upbeat."

"So, what's that feeling?" Lucille asked. "I'm sure you can think of a name."

"No ma'am, I can't imagine. It's a tiny buzz that starts—" Will tapped his sternum, "right here, and expands until you feel like your heart's too big for your chest, or maybe you suddenly feel like playing Capture the Flag. It has nothing to do with your—"

"Brain," she said. "I can't feel that right now. Because of Queen."

"No, it's not affected by sadness, necessarily," Will said. "Big feeling."

"Does *love* work?"

"Too common. And the feeling is not so much connected to a person."

"Love works for every big feeling, maybe even sad, like you just now said."

"Maybe. Guess I love people now."

"Doubt it." She circled her ear with her finger. "You're just crazy like the rest of us. Your kinfolks."

He memorized her freckled face inside all that fiery hair. Next time he saw her she'd be taller, like her father maybe, and would she forget all about Will, by next summer, busy with boys and life? He wanted for her: normal, everyday, easy.

Was there such a thing?

38

Open Water

The sun's glare made everything look practically prehistoric, like pages in history. Maybe the weepiness washing me had to do with the light. A tide of tears flooded my chest—there was no stopping tide, even if those feelings did belong buried.

Naomi found me in this dazed state. She and Marco and the little kids were ready to go.

The tear-tide overpowered me. In Belva's too-big dress and those oversized sunglasses, Naomi looked nothing like herself; she resembled a version of Belva. Today I wore white capris and a peach colored T-shirt. Peach. Not my color.

"Ready?"

Naomi's first word since this morning when she confessed her medical mistake. Not, "How are you feeling?" not "I'm sorry we need to leave." She probably didn't even realize how I bonded with Will, Belva, and Queen.

I'd completely changed on the inside. She knew nothing about me, not now. She'd been preoccupied but when wasn't she?

Across the way, at the market, Marco roamed, a hand on Mayzie's shoulder and his other hand on Jack's, offering help to artists. He glanced my way from time to time, as if wondering when I'd be ready to leave.

Never. I shook my head.

"Leaving is difficult, even for me," Naomi said.

"What does that mean, even for you?"

"Whose idea was it to come here in the first place? Mine. This place, well, the island, not Pinesboro. I still can't believe the island's gone."

Did Naomi care? With all her worries—losing her job, probably. And wouldn't even Naomi-the-fearless be afraid to enter a "facility?"

"You don't need to pretend—"

"Pretend? When have I ever pretended?" A cloud shadowed Naomi's face. "I hear they found some turtles stranded in nets—."

I'd never heard her even say the word *turtle*. She did like fishing and seining, though, so, I gave her slack for trying. "I never want to leave."

Now the expected adult lie: "You think that now, but . . ."

"You can't know. And you know you can't know." Dark was falling. I smelled fall on the river breeze, laced with the smell I'd always associate with Will—mud stink.

"You're right. No one can really know another person."

That's not what I meant, even if it was true. "For instance, you admit you need help but you don't really think you do."

"You are one hundred percent correct."

Too bad the light had faded; there was too much I couldn't see, and might never see.

She said something about wind, the dark, the rain and the trip home while I let her words sink in. Had she really admitted that? At least she wasn't lying.

I puffed my cheeks with air. "I belong here with Will." I almost added *with Dad*, but what I'd said already put me at risk of ridicule. Now she'd think it was a crush, which it was, but a father-type crush. "People are packing. Jack and Mayzie are running circles around Marco and Will, see? They'd probably like to stay, too. So would I. Why don't we?" I'd dreamed of renting a house. There were lots of Spanish-speaking families. Marco could get a teaching job.

Hers was a fake move, but, if she had expected me to say no, she'd been wrong.

She started to explain about what happened, but not to me, to the sky, the river or the horizon. Her eyes never met mine. Finally, she said, "Maybe someone would hire me."

But even I questioned my own wish—would the magic become ordinary if we lived here year-around, worked, and attended school, doing the dull dailies?

We walked along the pier jutting from the riverfront, staring at the water, where shiny dark shapes arced and dove.

"What are those?" I breathed.

"Dolphins. Playing."

We counted eight. "They're on their way someplace else, like us."

Far from the others, close to the dolphins and the river, I felt wild, longing to be alone in the darkness. Boats bobbed. The water slapped the padded pilings, reminding me of two weeks ago when I ate fresh figs at the waterside restaurant the night before Naomi left.

She sat on the dock and slipped off her shoes, using her foot to snag a rubber boat.

"Hey, Luce, let's take out this dinghy."

Why, she hadn't learned anything! Same old Naomi, acting out a whim.

"OK, never mind it's not yours. Isn't that stealing?"

"Borrowing. I can't leave without getting out on the water."

"You've been on the water. You took the ferry to Cumberland Island, which is more than I got to do. You're selfish."

"Don't remind me. Selfish people are never happy." She eased her leg then her body into the boat. "Never forget that. You're much happier than I'll ever be."

She lifted her arms.

I stepped into her arms and the boat, rocking.

"Watch me and row."

I sat, dipped my paddle in the water; the boat circled three or four times.

"Let's get the timing straight," she said. "I'll get us to open water."

"Open water! That's dangerous."

She rowed, and we zig-zagged away from the docked boats. The power of the water under the boat felt like an animal that might rear up any minute. OK, don't go far, I willed her, in my head, but mental telepathy had never worked on Naomi.

I dutifully dug my oar into water. A slice of moon, barely off the horizon, lit our jiggly waterpath. The low voices from the marketplace grew fainter until we heard only the drippy sound of oars plowing through water.

Naomi quit paddling, her oar locked sideways. I held mine across my lap, and we floated on the muddy river, inside its smells—a little rancid, a little putrid, but rich.

How much time passed? Why did I allow myself to drift with my mother, the most unreliable person I knew, the person I could never count on, floating on a dark river without a life preserver?

What was I afraid of? Not the water. Her. Her unpredictability, the crooked, crippled backbone of our lives. The horizon was nearly invisible, and there, in that unreachable distance, I saw I'd never be fully free, and that I was more like her than I wanted. I didn't want help, didn't need help, couldn't accept help, unless all options fell away.

Naomi steered the rubber boat around and back to the dock, where, embarrassingly, a small crowd, including jumping Jack and pie-eating Mayzie, gathered. Will and Belva, Marco. Even Renaldo. Oh. And now Trip.

"How'd you pick *my* boat out of all the others?" Trip squatted. "Throw me the rope." His voice didn't sound mean. Was that a smile on his face? Hard to see in the near-dark.

Naomi tossed and missed. Trip grabbed a post, and leaned over the water. He caught the rope and pulled us in. We stepped onto the dock. Everybody clapped. Now was that necessary?

END

Acknowledgments

Kin: *n. a person's relatives, collectively, kinfolk; family relationship or kinship; a people, a family; a relative or kinsman; someone or something of the same, or similar, kind.*

My short story, "All Corners of This Floating World," shape-shifted into *Everybody Here is Kin*, a novel that took years of writing and voracious reading. My heartiest, deepest thanks to the Shobes—Bill and Charlie and Alec—who always have my back. They inspire, inform, support, and fortify my life, my writing, and me; the late Merritt and Rita Shobe, whose connection to nature inspired the setting; my siblings, Charlene and Jimmy Nash, who gave me a lifetime of stories simply by picking on me while growing up; my parents, the late Bellewoods and Charles Nash, who, though maybe mystified by our chosen paths, nevertheless wanted us to fly.

I'm indebted to artists' residencies for time and space that bolstered my writing and confidence: MacDowell, Hambidge, The Ragdale Foundation, the Virginia Center for the Creative Arts, VCCA-France, The Tyrone Guthrie Center (Ireland), and the Thicket (Tolomato Island, Ga.)

Writing colleagues and friends and experts deserve kudos for reading terrible early drafts. Deirdra McAfee, writer, teacher, and mentor, tutored me, a journalist floored by the strange and often inscrutable world of fiction writing.

Thanks to Dr. Victor Thompson, archeology professor at the University of Georgia, who generously shared, in an interview, his expertise about native shell civilizations. My reading of *Sea Turtles of the Atlantic and Gulf Coasts of the United States* by Carol Ruckdeschel and C. Robert Shoop, grounded me in sea turtle biology. Countless books, pamphlets, historical documents, and maps further deepened my connection to Georgia's coastal islands.

Gratitude galore to the Wesleyan Writers Conference, where

Roxana Robinson's keen first chapter review kept me going; the Key West Literary Conference, where Claire Messud suggested third-person suited Will's voice; and to Connie May Fowler, whose suggestions strengthened the final draft.

I could not have managed without WriterHouse, Charlottesville's own literary hotspot. Or colleagues who read iterations, versions, chapters, cover letters, and elevator pitches for this novel. I am beyond grateful to Addison, Barb, Brad, Carla, Danny, Debby, Debbie, and another Debbie, Diane, Ellen, Heather, Ida, Jane, Janis, Jeannie, Kelly, Ken, Lane, Leslie, Lisa, Mary Kay, Martha, Margie, Mary, MaryAnna, Melanie, Meredith, Paul, Rachel, Sharon, Shelly, Tony.

I've probably omitted someone. Even on buses, trains, planes, or in grocery stores, I bored total strangers with plot and character problems. Thank you, whoever, and wherever you are, *I love you* and hope you love this book.

It will love you back. We really are all kin.

Betty Joyce Nash

About the Author

BettyJoyce Nash's writing has appeared in journals including *North Dakota Quarterly* and *Across the Margin*, as well as in newspapers, magazines, and online; her fiction has been recognized with fellowships from MacDowell (2013), The Ragdale Foundation (2015), and VCCA (2018). In 2014, she was selected as the Virginia Center for the Creative Arts fiction fellow to the Tyrone Guthrie Center in Ireland. She's taught writing at the University of Richmond, the Albemarle Charlottesville Regional Jail, and several community writing centers; she now teaches at WriterHouse, a nonprofit literary arts center in Charlottesville, Virginia.